Patches

A Novel

Margaret Mendel

PUSHING TIME PRESS

ISBN: 978-0-578-28770-6
ebook ISBN: 978-0-578-28771-3

First printing: 2019 Muse It Up Publishing

For information, please contact the author:
margaret_mendel123@yahoo.com

To Steven, my muse, my lover.

Roger and Pearl

MOM AND DAD MET AT a dance, fell in love that first night, and eloped three months later. Within a year, America was in the middle of World War II and Dad was drafted into the Army. By then I was born, and when Dad left for boot camp Mom had no choice but to move back with her parents. Looking at pictures of my young parents, Mom, seventeen, Dad, just turned twenty-one, they hardly look ready to marry, much less take on the world.

Eventually there would be three more babies, all girls. Over the years, my sisters and I watched the unraveling of any feelings that our mother and father once had for each other. It is difficult for us to imagine our parents young and in love, because we know the people they were destined to become.

Families have stories; tales told so often that they become a web of myths stretching out across the years. Mom and Dad told a story about something that occurred several days before Dad went off to boot camp. Sometimes this incident was told as a joke, though when heard from Mom's point of view, the story sounded more like an illustration of our father's mischievous youthful spirit. Each time they told the story, it felt like it might have been an attempt to reach back into a sweeter time when they were a newly married couple.

Dad usually started the story. "The three of us were driving home after dinner with the Millers." Being the first-born he included me in the story. "Your mom was hopping mad at me—said I'd gone too far this time." Though I was far too young to recall any of this, the story was told so many times it felt like listening to one of my memories. "We were on our way home," Dad continued. "I reached out to touch your mother's hand, and said, 'Come on, Pearl, don't be like that. It won't happen again. I promise.'"

When my sisters and I were very young, we remember our dad touching Mom when he wanted her to listen closely to what he was saying. But over the years, their touching eventually became accidental brushes in passing. Mom most likely angrily jerked her hand out of Dad's reach. I've seen her do this many times; he reaches out and she pulls away.

"You promise you won't do it, and then you always do something," she snapped. Though this tale is never told exactly the same way, my sisters and I know what our parents said to each other that night. We have slipped in the missing pieces from the millions of words we've heard them say over the years.

"How about Thursday?" Mom said. "You promised then, too. It's only Sunday and you did it again. Your promises mean nothing." At this point, Mom quite likely adjusted the blanket around the sleeping baby in her arms. When she and Dad argued and one of their daughters was close by, Mom reached out to one of us to fix a stray wisp of hair fallen from a barrette, straighten a ribbon on a pigtail, or fidget with our clothes.

Dad returned his hand to the steering wheel. "You're going to squeeze that kid to death if you don't watch out," he said. "Besides, the other day was just a joke, Pearl. I thought it was funny."

"Oh, sure, you thought you were a real comedian."

"Ah, come on, Pearl, it was just a harmless little old frog in that sock," he said.

Mom most assuredly gave Dad one of her furious looks. "You think it's funny to come home, put a frog in your sock, and wait for me to pick it up? Then you roll around on the bed laughing so hard you bust your britches, while I grab the baby and run out of the room. What's so funny about that? Huh? Tell me. I want to know the joke, too."

Mom gave him one of her looks, a look that over the years Dad learned to live with. Even back then Mom's soft blue eyes could harden into an angry, piercing, steely blue, as she clenched her jaw and pursed her lips so tightly together they no longer looked capable of speech.

Over the years, Mom perfected this look that made her husband and children want to hide. They were angry looks that made her daughters' hearts race so fast we had to look away for fear that the beating organ might burst. I realize now that behind those looks were our mother's regrets, anger and disappointments. This look that no one wanted to experience was an overflow of her own feelings, and I can only imagine how those emotions must have ripped through her as they raged out at us.

Dad was notorious for trying to explain himself easily with excuses. In his youth he thought excuses were reasons, though the years eventually rendered him excuse-less.

"You've seen frogs before," he said.

"You thought it was funny to see me scared," Mom snapped. "You didn't want to show me any frog. You like to play tricks on me. Well, they aren't funny anymore."

"They're harmless jokes. They don't hurt anyone. Where's your sense of humor? You got to admit it was pretty funny to see that old sock jump'n around on the bedroom floor." Dad might have grinned at that point, but only for a moment because Mom gave him one of her looks.

Dad certainly got a kick out of playing jokes on people, and even though he caught hell most of the time, he could not help himself. I've often wondered if his jokes during that time were a way of keeping his mind off the telegram from the draft board. Years later he'd admit to Mom how frightened he was about going to war.

"But you knew what you were doing tonight," Mom insisted. "You promised you wouldn't do it again and you did it anyway. Didn't you? You and your tricks." Her voice trailed off as it frequently did when she was tired of struggling to make herself understood. Many years later, while sitting in the kitchen drinking coffee with Mom on a cold winter day, she told me, "When looking out the side window of the car that night, I saw a ghost. It was your dad's reflection and the lights of an oncoming car passed right through his image in the window. It frightened me. It was like he wasn't really there. I wanted the war to be over. I wanted him home."

Mom never told Dad that she cried during the day while he was at work. Even after all the years of bickering and the anger that had grown up around them, Mom still talked about how, as a young bride, she wept thinking about her husband going off to war and how she would miss him. Not his jokes though. She certainly would not miss his jokes.

That night, on the drive home from dinner with the Miller's, Dad tried to reassure his young wife that he wasn't being mean to her. "How was I to know you didn't like those things?"

I'm certain Dad tried to look innocent, though when he said this he most likely appeared coy and probably not so innocent.

But Mom was not convinced of his blamelessness and her voice rose an octave when she related how she watched Ruth Miller remove a glass bowl from the refrigerator that night to put the finishing touches on the chicken and dumpling dinner. Mom told how, with a knife, Ruth carefully pierced something in the bowl and then gently pulled at the incision with her fingers.

"She tipped the bowl," Mom said, "and opened the egg sack of a chicken. Ruth put un-hatched eggs into the soup. It nearly made me gag when I saw those things bobbing up and down in the pot."

Each time Mom told this part of the story it appeared to rouse a visceral reaction in her. She made a smacking sound with her tongue against the roof of her mouth. Her taste buds still seemed disgruntled even after all these years.

"You don't eat dead chicken's eggs. It's like eating chicken guts," Mom said, her voice reaching a shrill tone as she recounted the memory that was obviously not so easily forgotten. "'Roger, I can't eat that soup', I whispered to your father. But he knew that." Most of the time when our mother told her side of the story, she related it as, "One of your father's stupid tricks."

"I tried to tell your dad what was going on, but talking to him sometimes is like communicating with a tree. He said he was too busy discussing the safety problems at the lumber mill to hear me. But that night the safety problems at work were of no interest to me. I was concerned about how to get out of eating that soup."

"I didn't hear you, Pearl, honest."

"Well, how come as soon as we sat at the table, you said, 'Oh, look, Pearl, little eggs. Did you ever see such little eggs before?'" Mom usually said this with as much sarcasm as she could manage. "Then you said, 'Let me give you some soup, Pearl.' I could have killed you. You gave me four of those eggs, and one of them had a red spot in it. It was fertile and supposed to grow up to be a baby chick. And you gave it to me."

Dad knew Mom wouldn't like the idea of eating those eggs. She had been raised to eat everything on her plate, especially when a guest at someone's table. At home, she cooked only what she wanted to eat and even though she was not a fussy eater, when they went out to a friend's house, she forced herself to eat everything, no matter how bad it tasted or what it was.

"And you didn't even have one of those things. Did you?"

"Yes, I did," Dad insisted.

"Then you pointed at them and said, 'Aren't they cute?' Roger, you're a pain in the neck."

It's never clear to my sisters and I what prompts the telling of something that happened so many years ago. I wonder if love is a memory that longs to be remembered. Does it slip back and forth through time? Does it squeeze out into the muddied present with remembered tastes, bits of humor and memories of moments so bitter and sweet that its retelling brings a strange longing? Did this story give our parents a brief respite from the ugliness that had grown around them?

Mom was exhausted by the time they arrived home. She has said many times that when she and Dad fought, the energy drained from her body like water from a spigot.

"I told you I was sorry," Dad said as they pulled into the driveway. The vision of them on a cold winter night is clearly embedded in my imagination as they turned onto the driveway that ended at the entrance to their little rented home in the country.

Dad always told us what a good-looking mother we had and that seeing her angry upset him. As very young children we remember seeing Mom and Dad kiss, or take time out for a quick embrace as Dad passed through the kitchen while Mom worked over the sink, peeling vegetables or washing the dishes. There were other times my sisters and I giggled when Mom sat on Dad's lap and whispered in his ear. These affectionate images have stayed with me.

As this story of when my parents were once a young couple nearly comes to a close, I imagine Dad putting an arm around our mother's shoulder after she got out of the car and that he kissed her on the forehead. I wonder did he softly say, "I'm sorry, sweetheart. I didn't mean to upset you." Mom never says anything about what Dad whispered to her that night. What she tells us is that when she went into the house, she walked around in the bedroom looking for more frogs in Dad's socks. Then remembering the little eggs floating around in the broth, she wondered how she had been able to swallow the soup. But, what was really on her mind when they got home that night was the draft notice. She knew it was going to be impossible to let go of her husband at the train station in two days.

Over the years, my sisters and I have patched together the bits and pieces of our parents' love story. We want to believe they were once in love. And I want to believe that as Mom unbuttoned her blouse that night, our father, a large framed man who towered over his young wife, came into the room, smiled, and said, "Let me help you with that." He had huge hands and his fingers were coarse and cold. They were always coarse, always cold, and it is easy to imagine they sent chills up our mother's soft girl's back. Mom, small framed and delicate, appeared petite standing next to Dad's strong, tall physic. She was such a fragile looking woman that it was easy to imagine she had hollow bones like a bird. Once, while Mom hung up bed sheets on the clothesline in the backyard, it looked as though she might blow away in the wind as the sheets billowed out around her like the sails on a ship.

Mom said Dad apologized that night for the frog in the sock, for the soup, and for anything else he thought she might be angry with him about. Between Dad's story about what happened that night and what Mom has related, Dad said, "When Sam told me what they were going to make for dinner, I didn't think you'd get that angry. You know Sam and Ruth are from the backwoods. They were simply being neighborly. They didn't mean anything by it. Maybe I didn't help things out too much. You forgive me? Please?"

Dad knew she would. She always did, though in the years to come, less and less forgiveness would be forthcoming. But Mom wanted to know, "Why do you have to play jokes so much?"

To Dad, jokes were fun and he had a hard time not pulling a prank. "When your mom and I were first together," he once said, "she liked my jokes. That might have even been what attracted us to one another. She said my joking made her laugh." But over the years Dad's jokes became mean-spirited and no one thought they were funny.

Mom said once he stopped apologizing that night, he kissed the top of her head. "He always did love my hair," she said. "Your dad said it reminded him of kitten fur. He was always touching and smelling it."

My sisters and I remembered, too, our father kissing the top of Mom's head. He sometimes stood next to her for the longest time, hugging her with his nose in her hair. It never made any sense to us why a grown man stood around smelling a woman's head.

Mom didn't tell this part of the story until my sisters and I were grown women, and by then Dad had been dead almost ten years. "That night he told me the secret about those horrible eggs." Until then, the egg story had only been a trick Dad had played on Mom. "He said, 'You know what those eggs were really for, don't you? They're supposed to keep the fire burning between us, so we can make more babies. Or, at least, keep trying to make them.'"

"I don't know how he did it," Mom said. "One minute he made me so angry I could kill him and the next minute I loved him again."

When we talk about the frog in the sock and those eggs floating around in the chicken soup, we don't talk about my parents as a young couple separating during wartime. We seem to be listening to a story about the tricks Dad played. But after Dad passed, Mom changed its telling slightly. She said, "That night your dad promised never to upset me again and that all he wanted was to make me happy. There were lots of promises. He was going to be a changed man." Mom sighed. "I'm sure he meant every word."

That night as they walked into the bedroom, something fell off the chair. Mom jumped back. She thought it might have been another frog trick. Dad looked at the garment on the bedroom floor and grinned a little. Mom grinned too, hesitantly at first, then said, "What am I going to do without you?" They both laughed. It was a nervous laugh. Mom said that if she had not laughed that night when they got home from the Millers, there would have been rivers of tears. I'm sure Dad must have been relieved to see his wife was no longer angry with him. Mom said the days were horrible before our father left for boot camp. She tried to memorize Dad's smells, his touch, and the feel of his chest against her cheek. That night she softly said, "I don't want you to go." "Shhhh," the young husband replied.

He must have felt Mom's tears on his chest as they lay together that night. But he did not break the quiet and tell her not to cry, or not to worry about him. He did not tell her that he could take care of himself. He did not tell her that everything would be all right. Instead, I wonder, did he kiss her hair?

The Recipe

SOCKS FALLEN, DRESSES FLAPPING, KNEES grimy with play-ground dirt, Pearl's daughters skipped around the kitchen table, singing. "We're going to have a picnic at school tomorrow. We're going to have a picnic at school tomorrow."

Wilma, her oldest, stopped in front of Pearl and asked, "Can we take something?"

"No," Pearl said. "We don't have food to give away." Pearl could not remember when the pantry was full or when the family did not have to brace against leaner times. "But I promised," Wilma said with a slightly pompous tone that demanded an explanation from her mother. Pearl knew no explanation would be good enough.

"Me, too," chimed in Jenny, the younger of the two. Jenny was the one who laughed the most easily and frequently mimicked her older sister's critical stance.

"Why not?" Wilma wanted to know.

"Pleeeeasssse," Jenny said, stretching out the word, long and thin.

"C'mon, Momma," Wilma insisted.

The two little girls took turns begging their mother to change her mind.

Pearl hated telling her daughters "no" so often. Looking at their pleading faces, Pearl's heart felt squeezed. "You can't go making promises," Pearl said. "Didn't I tell you to ask me first? Didn't I? Well, didn't I?" Pearl drove the words into the little girls, as if pounding nails into wood.

"But why?" Jenny asked, scratching a mosquito bite on the back of her left leg.

"Because I've got nothing here to make, that's why." Pearl sighed. "Stop this yammering. Go outside and do your chores."

Jenny began to cry. Her tears came as quickly as her smile. "Please, make something, or we'll be the only kids who don't bring anything." Jenny rubbed her eyes with grimy little fists leaving a faint dirty smudge circling one eye.

A tight clamping sensation crawled across Pearl's forehead. "I'm sorry," Pearl said. "We just don't have anything in the house to spare." Saying these words sucked the energy from Pearl, leaving an emptiness so deep it could never be filled. "Now go outside," Pearl said sternly. "And bring the clothes in off the line, then give the dog fresh water. Go on, get out of here and let me fix dinner."

Jenny and Wilma stood in front of their mother, hands dangling helplessly at their sides. All signs of happiness were gone. Their pleading echoed in Pearl's head. They didn't understand. Pearl had no comforting words for her daughters, only excuses.

When her daughters left the kitchen, Pearl began to prepare dinner. A large gunnysack of potatoes lay slumped against the side of the refrigerator like a dead body waiting for disposal. Pearl took an armload of potatoes from the sack, carried them to the sink and began to prepare the evening meal. Every night they had potatoes. They had them fried, boiled, or mashed with flour gravy. Many nights, they were made into a thin watery potato soup. Pearl cooked potatoes every which way possible in order to stretch it out to make a meal.

Even when Pearl was a little girl, barely tall enough to reach the sink, her mother called, "Pearl, come peel the potatoes for me. It's almost suppertime." And Pearl had been peeling them ever since.

Watching her daughters from the kitchen window, something about them reminded Pearl of her own childhood. The expressions on their young faces were so easily read. They had not yet learned to hide their feelings, and emotions slipped across their faces as if they stood naked in front of their mother.

Pearl knew these bothersome memories that were coming back were remembrances of a childhood that would not let her rest. Lately, she had begun to sound a lot like her own mother. "Where are those legs coming from?" Pearl heard herself say to Wilma the other day, just the way her mother had said years ago when Pearl was about Wilma's age. These memories were burdensome. Pearl had not wanted this kind of life. She had wanted to be a nurse, to travel, to move to a big city and go to parties.

Pearl went to the refrigerator and took out the slab of bacon that had been bartered for with eggs from the chickens that they kept. The piece of freshly cured meat smelled strong of smoldering wood and brine. Cutting the pork into small chunks, Pearl's thoughts of her past slid across her mind like clouds drifting along a never-ending horizon. Pearl lived a solitary life. The distance between the farmhouses wasn't what made everyone seem so far away, but it was the prickly and tangled isolation that had sprung up around her. These remembrances were not welcomed, but they were burdensome.

Chopping an onion, Pearl remembered as a little girl never having a new dress to wear. Classmates teased her because the hand-me-downs usually were poorly fitting, faded, and frequently patched. Some kids in school, the ones whose parents' owned the farms where Pearl's father worked, pointed and said she looked poor, making her always feel like an outsider among other school children.

Onions made Pearl's eyes burn and tear. "I sure as hell hate onions." She sighed. Dumping the wet potato slices into the hot pan with the onions, the bacon sizzled and spat out a stinging spray of grease.

Stirring the potatoes to coat them with the bacon grease, Pearl tried to recall faces of friends from school. Scraping the browning potatoes and onions from the bottom of the pan, not one face came to mind. When the potato slices turned a rich pan-fried brown, Pearl knew they were done and it was time to call the family in to dinner. Everyone moved about in the kitchen, washing hands and scuffing chairs across the floor, while Pearl broke several eggs over the potato and onion mixture. Stirring the mixture until the eggs stuck firmly to the potatoes, Pearl turned off the stove.

Jenny and Wilma sat quietly at the table. They picked at the dinner on their plates.

Roger, their father, came in and sat at his usual spot at the head of the table by the window where he looked out, nervously watching, watching. He was a big man with giant hands that swallowed the fork as he picked it up. He was never happy and meal times were especially miserable for everyone. Pearl dreaded them because if there was going to be trouble it always happened at the evening meal. That was the time for discipline, lecturing, and complaining. Something was always wrong. Her husband's booming voice rattled the dishes, and no one said a word once he got started.

Pearl waited for her daughters to talk about the school picnic. But they said nothing. Everyone ate in silence, as if the food in their mouths absorbed their words.

Roger quickly ate his meal and then went back to his workshop in the barn. Wilma and Jenny went to their bedroom to do homework. Pearl, left alone, cleared the dinner dishes. Potato peels were put into a pot to cook with the table scraps; this was the dog's food.

As Pearl stirred the mixture on the stove, an idea came to her. She could make a potato salad for her daughter's school picnic. It would be easy enough to prepare the mayonnaise herself. All the fixings: oil, eggs, and vinegar, were in the pantry. Glancing down at the gunny-sack leaning against the side of the refrigerator, Pearl knew there were definitely enough potatoes.

Opening the door to Jenny and Wilma's bedroom, Pearl said, "I thought of something you can take to the picnic tomorrow." Pearl want-ed to wipe away the disappointment from their faces the same way the grease had been cleaned from the pots and pans earlier that evening. Looking up from a lesson book, Wilma grinned broadly. The grin, al-most mischievous, seemed to be saying, "I knew you could do it."

Jenny let out a squeal and jumped up and down on the bed. The second grade reader bounced several times on the mattress and then fell onto the floor with a plop.

Pearl returned to the kitchen ready to prepare the potatoes for the salad. Even though a love-hate relationship had grown up between Pearl and the potato, the vegetable was always prepared with respect to keep in the flavor. That meant when boiling the potatoes Pearl did not peel them. So, the potatoes were scrubbed clean, put into a pot of cold water, and carried to the stove. While the potatoes cooked, Pearl began the mayonnaise by breaking several eggs into a bowl.

Lately, the memories that tumbled into Pearl's mind were both-ersome. They came of their own accord, scrambled images and in-cidents, each vying for immediate recognition. Pearl beat the eggs furiously. It seemed a hundred years since marrying Roger. The past came rushing quickly as she cautiously drizzled the vinegar onto the eggs. Pearl had just turned seventeen when Roger suggested they elope. Pearl mused that her young self thought she knew it all back then. Drop by drop, the vegetable oil was added to the egg mixture.

Roger was handsome, strong and energetic when they first met. Drop by drop, the oil disappeared into the eggs as Pearl beat the ingredients against the bowl with a fork. Roger and Pearl had both been full of dreams back then.

I thought he was Prince Charming.

They had only known each other three months when they married and Pearl wanted the honeymoon to last forever. But the world came crashing down around Pearl a year later when Roger was drafted into the Army. She wanted to die when he went off to boot camp. Perhaps something *had* died that day, because nothing was the same when he returned home. Pearl furiously beat the eggs until the mixture turned thick and creamy.

* * * *

Roger came home after the war a changed man. Depressed, he drank beer and whiskey all day, claiming it calmed his nerves. He whimpered in his sleep and often woke up soaked with sweat. One night, Pearl was startled awake with Roger screaming that his arm had been cut off. But the arm had been thrown over the edge of the bed and had fallen asleep.

Roger was angry at everything. Nothing pleased him, and he never again let Pearl into his world. Pearl was pushed farther away as her husband grew more brittle and aloof. He floated in and out of family events like an apparition, only coming into the house to sleep or eat. Life sure can play tricks on you, Pearl sighed, as she beat the last drop of oil into the eggs.

Pearl pierced one of the potatoes with a fork. They were done, and she took them off the stove, drained them and then put the pot aside to cool.

Memories continued to pour out at her from everywhere. They no longer came from inside Pearl, but the memories were now coming from the eggs, the bowl, and they were even coming from her hands.

Memories dripped down the walls, leaving dark, dirty stains as they slipped to the floor. She remembered feeling heartsick when Roger came home and pushed her out of his world. Her husband had made too many promises, and she had too many broken dreams. What a life, she thought. What's the use of it all? Pearl chopped the onions fiercely, ignoring the stinging fumes. She diced the bacon into little pieces and threw those into the hot frying pan. The pan soon glistened from the sizzling bacon grease. Pearl tried her best, but Roger was always angry with her. What had gone wrong?

They had enjoyed a few sweet moments when Roger first came home, but those times were ruined by the drunken furies and sullen, moody shadows that began to settle everywhere.

The onions sizzled and turned translucent. Slowly the snapping grease calmed to a simmer. In the momentary quiet, Pearl realized she had married someone who, like her old classmates, taunted and teased her. Pearl's husband now made her run for cover inside herself.

As Pearl put the food away in the refrigerator, she wondered why life had gotten so complicated; two children, two stillbirths, and now Roger had hurt his back and could no longer hold onto a job. *All I do,* she thought, *is piece myself together from scraps; nothing is easy, nothing sure, except making do with leftovers. Why do I keep trying?* She slammed the refrigerator door closed.

The children were asleep. Roger had come into the house earlier and without saying a word to her, went straight to bed. There were no sounds in the kitchen now except for the noisy memories that crashed about inside Pearl's head, memories that clung like babies at her breasts, sucking hungrily.

Sitting at the kitchen table, the house heavy with smells of the evening's cooking, Pearl realized her entire life had been spent waiting for her turn to come.

If I weren't so damn patient and good at making do with nothing, would I have put up with this life?

Pearl wanted answers. But any reason for why her life had turned out the way it had remained elusive. Any answers and reasons why life for Pearl had turned out as it had, floated away like steam and she yearned for something misplaced by time.

I've told Wilma and Jenny they have to learn to live with being poor, but what I really want to tell them is, "Run. Run as fast as you can to keep from caging yourselves the way I have." Maybe they're smarter than I am and won't put up with as much as I have.

Pearl sighed heavily, turned out the kitchen light and made her way to the bedroom.

Slipping under the covers, she lay next to Roger. Her husband no longer cried out in the night. That had stopped several years ago. Now he slept like a dead man, comatose, resentful of the living. The touch of his body made her angry. Pearl wondered where she'd be if Roger had not come into her life when she was so eager to believe that dreams could come true.

He had promised Pearl that she could go to nursing school after the war, after the babies. Now Pearl knew it would never happen. She did not want Jenny and Wilma to do what she had done, to hope for tomorrow, waiting, until one day they realized that they had waited all their lives, chained by elusive hopes.

At breakfast the next morning, Pearl watched Jenny and Wilma hum and chatter, as they got ready for school. She beat the mayonnaise back into its creamy consistency then poured the mixture over the sliced potatoes. With a large wooden spoon she folded the potatoes over each other, making sure they were well coated with the mayonnaise. The salad was given one last stir and it was ready for the school picnic.

Earlier that morning, Pearl had asked Roger to take Wilma and Jenny to school, with the salad. Roger grumbled, his face strained and tight but agreed. They did not really live together; they simply bumped into each other and, from time to time, occupied the same space.

Roger had lost another job, and Pearl knew her husband would spend the day fiddling with machinery in his workshop. Roger had no intention of looking for work today. As Pearl's family drove off with the potato salad, Pearl mumbled, "It's pathetic." But being able to send Jenny and Wilma to school with the salad made life feel a little better, even if it was like a speck of light in the thick dark cloud that Pearl lived in.

That afternoon, Wilma and Jenny came rushing into the house after school. They burst through the door and waved notes in front of Pearl's face.

"Here, this is for you. It's from my teacher," Jenny said, eager for her mother to take her note first.

"This is from my teacher, too. Read it, read it," Wilma said, and pushed her note into Pearl's hand.

Pearl took the notes and read each slowly. One note read, "Dear Mrs. Wilson, The potato salad you sent to school was the best I have ever tasted. Could you please give me your recipe? Very truly yours, Mrs. Curtis."

Pearl read the other note. "Would you please give me your recipe."

Pearl looked at Jenny and Wilma. They appeared charged with electricity as they jumped up and down and fidgeted.

"No one else got notes about their mother's cooking," Jenny said and watched her mother place the notes on the table.

Pearl smiled at Jenny. "But it's so simple to make. What's the big deal? It was only potatoes. Did you kids have a good time in school today?"

Pearl didn't wait for them to answer. "Go change your clothes. Then go out and do your chores."

Wilma and Jenny darted off chirping like happy baby birds. Once her daughters left the room, Pearl picked up the notes and read them again. They weighed nothing, yet there was a heaviness about them that could not be explained. Though she tried several times, the recipe was never written down and given to the teachers. Something always interrupted her. There was cooking, cleaning and it was time to harvest the garden and then there had been the canning that needed to be done.

Then one day, Pearl put the notes from the teachers into a shoebox tucked away in the back of her closet. Just as she had stored away her hope, she put the notes in a safe place, as if they were something to save, like a remnant of cloth. Pearl put them in the same place where Mother's Day cards, the frayed and brittle marriage license, and the hospital prints of baby feet were stored. These treasures were not so much to be remembered, as they were not to be forgotten.

Chicken Noodle Soup

GRANDMA WAS SHORT AND SHAPED like a dumpling. Sitting on Grandma's lap was like sinking into the perfume of this lovely old woman's life. She smelled of gardening, cooking, cleaning, regular church going, and mothballs—and there was even a faint aroma of Lava soap on those wrinkled hands when she brushed a lock of unruly hair from my forehead. The smells were welcomed, and they soothed my childhood.

Grandma was born into a family of German Mennonite missionaries who had moved to Russia in the late 1800's. Grandma told stories of villages burned to the ground during the Russian Revolution; about soldiers on horseback riding into the village, slashing swords through the air while she hid under the kitchen table. In one story Grandma was looking out from under a long lace tablecloth to see an uncle fighting, using a hoe against a soldier wielding a saber. This might have been one of the uncles who immigrated to Canada with her family, but she wasn't certain. The funny thing is that Grandma's stories did not always end the same way each time she told them. My sisters and I were the love of her life, but she hated our father. Dad was a Catholic. She could not accept the interfaith marriage and refused to give Mom and Dad permission to marry, causing them to elope. Grandma never forgave Dad for secretly whisking away our mom.

Grandma believed that only those who practiced the right religion went to heaven, and that Dad was going to hell because he was a Catholic. Fearful that Mom might sign a paper committing my sisters and me to a Catholic upbringing, Grandma said she prayed for our souls every night. Grandpa on the other hand, an easygoing, even-tempered man, only wanted our mother to be happy. He did not have strong convictions about who entered heaven and behaved civilly to his son-in-law. Eventually, Grandpa went deaf.

Dad told us it was Grandma's constant nagging that caused Grandpa's ears to naturally close up so that he wouldn't have to listen to all of Grandma's miserable words.

Besides being devoutly religious, Grandma was an ardent cook. She particularly enjoyed baking and making soups. I remember when she began writing a cookbook. The recipe cards, scattered across the kitchen counter for days and weeks, became speckled with batter and lightly dusted in flour as she tested and retested the recipes.

About this time, Grandma began to change, slipping German words into a conversation. No one seemed too upset or bothered by this. After all, she was translating into English recipes handed down from her German-speaking mother.

When we went to our grandparent's on Sunday, my sisters and I got to decide what Grandma would make for dinner. We always wanted chicken noodle soup. Dad, a meat and potatoes man hated Grandma's chicken soup. He especially did not like the noodles. But Grandma cooked to please my sisters and I, not our father.

So every time we went to Grandma's, we had chicken noodle soup. Every time we came home from Grandma's, Dad immediately took a couple antacid tablets, complaining how upsetting Grandma's cooking was to his stomach. Years later it became clear to me that Dad's heartburn was not from the soup, but from Grandma. Looking back, in my opinion, this may have been Grandma's only fault. If anything rang true in my life, and if I had to swear to its reality, that touchstone would undoubtedly have been Grandma's chicken noodle soup.

Sipping and nibbling on my memories, the odor of that soup, that simple concoction of water, fowl, and vegetables still resonates even after sixty-plus years. Grandma started this soup with the careful feeding of the chickens that lived in the coop in my grandparent's backyard. This flock of egg layers was fed quality seeds, grains, and the better table scraps. Grandma never went quickly into their coop, but approached the birds cautiously. Chickens should not be unduly excited, Grandma told us. A nervous chicken has trouble laying eggs and the meat turns tough. Knowing already what my sisters and I would request for Sunday dinner, Grandma went out to the coop and selected a dinner chicken. It was always an older hen that had stopped laying eggs. Grandma said these wise old chickens tasted the best. It always struck me as odd that Grandma thought wisdom had a flavor.

Grandma killed the chickens for our dinner. One, two, three and she chopped the head off with a startling exactness of her hatchet. It happened so suddenly that the beheading seemed like a natural demise of the chicken. I never associated death with this soup. Somehow, it felt as though these chickens willingly laid down their lives for the sake of Grandma's cooking.

The headless chicken was then plunged into boiling water to loosen the feathers so they could be removed more easily. Once in a while, my sisters and I helped to pull off the feathers. The chicken was hot and steam billowed up from it's body now covered in sloppy soggy feathers. The trick was to yank at the feathers quickly enough so as not to burn our fingers. Grandma taught us to grab and yank, grab and yank, until the chicken was a silly looking, skinny, naked bird.

Once the chicken had been plucked free of feathers, the next job was to remove the wispy covering of fine hair that grew out of the bird's bumpy skin. In order to remove this hair, Grandma rolled up a piece of newspaper, set it on fire, and ran it up and down the chicken's body. To this day, the smell of singed hair tickles my memory and I think of Grandma's chicken soup.

There was one part of preparing the chicken that was ugly. And my sisters and I never watched this. Grandma put the bird on the kitchen counter heavily lined with newspaper. At that point we left the room. When we returned back to the kitchen, all the innards had been taken out and neatly wrapped in the newspaper. The chicken, now hollow, lay on the counter breast-side down with its tail sticking straight up.

With one quick chop of a kitchen clever, Grandma hacked off the feet. They were scrubbed clean, and thrown into a pot of scalding hot water. The chicken was then cut into soup-sized pieces and put into a large soup pot filled with water. When Grandma thought the feet were clean enough to eat, she added them to the soup pot.

As sure as life brings changes, as sure as young becomes old, Grandma's mind stopped working properly. She no longer remembered who we were and most of the time mistook my sisters and me for our mother. No longer recognizing Dad as the demonic man who had taken our mom to the "evil altar" of the Catholics, Grandma talked to him as if no problem ever existed between them. Dad, not trusting his mother-in-law, wondered what tricks she would play on him next. But the tricks never came.

One night, I heard Dad say to Mom, "I think we've got to talk to your father about your mother."

My sisters and I were most likely not supposed to hear this, though when words are spoken in a lowered, discreet voice, children listen more intently. Or perhaps Dad's voice rose just a slight bit higher as he might have taken some pleasure in what he was about to propose.

"Your father can't take care of your mother anymore," Dad said to Mom. "She's unable to do anything for herself. The minute he leaves her alone, that woman goes into the kitchen to cook, leaving pots burning on the stove while she watches the TV. One of these days she's liable to burn the house down and kill them both." Dad said this very quickly and then waited.

Mom lit a cigarette. The flame from the match betrayed eyes that glistened with tears. "I know," Mom said. "She doesn't know who I am anymore." Then, in a voice so low it was barely audible, Mom said, "She got old so fast."

My parents often sat at the kitchen table talking about serious, grown-up things. As a child it was impossible for me to understand what grown-ups had so much to talk about. They appeared to do little else but work and talk.

Becoming an adult did not seem appealing, but it was while eavesdropping on these kitchen-table discussions that my sisters and I learned that something quite serious was wrong with Grandma. We no longer had chicken soup dinners. And Grandma's last batch of cookies tasted terrible. They were hard, like plaster. We couldn't even bite into them. So we licked at their salty crust, pretending to chew. Grandma didn't seem to know the difference. We giggled and put the rock-hard treats behind our backs, leaving the kitchen, careful not to let Grandma see the uneaten cookies. When we got outside, we laughed thinking it was all great fun.

Grandma began to act oddly in other ways, too. Grandpa had to watch her all the time to make sure she didn't hurt herself. Life was very difficult for him. She tried to sneak out of the house one evening while he was cooking their dinner. He had to force her back into the house and she was mad as a hornet at him.

Several days later Grandma whispered to me, "That man won't let me go anyplace by myself. What's the matter with him? I'm going back to my mother if he doesn't stop it."

I didn't know what to say. These situations frightened my sisters and I; frightened us in a way that we could not explain. But we no longer giggled when Grandma did silly things.

Then Grandma refused to feed herself. She spanked the mashed potatoes with a spoon, pushed the vegetables off the edge of the dish, and neatly tucked them under her plate. "I'm finished," she declared. At that point there was a lot of whispering. Grandma was wearing diapers by then, and my sisters and I heard that our grandma was doing other strange things, too, though we never learned what they were.

When Grandma stopped eating entirely, everyone agreed that Grandpa could no longer take care of his wife. Everyone agreed that the situation had become very serious. Dad stood beside our mom holding her hand. Several times we saw him gently wipe tears from Mom's face. All the battles once fought between Mom and Grandma had been slipped into a pocket of memory.

About this time, Dad, the thorn in Grandma's side, took charge. It all came about one night at the dinner table. Grandpa had gotten a neighbor to sit with Grandma while he came to our house along with Mom's brother and his wife. They sat around the kitchen table with coffee and cigarettes, talking intensely.

My sisters and I, watching television in an adjoining room, only heard part of the conversation. But we understood, well enough, that they had decided to put Grandma into a nursing home.

As the grownups sat around the kitchen table, Dad said he had talked to a few people, visited a couple of places and had found a home that seemed pretty good. Grandpa sat with his back to us. He lowered his shiny bald head, looking down at the floor almost the entire time the plans were being made. His shoulders sagged as though the air was slowly being let out of him.

As the evening went on, Grandpa appeared to get smaller and smaller, until it looked as if he might disappear.

"Grandma's going to be living in a good place," Mom said. And she promised that when our grandma was settled, we'd all go visit her.

Once Grandma had moved, Dad went to see his mother-in-law every other day, he said, to make sure she was being properly cared for. One night, Dad said to Mom, "She wouldn't let go of my arm and kept saying over and over, 'I want to go home. Please, take me home.' It was upsetting to see your mother like that. Over the years she's sure been hell on wheels, but nobody deserves to go out like that."

Mom said nothing, but sat very still, watching the smoke of a cigarette trailing into nothing. For the first time I saw how much Mom looked like her mother; the sharp, thin eyebrows, the hard strong lines of a thin mouth, a soft billowing of lines forming under the chin. Looking at my mother, Grandma's eyes reflected back at me.

* * * *

We never got to visit Grandma in her new place, and we never again tasted Grandma's chicken noodle soup. She died the next month. Yet the memory of all those lovely bits of food from my childhood that she prepared, float about haphazardly in my brain. The cookies, gingerbread, iced sugar cookies; rich jam filled butter cookies, they all swirl around in my memory as I faintly hear my grandma whispering her recipes to me. But it is not only the odor of the baking cookies or the simmering soup that linger in my memory. It was how lovingly Grandma prepared everything, even the noodles for the chicken soup. They were broad, thick, chewy noodles that tasted somewhere between a dumpling and pasta.

There was comfort slurping and chewing one of Grandma's noodles. Though it wasn't just comforting. There was a reassurance in those noodles, reassurance about Grandma's unconditional love for my sisters and me. The remembrance of Grandma's chicken noodle soup has become like a spice that lingers at the back of my throat, hauntingly present, never overpowering, infusing my life with a savory memory.

If I Die Before I Wake

FROM THE BACKYARD, MY SISTER Jenny and I could see a dairy farm with black and white cows, a forest where we picked wild purple irises with bright yellow tongues, and the home of a quiet family that Dad was always in a dispute with over the property line. In the backyard, we marveled at Mom's monster dahlias with blooms as big as supper plates.

Behind the dahlia garden, Brownie, our watchdog, spent his life chained to a fir tree.

Between our house and Mom's dahlia garden, grew a giant flowering Japanese quince bush, a project Dad started from a twig. It exploded every spring with millions of little purple flowers. Off to one side of the backyard, strategically positioned like a sentinel, stood our outhouse.

In the farthest corner of the backyard, on the border of our land and the quiet neighbor, a maple thicket grew with long branches jutting out like feather fans from a cluster of rotting stumps. The branches parted at one edge of the thicket, leaving an opening just big enough for Jenny and me to squeeze through. Inside the thicket, the ground, soft and sunken like a huge bird nest, made a space sufficiently large for us to sit. Everything was exactly the right size. Jenny and I sat in this thicket for hours, our magical hideout of leaves, branches and secrets.

From this hiding place, we spied on Mom as she hung the wash or picked the dead leaves from her dahlias. A thin woman, Mom always looked as though she carried a load equal to her own weight, either the laundry, one of our two younger sisters, or the bushels of vegetables she dragged in from the garden for canning. She worked like an ant, always dragging, lifting, or pushing something.

The dahlias were a different matter. Mom actually tiptoed into the garden. Jenny thought Mom did this to be quiet. But Mom said this was to keep from packing down the soil. Once she lifted a blossom slowly, cupping the giant flower in both hands, bringing it close to her, as though looking into a face. Then she smiled as though she intended to kiss the bloom. Sometimes our mother talked to the dahlias. Jenny never saw this and said that Mom wouldn't talk to flowers. My sister may have been right; Mom did not have time to spend talking to flowers. Our mother hardly had time to talk to us girls.

Dad seldom wandered into the backyard. Though we knew he ventured there once in a while to feed one of his special concoctions to the quince bush. Mostly, we heard him, rather than saw him, as he chopped down trees or drove the tractor preparing the garden soil for Mom's vegetable garden. And we heard him when he fed his one-legged pet crow, Mitsy.

The crow became one of Dad's experiments after he cut down a fir tree with a nest of baby crows cradled in a top bough. Mitsy survived the crash, but had broken a leg. Dad removed the broken leg, nursed the bird back to health, and kept the poor wild thing in a cage in his work shed. Mitsy was a noisy bird, always excited about something. The lopsided crow hobbled and flopped around in the cage all day while Dad went about his business. From our hideout, we sometimes heard Mitsy's shrill cawing gobble-gobble sound as Dad poked raw hamburger down her throat at feeding time.

Jenny and I never fought when we were in our hideout. We took turns cooking twigs and leaves and serving what we called princesses dinners. Jenny, younger than me by fourteen months, usually let me be the boss. In our hideout, things were different; Jenny could be the strong and powerful Queen, or Jenny could be the mother bossing me around, or we could both be lost children, huddled together, trying to outwit the wicked witch in the gingerbread house.

The air inside our retreat smelled sweet with the juicy bark of twigs, dusty leaves, dead bugs, and rotting stumps. These odors became a perfume that made us feel welcomed. These smells became our private air.

When Jenny and I grew older—or maybe it began to happen when we both had gone through a growth spurt and kept bumping our heads on the low branches of the thicket—our interest in the secret hideaway made us feel like intruders and we became bored with our make believe world. So we abandoned the hideout, and our younger sisters took command of the retreat. We saw them poke their heads out through the branches, watching Jenny and me as we walked down the road to run errands for Mom.

By the time we left the thicket, its odor still lingering in our hair, with long skinny legs and low-slung, gangly arms, Jenny and I looked more like spider creatures from the woods than girls. We walked away from our childhood and headed toward our father's world. He lived in a dark scary place. He listened to the news on the radio every night, informing us of every detail. The world had become embroiled in a cold war, he said. There were no actual shots fired. "That," he told us, "is just a matter of time."

One world leader banged his shoe on a table in a demonstration of his dissatisfaction during a major meeting. He threatened to set off a chain reaction of devastation, something that the world would never recover from. Dad convinced his family that the world would blow up. And Jenny and I, in our premenstrual, pre-acne, and post childhood phase, began to worry that we might not make it to our sixteenth birthdays.

Every night during dinner our father told us all the frightening details of what he heard on the radio.

"It is inevitable," he said. "The Atomic War is coming."

My throat clamped tight and I could not swallow my food. Part of what Dad talked about frightened us, while a more trusting part of me thought *Relax, so you have a crazy father, who doesn't!*

Then one night at the supper table, Dad announced, "We're building a bomb shelter." At that point, our father put our family into a life-and-death struggle with the world. One night he would say, "We may be the only survivors." Then several nights later, he said with a reassuring tone, "We won't be the only survivors. Other families are building shelters, too."

He made it all sound so frighteningly logical, though I wondered; how would we get together with these other families after the bomb?

Would we just get in a car and drive away?

Dad mistrusted everybody. He had always been at odds with one person or other—bosses on the job, in-laws, the neighbors, and now he was in a battle with world powers. The troubles in the world had pushed Dad over the edge of his already low tolerance for anxiety, into a place teeming with danger and terrible evil.

I believe he sincerely wanted to survive after the world had been blown apart. That way our father could start humankind over the way he thought it should be. It was difficult to fathom why he wanted to take his noisy kids with him. Honestly, wouldn't he have really wanted to leave his family to the bomb and start the world over by himself?

But Dad promised us life after total destruction. That frightened me. I could not imagine what the world might look like after the bomb. Jenny and I wanted nothing to do with getting home from school in time to have the massive door slammed shut, trapping us forever in a fallout shelter with Dad as its only leader.

However, I found a positive side, thinking about being a rare survivor when the world blew up. After all, the kids who gave me trouble in school were probably going to meet their end when the bomb went off because their fathers were not as crazy as ours. Their fathers had no plans to build them a bomb shelter to save their behinds. I imagined their arrogant bodies melted away forever, while our family sat in a shelter with Dad's promise of a high rate of survival. Kids like my sisters and I, with our nutty fathers, were going to populate the next world.

As the cold war accelerated, so did Dad's plans. He designed the shelter himself, he said, "To keep anyone from knowing what I'm doing." Fearful his shelter was going to be invaded by frantic mobs during zero hour, as the bomb melted all that had been known to humankind, he swore us to secrecy. With an ashen face, he told us over and over not to tell a soul what he had begun to build.

Dad worked frantically pulling together his plans. The shelter needed to be completed as quickly as possible. Dad decided on a location in the backyard. The fallout shelter was going to be constructed between the outhouse and the maple thicket.

Much to my disappointment, we were going to have a bomb shelter before indoor plumbing!

Dad used to say, "What good is indoor plumbing if you get your butt blown off." So every time I walked to the outhouse, with its ragged spider webs, flies that made zigzag sounds, and its unforgettable smells, instead of looking at the maple thicket and remembering peaceful play times, I trod past my impending doom.

One day Dad brought home a chemical toilet as though it were a toy to delight in. He took it out of the box, placed it next to the refrigerator, and invited Jenny and me to sit on it. "Try it on for size," he said, grinning. He seemed to be having fun with this business of the world's ultimate destruction, while I thought I would rather die than have to use that thing in the shelter with everyone watching.

Then early one morning a bulldozer and backhoe arrived on our property. All day the workmen scraped and dug deep into the earth until they had dug a giant hole in our backyard for the shelter. It was an ugly, ominous gaping pit where I fantasized Dad would throw his wife and kids.

After that it didn't take long before our father set out to build the frame for the shelter in that hole. With Mom as his helper, they lifted, shoved and pulled rough timber planks for the frame, and then dragged the steel cables for reinforcement back and forth across the yard. Mom did not appear to be frightened like Dad. Mom consented in her silence to participate in the construction of the monster being built in our backyard.

Each day, watching this project growing, Jenny and I wished this wretched thing would fall down, collapse in on itself the way we imagined the world was going to do when the bomb struck at last.

Cement trucks came and filled the bomb shelter's frame. I became constipated as Dad continued to build a wall of fear around our family. He was caught up in the madness of the times and began to act as though it was common knowledge that the world as we knew it, was coming to an end.

The first time our family went into the shelter after its completion, we descended the stairs with Dad holding a flashlight, the dead, still air, quieted by the twelve-inch-thick concrete walls. It was as though we followed our dad down into a tomb. Fear of the dark nearly overwhelmed my sense of reality, and though able to keep my fear under control, our youngest sister, desperately caught up in her imagination, ran back up the stairs, screaming.

"I saw something waiting for me," she whimpered at the dinner table that night.

Dad expected his family to live in that hellish hole, with the hope of re-establishing life after the destruction of the world. There was no doubt in my mind that every member of our family would be insane by the time we resurfaced.

Dad sank deeper into this madness and decided the best way to feed his family at the end of the world was for Mom to can the food and store it in the shelter. So, every summer for years after the structure was finished, while we waited for the end to come, Mom canned food from the garden and placed it in the shelter, feverishly stocking the larder every summer and autumn.

Jenny and I doubted that all the preserved food in the jars lining the shelves of our refuge could survive a bomb blast like the one Dad expected. Those jars, rattling and shaking, would certainly shatter during the mayhem, falling from the shelves leaving us sitting in the autumn harvests of jams, green beans, spiced pears, pickled relishes, and potted chickens, while the rest of the world melted away.

Dad continued to listen to the news in the years that followed the completion of the bomb shelter. We knew he waited for signs of when the bomb might be dropped, as though someone would give a date. About that time, Mom decided we should have indoor plumbing while we waited for the world to blow up. Dad, having nothing else to do—considering he had already built a masterpiece—agreed to begin the bathroom and with that gesture, we moved into the same time period as those around us.

But before a door was even hung on that monumental lavatory, the state highway department declared ownership of our property through eminent domain. A road was going to be built right through our home, over Dad's bomb shelter, and through everything else.

Dad fought the highway department with the same tenacity he put into building the bomb shelter. This time he got a lawyer. He gathered lots of paperwork and did everything in his power to keep the state out. In the end, Dad lost his case. The State evicted us from our land, and Dad had no choice but to abandon his hope for a better new world.

Some years later, in our new home, after I thought Dad's wounds were healed, he said, "I sure would like to have seen the looks on the faces of that demolition crew when they dug up that old bomb shelter. I'll bet she was a tough old bugger to take out." He grinned. "No, what I'd really liked to have seen," he said, "was when they ran into the hole where that outhouse used to be."

I knew he still wondered if the world would ever blow itself up. But he didn't have the energy to build another bomb shelter. Mom, out of habit, continued to can her garden crops, storing them on the back porch, and didn't plan too much further ahead than the next canning season.

And me?

Well, I made it past my sixteenth birthday. Jenny and I don't talk too much about that time anymore. But our youngest sister is still convinced there was a ghost down there that day and for decades was haunted by nightmares about what happened when we descended into that fear-provoking structure.

"If there was a ghost," I tried to reassure her, "he's sure to have been run over by the cars on the highway—the one they built over that old place."

She took little comfort in my words. "Ghosts are slippery," she said. "They can't be run over."

Anyway, it made me feel a little better thinking the highway did some good after changing the course of our dad's life.

Nash Rambler

FRANK DROVE HIS FATHER'S NASH Rambler through the intersection, neither slowing down nor looking to see if there were oncoming cars. At the same time, he changed stations on the transistor radio hanging from the rear view mirror.

"So, Wilma, you like Elvis?" Frank asked and tuned in a station with the least amount of static.

"Yeah, I like him." I said, gripping the seat as the Nash Rambler came to another intersection.

"Love me tender, love me sweet, never let me go," Frank sang along with the radio, mimicking every quivering Elvis note, even wrinkling his forehead and curling his upper lip, exactly as I had seen Elvis do on the *Ed Sullivan Show.*

Frank, a sailor on leave, was my first blind date. Joe, Frank's father, suggested we go out. My initial response was to say, no. Dad hadn't let me date in high school. I'd only been on a couple of dates since starting college and they were double dates. A blind date, and with a sailor, that was an entirely different matter. But Joe was a nice man, always a gentleman, and hopefully like father, like son. Besides, a girl's got to get her feet wet sometime. So, I agreed to go out with Frank.

As we neared the drive-in movie, about fifteen miles out of town, uneasiness came over me thinking about being alone in the car with this stranger. I had just turned nineteen, on my first blind date and wasn't sure how to act. Though there was no doubt in my mind what should not be done. Dad had pounded that into my head enough times over the years.

Dad had a very strong opinion about morals and was always going on about something; how my sisters and I should dress, how we should sit and how we should act around boys. He called all the girls in my high school "little whores" and thought all girls were up to no good, every last one, even my best friend, shy Rebecca. Dad said he could see it in her eyes that she was headed for trouble.

And according to Dad, boys and men were only interested in one thing, sex.

So now alone in the car, and with a sailor, even if the situation made me uncomfortable, I'd decided to make the best of the evening and have fun. Though leaving my car door unlocked during the movie seemed a good idea, just in case there was a need to make a hasty retreat.

As the Nash Rambler zipped through another intersection, Dad's warnings came to mind when he learned about my acceptance to the local college. I'd saved money for a year working as a power sewing machine operator after graduating high school. Then without telling Dad or Mom, a friend helped me get a position as a teacher's aide in the State School for the Deaf, to work for my room and board while attending college. Even filling out a college application remained a secret until the acceptance letter arrived.

"You don't need to go to college," my father grumbled. "Learn to cook, or take secretary classes."

Nearing the entrance to the drive-in movie, my only other date while in high school flashed disastrously in front of me. Charlie Lux, a short, plump boy, with stubby fat fingers that always had farm dirt caked under his nails asked me to the Senior Prom. All the boys in my class knew Dad wouldn't let my sisters and I date, but Charlie asked me anyway. Even though Charlie was at least three inches shorter than me, and we'd look ridiculous on the dance floor, I desperately wanted to attend the prom.

Regardless of the disappointment that I'd be going to the prom with Charlie Lux, I begged my parents to let me go. Much to my surprise, Mom and Dad gave their permission. Mom took me shopping for a prom dress and ended up purchasing a strapless, lime-green horror with a matching little lace bolero jacket, the only dress in our price range.

Frank drove the Nash Rambler into the parking lot of the drive-in. Being alone with Frank made me uneasy and made me worry that something stupid might happen, like that night after the prom, when Charlie took me out for a burger.

While we were eating our burgers, the weather outside had changed dramatically. A blustery autumn wind blew through the parking lot. The wind was so wild that at one point the skirt of my prom dress nearly flew over my head. Finally we got to the car. Charlie opened the door for me. The car seats were freezing cold. As Charlie reached the driver's side of the car, with the wind blowing his hair every which way, I took pity on him and reached across the seat and unlocked the door for him.

Most of the evening I spent pulling up the uncomfortable scratchy, strapless dress. All night it kept slipping down and I kept pulling it up. But then much to my surprise, when I leaned over to unlock the door for Charlie, that lime-green horror did not move, and my breasts slipped right out of that wretched dress with both of my girlish nipples poking out between the bolero jacket and the sharp wires of the strapless gown.

Charlie Lux's eyes nearly popped out of his head when he saw my boobies. Furious and humiliated, there was nothing else for me to do but quickly pull the dress up over my private parts. Poor Charlie looked confused. His face turned beet red, the wind still whipping his mass of hair around on the top of his head, as he stood outside in the cold seeming not to know whether or not he should get into the car.

Then once inside, Charlie fumbling with the keys, the car wouldn't start right away. He never looked at me again that evening. He focused on the steering wheel or the road in front of him, but he never once glanced in my direction. Who knows if Charlie had seen live breasts before this? Yet it wouldn't surprise me if he'd seen plenty in magazines. Even though this was an unfortunate experience, and I certainly wished it hadn't happened, in an interesting way it made me feel a new kind of power. And I certainly never told my parents what happened that night.

Tonight though would be different. There was no strapless dress to fiddle with, and my jeans and t-shirt felt comfortable and totally appropriate. The only problem was Dad's constant warnings that kept rattling around in my head. My date with Frank certainly wasn't going to be any fun if Dad's cautionary tales about the devious minds of men kept intruding.

Frank turned out to be as choosy about where he parked in the drive-in as he had been in selecting a radio station. We drove around for the longest time looking for what he called the right spot. Frank seemed to do everything with sincere deliberation, the way he rolled up the back of his collar to meet the bottom of his close-clipped hair line, the neat placement of his pack of Lucky Strike cigarettes folded into the sleeve of his freshly pressed shirt, and the way he meticulously hooked the speaker onto the window of his father's Nash Rambler.

The couple in the car next to us was kissing and that made me wonder if this would give Frank ideas. Not that Frank needed anyone to give him ideas. Glancing at the couple, I wondered what the girl's parents might think if they knew what their daughter was up to. Oh, my God, now I'd begun to sound like my father.

Frank opened the car door. "Let's get popcorn."

Walking to the snack bar, Frank held my hand. His was about the same size as mine. His felt cool. Mine was warm and clammy. The closer we got to the snack bar, the warmer his hand became. When we reached our destination, he let go of my hand; it felt cold, almost startlingly isolated from the rest of my body. "What do you want to drink?"

"A coke," I said, rubbing the palm against the leg of my jeans.

Walking back to the car, Frank carried the tray of food, occupying his hands this time. All the cars we passed by had couples in them, kissing. This made me feel tense and on guard. Why couldn't I just relax and have a good time?

The windows of the car next to us were now fogged up. The car looked empty. Music played loudly from the speaker. Then the slight vision of a head popped up in the back seat. Then it was gone again.

"Oh, shit," I said.

"What?" Frank asked.

"Nothing. I didn't say anything." I climbed into the Nash Rambler and adjusted myself in the seat. Glancing once again at the neighboring car another head popped up. Then that head disappeared, leaving only a smeary streak on the steamy window.

The music from the speaker stopped. There were a few seconds of silence, the floodlights went out and the movie screen lit up.

The size of the little Rambler made me confident that Frank and I wouldn't be able to get as involved as the couple in the car next to us. This little car didn't even have a back seat. After giving the situation some thought, it was clear to me that the Nash Rambler was the right kind of car for me.

I settled into my seat, eating popcorn and drinking my coke as the cartoons ended and the feature move, *The Birds*, began.

It didn't take us long to finish the popcorn. Frank tipped the container sideways. "All gone," he said. Then reaching over to my side of the car where the speaker had been hooked, he said, "Sounds a little muffled?" He fiddled with the speaker. "No, that's as good as we'll get it." And then as Frank moved away from the speaker, he swung his arm over onto my shoulders.

I went stiff with both excitement and fear and took his hand off my shoulder.

"No!" I snapped, putting his hand down on his lap, intending to let it go, but Frank did not release me.

"Well, at least let me hold your hand," he said, and gave my hand a gentle squeeze.

The movie opened with a beautiful blonde driving a car while two doves sat next to her in a cage on the front seat. We chuckled as the birds in the cage swayed from side to side as the woman dramatically took the curves of the twisting road.

"I wonder if birds throw up," I said.

"I don't know. Looks like they might," Frank replied. He gently rubbed the top of my hand. It was a sweet gesture that made me feel relaxed.

The woman in the movie parked her car in front of a gas station and went into a coffee shop. The patrons were talking about the crazy things that birds in the area had been doing lately. So far the blind date with Frank had gone nicely and any uneasiness I felt earlier had begun to slip away. Then, as though winged devils had fallen from the sky, birds—black birds, large birds, small nondescript birds, sea gulls—swooped down, attacking this small coastal community.

I sat up in my seat, startled. At that moment, Frank put his arm around me. "Don't worry," he said. "It's just a movie."

At first, instinct dictated to take his arm away. But then, my next thought was, how harmful could it be to let him do this? So, we sat safely tucked away in the little Nash Rambler while the devilish swarms of birds pecked at people, smacked into telephone booths, and caused fires. The gas station exploded. All this mayhem made me feel a little creepy. Looking around I wanted to make sure our windows were rolled up. Then glancing at the car next to us, with the couple nowhere in sight, it made me wonder what if an insane flock of birds swooped down on us at that moment, would this couple even notice?

As the birds grew ever fiercer, seemingly intent on the destruction of humankind, Frank pulled me closer to him. We had not spoken much since the movie began; in fact, every time either of us said something it sounded odd, like our words echoed strangely off-key with the movie dialogue. It felt as if we were sitting snugly inside a capsule, watching the destruction, yet safe and protected. Then as mysteriously as the birds had arrived, they flew away again. The tension let up slightly. And while the beautiful movie star sat outside a school, we watched birds gathering behind her. They quietly gathered on telephone poles, settling in clusters on the roof of the schoolhouse, and they grouped thickly on the playground equipment.

"I wouldn't stay there, if I were you, lady," Frank said, and gave my shoulder a playful squeeze.

The woman lit a cigarette. She took a puff, slowly letting out the smoke. Reaching down to put the lighter back into her purse, the woman glanced over one shoulder and saw the birds gathering behind her. Cautiously, she got up, moving toward the school building.

"Oh, no," I said. "Now we're going to watch birds pecking at children."

"Yup, we're going to watch'm get eaten up. Mmmm, yummy, yummy," Frank said, and leaned his head closer to mine.

As we sat safely in the Nash Rambler, the children burst out from the school building, screaming. Birds chased after them, pecking at their heads, their ears, tugging at pigtails, gouging big chunks from their faces.

About this time our windows began to fog up. Frank wiped the glass clean with a piece of cloth from the glove compartment. I glanced at the car next to us. The vehicle looked abandoned.

When the birds were finished chasing the children and a teacher lay on the ground pecked to death by a flock of crows, Frank leaned over and kissed me on the mouth. My first response was to move away and resist. But it felt good to be kissed. I had always wanted to be kissed. When our lips met, I felt a tingle on, of all places, my nose.

"That was nice. You taste real sweet," Frank whispered.

"I do?" My response sounded so lame.

We kissed again. This time longer and harder. He swung his free arm around and pulled me tightly against him. Then slowly Frank eased his tongue into my mouth. It felt coarse and warm and I wondered what to do with it. My head pressed up against the back of my seat, Frank maneuvered his body so that he lay across me.

I suddenly became acutely aware of the sounds around me; the swooshing noise of the leather seats as we moved about in the car, the soft rustling of our clothing, our heavy breathing that wheezed through our nostrils as we kissed. The intimacy of the kissing intensified the sounds around me and I fell into a trance, dizzy and light-headed.

We slid lower into the seat. But when my head bumped against the speaker the spell was broken. I pulled away.

"Let's watch the movie," I said.

"Why?" Frank rubbed his mouth across my ear.

Chills crept up my back.

"Come on, stop it," I said.

Frank sat up in his seat, and put his arm around my shoulder. He no longer frightened me and we snuggled closer together. Many things had happened in the movie while we kissed. For some unknown reason nature had unleashed its anger on this small California town. What horrible wrongdoing had this community been guilty of? Were the citizens being punished? What mysterious secrets lay behind the locked doors of these seemingly humble people? Or, had the birds gone mad all over the world, and the citizenry didn't know it yet?

While these questions bounced around in my head, Frank pulled me closer to him and put his other hand on my knee. We sat perfectly still watching the movie. The characters in the movie escaped the birds and were securely settled in a house. A man, a rescuer of sorts, along with several other people and the beautiful blonde lady were hunkered down in the house while the birds continued to swoop and dive, wreaking havoc with the outside world. The blonde woman, the only person awake, heard scratching sounds coming from a room down the hall. Cautiously she walked toward the noises.

At the same time, Frank slowly moved his hand up and down my thigh. Then his fingers crept toward my inner thigh as the woman slowly walked down the hallway. Frank's hand reached my crotch by the time the woman stood in front of a closed door listening to the soft pecking and scratching sounds coming from inside the room.

Clamping my legs tightly together, I said, "No," and immediately moved Frank's hand away.

The woman opened the door. "Don't go in there," I said, snuggling in close to Frank.

She stepped into the room. Slight fluttering sounds came from somewhere in the darkness. There was no doubt in my mind that the birds were lurking in there, waiting for her. My body tensed with excitement. Then in less time than it took for my heart to flutter one beat, birds flew at the woman, pecking and pecking and pecking at her, leaving bloody gouges on her face and her arms. She fell to the floor in shock and horror.

All the while, Frank's hand moved up my thigh. "Why did she go in there?" Frank asked, breathing softly into my ear.

"I don't know," I replied. "Maybe curiosity."

"What did she find?" he asked.

Frank took his hand from my thigh and pretended to peck at me by giving me light pinches. "Birds," he said in a screechy voice. "That's what she found. Birds. Lots of 'em, pecking her all over."

Frank pecked at my leg and made me laugh. He pecked at my shoulder, then my neck, my face, gently pecking, quickly, as I tried to catch his hand. Pecking my collarbone, he leaned over, kissed me on the lips, and moved his hand to my breast. He held me firmly, while

I became caught between the excitement of seeing a woman being nearly pecked to death by birds and my own stirring of passion.

A rush of new sensations washed over me. In the background we vaguely heard the woman being rescued by a man, the "rescuer" from earlier, with whom she might be falling in love. My breasts tingled. My entire body vibrated. My crotch strangely throbbed, my mouth felt slippery and wet against Frank's lips, and I began to experience a loss of control. Frank slipped his hand under my t-shirt, slowly moving up toward my breasts while the beautiful woman screamed and flailed her arms trying to prevent the birds from pecking her to death.

All the while, Frank's hand moved slowly under my t-shirt. Grabbing hold of his hand there was a need for me to protect that soft mound of flesh against being touched. Frank tried to force his hand farther up.

We wrestled for a while and then out of breath, we leaned back in our seats in time to watch someone bandage the woman's bloody wounds. Soon, everyone rescued from the house walked outside into a strange twilight, an ominous world filled with birds sitting everywhere, on rooftops, on cars, on telephone wires. The world had changed. The blonde woman, still reeling from the attack of the birds, appeared terrified as a flock of crows fluttered onto the white picket fence near her.

Just then the door of the car parked next to us opened. The couple stepped out into the damp night air. They walked to the snack bar arm in arm, the girl's head resting on her boyfriend's shoulder. They looked so very much in love, and I wondered if Frank might fall in love with me.

During the second feature, Frank and I wrestled several more times over whether he could touch my breasts.

"I won't hurt you," he said, almost pleading.

"I know, but it makes me feel uncomfortable."

"It makes me feel good," he said.

When the last feature ended, a voice boomed over a loud speaker. "Okay, you guys, time to go home. Don't forget to unhook the speakers." Floodlights soon glared across the drive-in field as bright as if it were midday.

The windows of the car next to us had fogged up again with no sign of life. Our neighbors hadn't watched much of the movie, I was sure of that. Then realized we hadn't seen much of the second feature either.

Frank drove me back to the School for the Deaf, parked outside my dorm, and put his arm around my shoulders. A gentle rain began to fall. The air inside the car felt intimate and far too dangerous.

I took Frank's hand away. "I've got to go. It's late."

"Oh, come on, let's stay here for a while," he pleaded.

"No," I said and opened the door to get out.

Frank grabbed for me. Though while resisting, a part of me realized what great fun the evening had been.

But Frank wanted more.

I wanted more, as well. Pulling away from him, I said, "I can't."

"I don't want you to go." He reached out again to touch me. Quickly getting out of the car, I ran up the front stairs.

"I have to get up early," I called back.

"I miss you already," Frank shouted.

Running to my room and quickly looking out the window, I got one last view of the Nash Rambler's taillights as Frank drove out onto the street.

That night, Frank wakened new feelings in me. I chuckled to think about how we twisted around in that little car, trying to get closer. And then when trying to remember what the second feature had been, the only thing that came to mind was Frank's kisses, and that made me smile.

Gossip

TIME MOVED QUICKLY. BEFORE I knew it, my fist year in college was coming to an end. I fooled around too much, skipped too many classes, slept late more than a serious student should have, and my grades suffered. The school administration put me on academic probation, but I vowed to do better next year.

After a few more dates with Frank, he sailed off to the Orient. He wasn't sure where he'd end up, though he suspected it would be on a troop transporter headed for Vietnam. One night before Frank shipped out, he said, "Wilma, I promise to write you." Though he never gave me his military mailing address. Then a couple months later his father casually told me that Frank met a woman in another port and that it sounded pretty serious.

It wasn't too long after that I met Ed. He was an older man, a Veteran of the Korean War and going to school on the GI Bill. Ed was tall with short, curly, ash-blond hair. When we took walks, Ed's long stride forced me to take two steps to keep up with one of his. I fell in love with his ocean blue eyes that sometimes looked emerald green. A perfect gentleman, Ed never forced himself on me. We went out to dinner. We saw movies. Sometimes we took long rides in the country. There was a mystery about Ed. He never spoke about his past. We never talked of marriage, yet I think he cared a great deal for me.

Even though I was reckless with my study time, there was still money in my savings account, enough to cover next year's tuition for two semesters, and I made plans to return to school in the fall. I knew full well that an education was the only hope for improving my already too-hard lot in life.

* * * *

Then one day when Dad picked me up for a weekend visit at home, he told me that he needed my college money.

"Wilma, I hate to ask," he said. "But remember those gadgets I bought when we were building the bomb shelter? Well, I got them on credit. Now they want their money or else."

The gadgets were called dosimeters. Dad, convinced that the atomic bomb would be dropped, purchased cases of these hand-held radiation readers. He thought he'd make a lot of money selling them to the neighbors. As it turned out, Dad had been the only one for miles, maybe the only person in the whole state of Washington, who thought they were necessary. There had been no atom bombs, no radioactive cloud hovering above us. The boxes of dosimeters were useless. They sat in the attic since that time gathering dust. The manufacturer wanted its money and sent collectors to hound Dad.

My father's physical and mental health continued to deteriorate. He could no longer hold down a job. And now he was fighting with the Veteran Administration for a partial disability pension. In the meantime, my mother and sisters were on state aid. Mom, depressed, slept all day.

The reality of my family's situation struck hard when Dad asked for my money. This money had been my ticket out of the kind of life that had dragged Mom down—the life that fostered both anger in me at my parents while at the same time a terrible pity for each one of them.

Caught between duty and my freedom, in the end I chose duty and gave the money to Dad. After finals, I moved back into my parents' home and said goodbye to college life. Ed and I broke up. It was a sweet farewell with gentle kisses. I cried a little, more from the sadness of losing my freedom than from ending our affair. Life had turned upside down on me. Older and wiser, now I knew exactly what would be missing from my life.

Getting my old job back at the garment factory was easy. They assigned me to the same department I'd worked in before going to college. My old co-workers were happy to see me. The same women sat at the same sewing machines, still working on the same line of clothing. Nothing had changed.

Well, that wasn't exactly true. Something had changed. Caroline, the supervisor of this section, and my old boss, had been involved in a big scandal in my absence. Caroline's husband had committed suicide. For a while, the authorities suspected that she might have murdered him. I'd read about it in the newspaper. Now I'd hear all the juicy details. Gossip might not make my situation any easier to take, though the story making the rounds was a bit of a fun distraction.

So on an early day in June, I began my eight-hour shifts of huddling over a sewing machine, quickly zipping out the expensive line of clothing the factory produced. My body used to having the freedom of moving about during the day, now had to get used to sitting in one place for eight hours mindlessly performing rote tasks. From now on hundreds of garments were going to pass through my hands.

Day after day, I would do the same stitch, handle the same fabric, the same color, in an endless stream of production. It didn't take long for the women to accept me back into the fold. We talked and giggled above the monotonous roaring sounds of the sewing machines.

Caroline walked down the rows of machines, like a straw boss on a chain gang. When she came around, everyone stopped talking, hunkered down, and worked faster.

"She thinks we only talk about her," Janet, the woman sitting at the sewing machine to my left, told me the first day back on the job.

"Paranoid," I said.

"Or guilty," Janet responded.

Lunch and coffee breaks were exactly as I remembered them with all the women chatting, joking around. Though now, from time to time, we speculated on how Caroline managed to get rid of her husband.

"The authorities said he died from sleeping pills and alcohol," Bertha, Janet's buddy, said with authority. "If you ask me, Caroline slipped the pills into his soup. Then, before he got too groggy, she began pouring him drinks. Alcoholics would drink in their sleep if they could."

Bertha was married to a "cocktail," as she called her husband, and everyone knew she had the inside scoop on handling men who drank too much. Bertha also hated her husband. I wondered if she had considered getting rid of him the way everyone thought Caroline had done with her own man.

"I've said it before," Janet replied, as though she were informing me of the truth. "I don't see how any husband could keep his sanity living with a woman like Caroline. Tight-assed and cold, she'd drive anyone to drink."

In the break room, the supervisors had their own table, near a bank of windows where the sun poured in on those rare sunny Northwest days. Most of the time though, this winter, the women who had risen to the rank of management, sat with a dreary haze at their backs. Caroline, instead of sitting at the table with her supervisor buddies, as I remembered she used to do, went outside to smoke a cigarette. She spent a lot of time on a pay phone just inside the entrance of the factory.

I had recently taken up smoking myself. So while a few minutes still remained in a break, I rushed outside, sweater thrown over my shoulders, and stood with the other smokers to take a quick drag on a cigarette.

With the pay phones so close to the front doorway it was difficult not to listen in on conversations. I frequently overheard calls being made, some a bit startling and really none of my business.

"Get your butt out of bed and go to school," one woman shouted into the phone during a morning break. It sounded to me like single mothers had a lot of trouble with their kids. Or I'd stand by the door, cigarette in hand, puffing away my life, listening to a woman fight with her husband. Smokers were privy to quite a few secrets here, even if we only heard snippets.

Caroline made her calls discretely, however. She'd whisper into the receiver, one hand cupping the mouthpiece. Though she'd have said it was no one's damn business what she was saying, it didn't take a genius to figure out she was up to something. Most of my thoughts during the day pivoted around Dad not working and Mom sleeping the days away.

Caroline was only a brief distraction. I buried myself in the work much of the time, always trying to earn more money by beating the piece-rate quota.

Once in a while, Ed slipped into my daydreaming. He hadn't asked me to marry him. If he had, I'd have said no. It was quite likely he had another girlfriend, or maybe even a wife, because he was always busy on weekends. When we said goodbye in the end, I knew we'd never see each other again. Now, in the middle of my drudgery, Ed was a ghost of man who only occupied my thoughts from time to time.

Hunched over the sewing machine hour after hour, my neck became stiff and my shoulders ached. It wouldn't take long before my shoulders would become hunched over like all the other women in the factory. And eventually my skin would resemble the old-timers with a pasty, dry look that resulted from all the lint and dust floating around in the air. Everyone had a glassy stare, and in my opinion it was from the constant focus on the material passing beneath the presser-foot of the sewing machine that caused this look.

After six months on the job, the mirror began to show the changes that were taking place in me.

Eight hours a day I lived in a blizzard of zippers, waistbands, side seams, padded bra inserts for swimsuits, or back pleats of skirts. Scissors in hand, buried behind mountains of fabric, eyes intent, necks bent, we all worked in a frenzy of flapping fabric.

I had been back on the job about seven months when Caroline brought me a new assignment.

"Wilma," she said, one hand on her hip, a bundle of fabric carelessly slung through the crook of her arm. She put the bundle on my sewing machine. I cringed. She placed in front of me the dreaded stiff, rubbery fabric that the men's swimsuits were made of.

"Sew the emblem here." She handed me the flimsy company logo, then pointed at a pinhole that had been burned into the fabric indicating the logo's placement.

I sewed the logo onto the fabric, slowly and carefully, with my zigzag machine. "What do you think?" I asked when I finished.

"Looks fine." Caroline never showed emotion. She never gave praise for a job well done. "The quota's seventy-five dozen," she said with an authoritative tone, then turned and walked off.

I'd never be able to sew seventy-five dozen a day, no matter how hard I worked. The fabric, infamous for being uncooperative, puckered and stretched, as I knew it would, or I'd run off the edge of the logo. Either way, I frequently had to rip out the stitches and start all over again.

Caroline frequently came by my station, inspecting nearly every finished piece.

"Good work," she'd say. "How many have you done?"

I'd tell her, and she'd go away.

One afternoon when stepping out for a quick cigarette break, I saw Caroline talking on the pay phone. My smoking had grown to nearly a pack a day by now. I couldn't wait to light up. Caroline came outside and lit up a cigarette. She stood next to me. Her red eyes betrayed her tears. Caroline struck a match with an angry snap, and sucked in a deep, long pull of smoke. She sure looked like a smoker with deep troubles to me. Every day now, the only thing Caroline said was, "How many? How many? How many have you done?"

The most I could do was twenty-five dozen a day. "That's not good enough." Caroline folded her arms and looked down at me from over her glasses, a habit that totally got on my nerves. "It's an easy job. You can do more. Now get going," she said, with that ever-present critical tone in her voice.

"Bitch," I muttered under my breath when she bent over to inspect Janet's work.

Sewing faster only made the needle run off the edge of the logo, or the fabric puckered. Speeding up didn't make the operation prettier; it only made the job look sloppier. But Caroline wanted me to step on it, and though I could produce a little more, reaching the quota was impossible.

"You've got to go faster," Caroline demanded each time she came to inspect my work. So I made them faster, and the quality of my work, of course, went way down.

When Caroline looked at the work, she said, "As long as you can make the quota. The inspectors don't care what they look like. These are going to be cheap garments that'll go into sale bins."

"Okay," I said, and taking Caroline at her word, pushed the work out no matter what it looked like.

The job got a little easier, though the logos on the men's swim trunks didn't look great. But everyone seemed happy and eventually

I reached the quota. When Caroline saw the end products with the zigzag stitch going off the emblem, a pucker here, a run-off there, she assured me, "They're fine. Just keep pushing them through."

That's exactly what I did.

One day, after working three and a half weeks sewing the damn logos onto the men's swimsuits, I went outside for a cigarette break, and saw Caroline get out of a car. A man driving the car shouted, "If you think I'm going to take the blame, you're crazy." Caroline slammed the car door.

"Get an earful?" Caroline snapped as she hurriedly passed me and went into the building.

I didn't care what was going on with her. There was enough in my miserable life to contend with. Though the situation with the man in the car did pique my interest, and I told Janet about him.

"I'd seen them together before Caroline's husband died," she said.

Janet always in on the latest information, said, "What do you think now? Did they kill the husband?"

"Beats me, but nothing surprises me around here," I said. There wasn't time to think more about Caroline and her dead husband. The buzzer rang which meant the break was over and it was time for me to sew those lousy decals on the swimsuits.

The next day, by lunch break, the entire factory buzzed with a new piece of gossip. Everyone now said that I had overheard Caroline discussing with a man how they'd killed Caroline's husband.

"How could you do this to me," I snapped at Janet. It couldn't have been anyone else who started this newsy bit of information.

She shrugged her shoulders. "People just like to gossip. Maybe it got a little out of hand."

"Maybe?" I shouted. "Maybe, a little out of hand?" I couldn't believe it.

"Don't worry. It'll blow over. It always does," Janet assured me. "There have been plenty of rumors."

But in my mind nothing good could come of this. Janet might have been right. It might blow over in a couple of days, yet from the look on Caroline's face, she seemed pretty upset about something. She threw dirty looks in my direction all morning, though she hadn't said a word to me.

That afternoon, Caroline came down the aisle pushing a large canvas bin—the kind of bin that everyone in the plant knew meant trouble. These bins came from the inspection station, and they only brought bad news. The anger on Caroline's face wasn't hard to read either.

She parked the bin at my machine. "What do you mean putting this kind of stuff through?" She grabbed a handful of the fabric pieces from the bin, shook them in my face. "What were you thinking?" she demanded, her voice, shrill, vibrated with anger. She threw the fabric back into the bin.

I picked one out of the bin and looked at it. "I showed you what they looked like," I said. "You told me to put them through like this." Gritting my teeth it was all I could do not to call her a liar.

"I never said any such thing. You never showed me any of this." She spit the words at me. Her face turned redder and redder by the minute. "You'll have to fix every one of them. Now get at it. Two more bins are waiting for you when this one is finished." She walked away shaking her head.

By now I had sewn logos onto thousands of men's swimsuits. If what she said was true it would take me forever to fix them.

"What the hell is this?" Janet asked, pointing at the bin. She knew what they were. Repairs. "Look, kid, we've all been there," she said in what might have been her attempt at a comforting tone. "You'll have this done in no time." I didn't tell her there were more where these came from.

Clipping and pulling out threads, then sewing the logos back on, bored me to death. I began to think about killing someone. Not with overdoses of sleeping pills and alcohol, like Caroline had been suspected of doing. No, I wanted to get my hands around someone's neck and squeeze the life out of them. Not just someone—Caroline.

I no longer went to the break room, but stepped outside to smoke a cigarette on my break. Caroline would sometimes be out there, too. She'd glare at me and then turn her back. There were no more secretive phone calls, and the man in the car never showed up again.

The whispering gossip now focused on me. I had become the news of the day. The story got around that Caroline had never seen such sloppy work. I'd heard that some of the women saw me as the biggest goof-off in the plant. The repair work went on for over a week. Then even before the bin of repairs was completed, Caroline wheeled in the other two bins, each one filled to the top with repairs. Self-pity and anger raged in me like a violent storm. I had to get out of there or I'd die. I had begun to mumble.

"What'd you say?" Janet asked.

"I'm going to kill someone," I responded, throwing Janet an angry look. She quickly turned away. Janet never apologized for starting that rumor. She never tried to stop it, either.

Two weeks later, the repairs were still not finished. Caroline, irritable and cranky, constantly peered over my shoulder. She never said a kind word of encouragement and told everyone that I'd caused production to go down in her department. For that, Caroline had no forgiveness.

But there was an interesting consequence to the rumor that I had supposedly started. Caroline made me her revenge. The gossip about Caroline killing her husband no longer ran rampant through the factory. The supervisory buddies that Caroline lunched with, including the woman from the inspection department who kept me buried in repairs, now huddled conspiratorially with Caroline. She was once again allowed into the realm of the supervisors' table in the break room. While Caroline was coddled and taken cared of, I became the outcast in the factory.

Repairs had no quota and I worked my tail off for the base pay. This was never going to change. Caroline's job now was to make sure my work life was hell. Eventually, I knew she would assign me to the most difficult jobs. I'd get the garbage work and never be able to make the quota. Caroline intended to make sure that I'd never make more than the base pay.

There was no choice for me but to quit.

Calling in sick that next day, I went to Portland by Greyhound bus. Making an afternoon appointment with an employment agency, it didn't matter what kind of job they could find me. I just wanted out.

They sent me on an interview, and much to my surprise, by the end of the day, I had a job as a file clerk in an insurance company. Next, I needed to find a room, someplace close to my new job. A rooming house eight blocks away from where I'd be working had a sign advertising a vacant furnished room. I took it. I said nothing that morning about looking for a new job or about moving out. Dressing a little fancier than usual, I went off to catch the Grey Hound Bus. I didn't ask for permission, which Dad, even now, thought I needed in order to live my life.

While helping prepare supper that night I said, "Mom, I got a new job and found a place to live in Portland. I'm leaving." My heart pounded so hard when I told my mother what I was about to do, that it was difficult to say much more than this.

"What do you mean, you're leaving?" she asked.

"I'm just going."

Mom became very quiet and didn't say anything else. I wanted to believe that she cared, but knowing her passivity and depression, my mother showed little interest in my moving out.

When everyone was seated at the supper table, taking a deep breath, I said, "Dad, I found a new job today, and I've got a place to live. I'm moving to Portland."

I waited for him to jump up, to pound the table, to shout at me about all the evil people who were waiting for me out there in the world.

Instead, Dad tightly squeezed a slice of folded, freshly baked bread, crushing the butter inside so that it would not fall off when he took a bite. "Well," he answered. "I thought this would happen sooner or later. I knew I couldn't keep you forever."

I had been ready to defend this move to my death. He said nothing more. He ate his dinner, drank his coffee in silence, and then went outside.

The following morning, before sitting at my sewing machine, I stopped by Caroline's desk and said, "I'm giving you one week's notice."

Caroline threw me a familiar mean look. "Yeah, well, you're not cut out for this kind of work, anyway." She said this as though it were a fault. I wanted to laugh in her face. "You'll be doing repairs until you leave. Now sit down."

I walked past my coworkers. Their strained eyes followed me. "What happened?" Janet asked.

"I just quit," I said, smiling.

Janet started to say something, but stopped herself. Caroline began to walk down the aisle in our direction. I picked up a blue piece of fabric and began to clip the threads as I sang, "Two women sitting on a dead man's chest. Ho, ho, ho, and a bottle of rum."

I wonder from time to time if I didn't owe Caroline a debt of gratitude for her help. Who knows how long I'd have put up with that job before I'd have gotten the courage to quit if it hadn't been for her?

Freedom

AFTER MOVING OUT OF MY parent's home, Franco-American spaghetti from a can became my freedom food. My desire was to never develop cooking skills for fear of falling into the trap that, to my way of thinking, had dragged my mother down. But understanding full well that it was necessary to eat, my meals would be acquired without responsibility or cares. I would eat in cafes and restaurants. I would eat from cans. Eating from a can became a newfound liberty.

However, my taste buds were, still eager for new taste sensations and it was during this time that I fell in love with the Reuben sandwich. This sandwich was a real treat for me. I ordered it so frequently, that I smugly thought it should be named the Wilma Reuben. Much like my first sexual stirring, this sandwich remains in my memory where other unique foods have tried but failed to bring me back to that ecstasy of the Reuben of my youth.

I first ordered this sandwich in a coffee shop not far from my rooming house where the Italian-American meals from a can became my mainstay for dinner. Initially, this sandwich was an innocent flirtation. The Reuben contained all my favorite salty foods: sauerkraut, corned beef, Swiss cheese, all piled high between two slices of hearty rye bread smeared generously with a hefty portion of Russian dressing.

I had no idea at the time that this sandwich might become an obsession for me, that over the years I'd search out this repast, hoping to taste again those early days of my adulthood. If I could only find another triple-decker, like the one I had in Portland, Oregon, when just turning twenty-one years old and newly on my own, I would truly be in paradise. But looking back, a question lingers in my mind, did that Reuben sandwich ever really exist—or was it the freedom itself that tasted so good? If this brand-new freedom had only brought me wonderful experiences, I would have moved through those days unscathed and jubilant. But frequently life turns from sweet to bitter in an instant, with only dark, vague warnings that usually go unheeded. I wanted to leave the farm girl behind. She was a burden.

My new surroundings made me feel as I imagined a butterfly might feel as it emerged from a cocoon, wings filled and perfumed in beauty, wings that, but for an instant, were weak, untrained, yet wings that knew instinctively how to fly.

Walking home from work in the evenings, it often felt as if the earth charged me with sparks of magic. Everything excited me. My new life had no limits. The world belonged to me. I often stopped for a cup of coffee and read a book in the same coffee shop where I ate my Reuben sandwich as often as once or twice a week.

One day, while I read a second-hand paperback, a man came to my booth and sat down across from me.

He smiled, and then called for the waitress to bring him a cup of coffee. "You look lonely," he said. "How about I join you."

The waitress brought him a cup of coffee, and then as she turned to leave, he pulled at her apron string, and said, "Thanks, doll, is there something I can do for you?"

The waitress gave him a wink. "Not now, maybe later," she said, then turned and went back behind the counter.

"She's a good kid," he said.

"Yeah, she seems nice," I responded, not knowing what else to say. The situation made me feel awkward and I went back to reading my book.

"What are you reading?" He pushed my book up to check the title. "*The Grapes of Wrath*. Is it any good?" He poured cream into his coffee. "I haven't seen you around here before. You new in the area?"

"Yes." Distracted from my reading, I watched him stir his coffee.

"You really are a beautiful woman." He put his elbow on the table, resting his chin on his fist. "You've got the prettiest eyes I've ever seen."

My face flushed.

"Oh, I embarrassed you," he said. "I'm sorry." He placed his hand on top of mine. "I just thought a pretty woman like you should be told how nice she looks."

I smiled, shrugging my shoulders. "Thank you."

"Let's start over. My name is Willie. What's yours?" He still held my hand. "Wilma," I said, feeling the hotness leave my face.

"Well, what do you know about that, we almost have the same names. I'll bet we're going to be good friends." His attention disturbed me. No one had ever approached me this way before, but as my face once again became cool, my control over the situation returned.

Willie's dark blond hair, heavily greased and swept back into a fashionable DA, grew a bit raggedy down his neck and brushed against his pulled-up collar when he moved his head from side to side. His off-white shirt, a little skimpy for the current cool weather, made it easy to read the Lucky Strike label through the fabric of his front pocket.

I closed my book, removed my hand from his and took a swallow of my coffee.

"You live around here?" I asked.

"Yeah," he said. "In the hotel down the block, on the third floor." He took the pack of Lucky's from his shirt pocket and offered me one.

"Thanks," I said, and took one of his unfiltered cigarettes. My preferred smokes were a milder, menthol brand. When I inhaled this guy's Lucky, the harsh smoke dragged painfully against my throat. But I kept smoking.

"So you live around here, too?" He leaned sideways in the booth, putting his back against the window and lifted his feet up on the seat.

"Yeah," I said, feeling slightly more at ease. The cigarette seemed to have broken the tension.

"That's great, we're neighbors," he observed. "Say, why don't we go to the movies this afternoon? There's a great double bill around the corner."

"I don't think so." It seemed fine talking to this stranger in a well-lit coffee shop, but wondered if I might have been a little too friendly.

"Why not? I'm a nice guy," Willie said. "All the girls'll tell you that." Willie took a few drags on his cigarette, knocked the growing ash into the ashtray, looked up at me and smiled. "What can happen in the movie?" Willie asked. "Nothing, that's what can happen, nothing at all." He took hold of my hand once again. "You're just so pretty I thought you'd be a sweet lady to take to a movie." He looked straight into my eyes, then he took hold of my hand again and began to gently rub it. "I won't hurt you. We're just going to the movies. Come on, we'll have a nice time. Look, we're neighbors, we were destined to meet. Now that we have, we're destined to go out, too. Hey, we even almost got the same name. Let's go to the movies. The first show is about to start. Come on, finish up your coffee. Let's go."

Without thinking about it again, I gulped my coffee. "All right," I said. After all, I thought, what was the harm in going to a movie. Willie seemed fine, and he thought I was pretty. That felt kind of nice, too.

Willie insisted on paying for my coffee and put two dollars on the table. But when he stood, it surprised me that he was actually quite short. He looked taller and bigger sitting across from me in the booth.

As we left the coffee shop, Willie put his arm around my waist.

Removing his hand, I said, "No, or I won't go to the movies with you."

"All right," he agreed, slapping his own hand, pretending to punish himself. "Whatever you say."

Asserting myself made me feel confident that Willie would behave himself in the movie. Living on my own seemed to be working out quite nicely.

The movie was already in progress when we arrived. Looking for seats in the darkened theater, we kept bumping into each another. Willie brushed against my breasts several times, but excused these accidental encounters to the darkness. Once we found our seats, Willie put an arm around my shoulder.

"Stop it," I said and removed his arm. "I want to watch the movie."

"All right. All right," Willie said.

Several minutes later, he again attempted to put his arm around me. Then taking hold of his hand, I tightly held it securely on the armrest. "Now keep it here," I said sternly.

Willie tried to pull his hand away, but my grip held it firmly in place. "You're a strong thing, aren't you," Willie whispered.

Holding Willie's hand on the armrest throughout the movie made my hand tired. And being with Willie had not been as much fun as

I thought it would be. He attempted to get loose several times, but I refused to release his hand. I thought my experiences on other dates had given me a good understanding of what to expect. Though Willie seemed more determined and less cooperative than the other guys I'd dated. In fact, his behavior made me feel a little creepy.

By the end of the first movie, I had no interested in seeing the second film. Willie was fine with that, too, and we left the theater. The sun had set by now and deep shadows hovered in the creases of the closed up shops. The damp, chilly night airs made me shiver. Though walking in the cold, as unpleasant as it was, felt more comfortable than sitting in the theater with Willie.

"Well, what should we do now? Willie asked. "Want to go for coffee?"

"No. I'm going to go back to my place."

"Great, I'll go with you."

"No, that's all right. I've got things to do."

Willie was too clingy and though I didn't want to hurt his feelings, I wanted to be free of him.

"I'll walk you home. After all, we are neighbors."

Something in his manner made me feel uncomfortable. What bothered me wasn't anything specific, but maybe his smile, now more of a smirk, did not seem as sincere as when we first met in the cafe. Or, maybe the problem might have been that he always wanted to touch me—but I wanted this date to be over.

Willie refused to call it a night at the front door to my rooming house, insisting on accompanying me to my room. I thought, what would be the harm in that. But walking up the one flight to my room, Willie followed too close, nearly tromping on the heel of my shoe as we ascended the stairs.

Unlocking the door to my room and then turning to say goodbye, Willie pushed his way in and quickly closed the door behind him. At that point, there was no doubt in my mind that letting Willie walk me home had been a big mistake. Though it seemed as though the situation was still under my control.

"What are you doing?" I shouted. "I want you to go. Get out." I tried to grab the doorknob.

"I want to visit with you some more," he said, grabbing one of my hands. His grip, much stronger now than it had been in the theater, frightened me. My heart beat furiously. I could not catch my breath. No matter how hard I struggled, Willie would not let me go.

I tried to push him away with my free hand, but Willie grabbed hold of that hand, too. Then, securing both hands behind my waist, he pulled me tightly against his body. His mouth pushed hard against my lips, his teeth crushed against me like a hard strip of metal.

For the first time I really smelled him, inhaling the odor of his cheap hair grease, his shirt now rank with sweat and the smell the cigarettes that I heard crinkling in his shirt pocket while he held me crushed to his chest. In this desperate moment, my only thought was to get free and shove him back out into the hallway. Pushing and flailing, my anger at Willie made me feel strong. But Willie never relented. He continued to hold me firmly, kissing me ferociously. And then he pushed me to the floor.

"You know you want it," he said, his voice raspy, his breath, foul with the smell of tobacco and coffee.

My heart pounded fiercely. The arteries in my neck, my throat, my entire body pulsed with fear. I felt like an animal caught in a trap. It had seemed like fun to go out with a stranger. He said I was pretty. Which made me feel good. Now on the floor, I kicked at him, tried to bang my head against his, struggling with all my effort, but Willie never let up on his grip. "No! Stop it! Get off me! Let me go!" I shouted.

Forcing his stinky cigarette stained hand across my mouth, Willie muffled any shouting. I fought with a fierce energy, drawing strength from a place within me that I never knew existed. Willie lay on top of me. His grip would not loosen and my arms remained beneath me, useless like two broken sticks. Willie pulled up my skirt, grabbed for my panties and yanked them down past my knees.

Stupid! Stupid! How could I have been so stupid? My mind went wild. My thoughts shattered in a thousand directions as Willie's mouth pressed against mine making it impossible to scream. Carpet burns heated my naked arms as I struggled to free myself. How stupid of me to believe that I could have walked away; first at the theater, then at the door to my room. With my panties pulled down to my ankles, my heart pounding beyond belief, my mind wild with fear and anger.

Then Willie grunted and buried his head in the crux of my shoulder. My nostrils filled with the rank smell of his breath, and then when the violation had been completed, he fell limp and whispered, "Sweet."

Lying in a wet puddle of my bloody virginity, angry and ashamed, I blamed myself for what had happened.

Tears eased down from the corners of my eyes. They trickled onto my temples, then down into my hair, crawling across me like a troop of bugs making its way to the carpet below.

Willie released me and quickly got up from the floor. His body looked misshapen and foul in the dark. He went into the bathroom. I heard water running in the basin.

Numbness washed over me. My breathing slowed, my pounding heart slackened, my body no longer throbbing and I grew cold as though the floor beneath me had turned to ice. I shivered. Sitting up, the shivering got worse. My hands trembled violently and for a few moments I had no idea where I was. Then Willie returned from the bathroom. I panicked. Frantically I tried to remember where I kept a knife, a sharpened pencil, anything capable of doing harm.

Willie looked down at me. I thought he was going to say something, but then he opened the door and walked out.

Slowly standing, I could not move from the middle of the room for the longest time. Then gathering my courage, turned on a lamp, I saw the bloody spot on the floor. I locked the door and then meticulously washed myself.

It was impossible to remove the bloodstain from the carpet even using several different cleansers. Once in a while, when entering the room, I found myself stepping over the slightly visible discoloration.

I never told anyone what had happened and except for the dark spot on the carpet, most of the time the event with Willie that evening has been shredded from my mind. This experience taught me a great deal about freedom and trust. But unlike the Reuben sandwich on which I continue to ruminate over to this day, the memory of Willie is tucked away in the back of my brain in one of those wrinkled crevices in the cranium where memories can lurk undetected for years, and perhaps even a lifetime. Willie was a predator and I was his victim, plain and simple as that. But I do know that if a knife had been within my reach when Willie came out of the bathroom, this little tale of misery might have had a different ending.

The Wedding

CLOUDS, ILLUMINATED BY A FULL moon, streaked across the Oregon night sky smudging the darkness with a glowing gray light. I rushed home from my life drawing class at the art museum. James was dropping by tonight to read his poetry to me.

I had lived in Portland six months and two weeks ago mutual friends introduced me to James. From that first night we both felt as if we had known each other all our lives. You wouldn't call James handsome, but he was cute, with his sparse brown mustache and a mass of hair that got slicked down with a heavy portion of Brylcreem. James, very tall and a bit on the skinny side had extremely long feet. His feet were so big in fact he slightly resembled a T-square. But his warm, friendly smile with sad, light blue eyes made me feel as though he could look deep down into my soul. I ran up the stairs quickly to straighten out my place before he arrived.

Books and piles of sketches from my art class were haphazardly scattered everywhere. It didn't take long to tidy-up the place by cramming some of the books and sketchpads into a closet.

When James knocked on the door, an excited thrill ran through my body. We drank cups of peppermint tea and sat cross-legged on the floor while James read his poems. He read with a practiced, deliberate style, pausing after each poem. Turning the page, he would take a deep breath, and then began to read again. The verses were clever, with beautiful depictions of auburn fall days, rickity-tickety sounding cars, music that vibrated inside the cranium, and poems about lovers dying together in their sleep. Though I breathed in every word, every stanza, what really made listening to his poetry so special was listening to the person read from what they actually had written. James embodied the artist, the creator I wished I could become.

"You express yourself beautifully," I said. James smiled and then read me another poem. The poetry wrapped around us, making the evening magical.

When James finished reading all of his poems, he closed the notebook. "Well, that's it," he said. "You've heard all of them now." James looked down and gently ran his fingers over the edges of the pages.

"They were beautiful."

"Thank you. Which one did you like the most?"

"I liked them all."

We sat in the middle of the room, both of us quietly self-consciously saying nothing for a while as I inspected the poems in the folder. James glanced nervously about the room.

* * * *

That evening, we took a long walk. Our hands shoved deep into jacket pockets, our breath synchronized as we exhaled into the cold winter air. The following day my job as a file clerk flew by and I easily alphabetized the insurance claims. The papers floated like feathers into the file cabinet with gall bladders mingling discretely with childhood illnesses. While I filed the pleas for payments and reimbursements, I pictured James sitting cross-legged on the floor reading his poetry to me.

* * * *

Most evenings I worked on assignments for my art class. The coarse-textured drawing paper, the smudge of charcoal on my fingers, the smell of art supplies that lingered in my room awakened in me a long hidden desire to draw and, eventually, to paint. Until now, being an artist had only been a dream, a faint whisper, and a secret hunger for something beautiful and unattainable.

It didn't take long before James and I were spending every evening together. Rushing home after work to draw for an hour or two, I then waited anxiously for him to arrive. Some nights we sat in my room talking for hours, or we strolled through the Portland nights. On the weekends we sometimes drove to the coast and watched the waves rolling across the shoreline or we'd sit on a foggy beach huddled together under a blanket. Within a month we declared our love for each other—though I think we had fallen in love the first night we met.

James dreamed of one day living in San Francisco. We talked about moving there together.

"Once you establish residency in California, school costs almost nothing," James said. At that point James' dream became my dream.

We kissed to seal the deal. James made me feel comfortable and beautiful when he held me in his arms. Life became magical from that moment on. There was no longer the fear in the back of my mind that I might end up like my mom—poor, with children hanging on me. James brought promises of an education. He would be a tender, loving husband, an intellectual, not a physical laborer who never earned enough money to pay the bills.

My dreams were going to come true and my head filled with only good times ahead. James would help to make them come true. Our home would be filled with nice furniture, not a car seat taken from a Volkswagen bus and used as a couch, the way Mom was forced to do. I never wanted to see another potato again as long as I lived. I would have children when I wanted them, not when they happened along.

The more my imagination unveiled the wonderful future before me, the angrier my feelings were toward my mother for not being able to control her situation. Mom's life could have been easier, from my perspective, if she had only tried harder. Telling Dad about my plans to get married might be a bit tricky. James met my family a couple times, though the meetings did not go well.

As soon as we arrived Dad went outside, closing himself up in his work shed. Then returning several hours later Dad ate dinner with us, gulped down a hot cup of coffee before returning to his solitary retreat. He hardly spoke to James, except to ask what he did for a living.

"He's not a man," Dad snapped when he learned of my plans to marry James. "He's a kid." Dad's face turned red as he became angrier by the minute.

"He is too a man," I protested. "Just because he works in a hospital, that doesn't make him less of a man."

Dad, as cranky and stubborn as he was, I knew would never change his mind about James. Dad clenched his teeth. The muscles in his jaw pulsed. "He's a skinny, snot-nosed kid. He'll never grow up," Dad shouted.

"How can you say that? If you took time to know him, you'd feel differently."

Getting Dad's approval meant a great deal to me, though it was clear that would never happen. "That boy's not going to grow up until he's an old man. You can bet on that." Dad lit a cigarette with trembling hands.

Lately, his hands had begun to shake a lot. It wasn't just his anger that made his hands so unsteady. But at this moment, I was shaking myself. "I love James," I said. "I don't need your consent to get married."

Mom said nothing. She didn't cry either. She looked paler, thinner than usual. I wished she'd say something. She didn't though. She sat listening, drinking coffee, smoking cigarettes, and said nothing. There was a time when she cried at everything. Now she sat silently while Dad ranted. I felt alone, distant from my family. Glancing at Mom, she looked empty. My mother's eyes, dry and vacant, her hollowed cheekbones made her look as though she were floating away behind a cloud of cigarette smoke.

"Well, young lady," Dad said, "go right ahead and get married. Just don't expect me to be a part of it."

"You mean you wouldn't come to my wedding even if you knew I was happy?"

"You want to get married, go right ahead and do it. But without me." Dad got up from the table and left the room. The back door slammed shut. Dad usually did this in one of his fuming rants—slam doors, pound on tables. Anger drove Dad to the backyard frequently, cursing, banging and throwing things around. Everyone left him alone when he stomped out the door, and that was exactly what he wanted. I couldn't understand why Dad disliked James. Why couldn't my father be happy for me? But then Dad didn't want anyone to be happy, because he could not escape his own misery. I'd show him, and made a promise to myself to be the happiest person ever married.

"What do you think, Mom?" I asked.

My mother did not respond immediately, and then in a very familiar weak tone, she said, "I don't know. James is pretty young." "We're over twenty-one. You married Dad at seventeen. You're still married."

That didn't seem like a good response. Though it was the best I could do considering my mind was filled with so much anger at my father. But marriage would be different for me than it had been for Mom.

My mother and I sat silently for a short while.

"Do you think Dad will change his mind about coming to the wedding?" I asked.

Though the answer was already known, the question needed to be made public. "I don't think so," Mom said. "You know how he gets. Your father doesn't like to change his mind. He thinks you're making a big mistake."

Smoke trailed up from Mom's cigarette. The grey tobacco cloud hung loosely over my mother's head. And then she lit another cigarette from the dying butt in her hand. The constant inhaling of poisonous smoke, the swallowing of her pride, the gulping of her words, the squelching of her feelings; I had watched her do these things for so many years, and now I sat with her at the edge of my new life, and all she could do was exhale smoke that rose to hang over her head like a ghost. I knew she understood more than she would ever tell. She had to.

"Will you come to the wedding?" These words were really not a question, but rather an invitation for my mother to break free from Dad's displeasure with me.

Mom slowly brought the cigarette to her mouth. She sucked a huge mouthful of smoke into her lungs. The ash glowed red and made a nearly imperceptible sizzling sound. Not everyone hears the hissing that a cigarette makes, but so often sitting with my mother, that would be the only sound that bounced between us. Then she tapped the cigarette against the side of the ashtray, something my mother had done for years, a deliberate action that seemed to occupy her full attention as she looked away from me and gazed out the window.

* * * *

Years later, Mom told me how much she hurt for me that day, that she didn't know of any way to make things better. So she swallowed any feelings she had and hoped that my life might work out the way I wanted it to. But that day when announcing my impending marriage to James, Mom seemed to have no thoughts, no thoughts about anything, and anyone who saw her reaction might have wondered if she was empty.

What did my mother think about when she sat so quietly? Did she remember a time when she had reached out for her own dreams?

"Mom, will you come to the wedding?" I asked again.

"No," she replied. "If that's the way your father feels, he'd be easier to live with if I stayed back, too." Mom slowly looked away from the window. Our eyes met, her's cold or sad, it was nearly impossible to read her expressions any more.

That evening I got on a Greyhound and traveled back to Portland. The gasoline fumes and the smell of the air freshener from the toilet at the back of the bus made me nauseous. My stomach churned. Closing my eyes, an image of Mom sitting in a cloud of cigarette smoke bubbled up in the back of my brain and my head felt heavy against the back of my seat. The closer the bus got to Portland, the more the afternoon with my parents seemed like a bad dream.

When the bus pulled into the station, the streetlights were just coming on, giving the city a warm, welcoming glow. Tired travelers sat on the wooden benches in the indoor waiting area. An older couple sat by the coffee vending machine, leaning against one another. Several sailors slouched in seats, arms folded across decorated chests, hats pulled down over their eyes. I imagined they all dreamt of the journey's end, whatever that would be.

A young woman—she couldn't have been much more than a girl—sat on a bench in a far corner, holding a small child on her lap. And though it looked as if she might be younger than me, she had a tired old woman look about her. With a greenish hue to her skin, the deep dark circles under tired eyes and her dishevelled clothing, this young woman looked like she had been on the road for years.

The child on her lap grabbed onto the woman's sweater, pulling herself up to a standing position. The young woman held a baby bottle in one hand and, with the other hand, braced the child against a fall. When finally the child managed to get to a standing position, the baby hung onto the mother's shoulder bouncing up and down as if on a trampoline, all the while making deliciously comical drooling sounds. I watched the mother and child for a few moments. I wanted to ask the woman if she would like me to hold the baby for a while, to give her a rest. But, deciding against this, instead went on my way, and as I passed, heard the mother softly humming.

Back in my room, the vision of the young woman haunted me and I decided to sketch them from the picture in my mind. Finishing the drawing and stepping back to take a longer look at what had been created, the image astounded me. The woman in the drawing closely resembled my own tired mother. It was Mom's image that stayed in my mind.

That night, while lying in bed, my mind kept wondering back to the young mother and her baby. It was difficult for me to separate my feelings about Mom from the expressions on the young woman's face at the bus station. They were the same. Life had sucked them both dry. Yet they held onto their children and hummed with them, sat lifeless and protected them against falling, sat lifeless and fed them, and sat lifeless, and sat lifeless, until they were lifeless.

Finally falling asleep, I was disturbed by dreams several time that quickly dissolved in the darkness. But the bright sunlight of a Sunday morning brought relief from the troubles of the day before. James and I were to meet up with his parents later that afternoon and have a picnic in a nearby park. We both agreed to tell our parents about our marriage plans on the same day. James' parents were quiet, gentle people, and I couldn't imagine that their reaction to the marriage would be the same as my dad's.

When James arrived, he listened sympathetically about my parent's reaction to our plans. There were no tears. The story came out of me in a matter-of-fact way. How Dad had spoken, his angry words.

"Your father's a cruel man, Wilma," James remarked.

"Yep. How did your parents take it when you told them?" I asked.

"They weren't too thrilled. They think we should wait."

"I don't know. Should we?" I asked.

"No. Why?"

"I guess you're right. Our love almost seems too perfect. Doesn't it?" I said.

"Yes, and when we get to San Francisco we'll have everything we want. Our lives are going to be just great."

James took me in his arms. He made me feel loved and wanted. He protected me from the forgotten troubling dreams of the night before, and the fear of becoming like Mom. Snuggling in his arms, the warmth of his body penetrated mine. James with his love, opened feelings in me never experienced before, feelings of belonging, happiness, and of dreams coming true.

We went ahead with a simple civil ceremony, having decided not to be married by a priest as James' parents had wanted. Charles, James' oldest brother, took our wedding picture with a sunny Oregon sky at our backs.

Everything seemed beautiful that day. I wore a dress I made at a friend's house because Mom and Dad stood firm about having nothing to do with the marriage, refusing to even let me even use Mom's sewing machine to make my wedding outfit.

James smiled at the camera, his hand warm against the curve of my back. I thought we made a handsome couple, standing tightly locked together, bracing ourselves for an adventure, frozen in a picture of a happy time.

I spoke to Mom the day before the wedding, hoping that she might change her mind. "No, I won't be coming. Your Dad's not feeling well again."

My new in-laws hosted a small reception. Most of the guests were from James' family, aside from a few of our friends. No one from my family attended. That night in our apartment with my head on James' chest, I said, "I'm never going to leave you, never." Hugging James I felt desperation deep in my bones.

"I'll never leave you, either," James said. He kissed the top of my head. "If you ever leave me, I'll die," I continued.

"Ah, I wouldn't leave you," James answered. "How could I leave you? I love you too much."

I felt an overwhelming urge to enter James' body, to crawl inside him and to stay there forever, wishing that our love could melt us into one person. The following weekend James took me to the Greyhound Bus station. It was time for me to visit my parents, this time without James.

Mom was in the kitchen stirring a pot of soup on the stove when I arrived. The smell of the soup reminded me of all the food that Mom had ever prepared. The odor of rich bone broth and the pungent sting of sliced onions permeated the house.

I kissed my mother on the cheek. "Where's Dad?" I asked.

"In the backyard." She wiped the table with a damp cloth, and then poured two cups of coffee. "So, now you're a married woman?" she said, sitting in her usual chair by the stove.

"Yes, I am." Mom lifted her cup, took a sip of coffee, and then lit a cigarette.

She and I had done this hundreds of times before, the sitting in silence, seeming to have nothing to say, while millions of words scuttled about in my head.

I sat with Mom, watching out the window, waiting for Dad to come into the house. The door to the back porch opened. Dad kicked his shoes against the outside sill of the house, knocking dirt from the soles of his boots. My heart raced with trepidation. He came into the room. Our eyes met. Dad turned away, and washed his hands in the kitchen sink.

"You a Mrs. now?" he asked. "Yes," I said.

"Well, what's done is done." Dad dried his hands, poured himself a cup of coffee, and sat at the table.

I had come to visit my parents thinking we had unfinished business to take care of. I had even prepared a speech about how well the wedding turned out. I wondered if they wanted to see the pictures. Dad took a long drink of his hot coffee. He never looked at people, but burrowed into them with his piercing pale blue eyes, looking for secrets, seeking evidence from a shifting glance that something had gone wrong. Over the years I'd learned how to hold my head, how to focus my eyes, only allowing him so far into my world.

"You staying for dinner?" Mom asked. "No."

Mom got up from the table and went to the stove. She took up a spoon and stirred the soup. So much was familiar about this house, the smells, the sounds, and even the ringing of the metal spoon that Mom tapped against the soup pot; it all had a place in my memory. This was my family, yet somehow I felt like an observer. Now it was time to build my own life. It was time for me to step away from my parents, and leave childhood behind. Life in this family was complicated and knowing Dad, he had not finished saying his last words to me about my marriage to James.

Waiting, watching Mom fuss around in the kitchen finishing with dinner preparations, my nerves were getting a bit frayed. Mom, too, knew that Dad had a few more words for me.

Then it came—Dad's last words before shutting me out. "If it doesn't work between you and this guy," he said, "I don't want you to think you can bring your bawling brats around here for your mother and me to take care of. You made your bed, now, young lady, you lie in it." He had not shouted these words at me, but delivered them with a cold, direct hit.

It had never entered my mind to ask for his help.

Mom looked at me, then at Dad, but she said nothing.

I looked down at my watch. "The bus'll be coming in fifteen minutes," I said.

That wasn't true. It was more than half an hour until the next Greyhound was due. But I had to get out of there. The smells of the cooking, the coffee pot on the stove, the ashtray filled with cigarette butts, everything had become suffocating.

"I'll see you," I said and put on my coat.

Mom looked up from the stove. "Okay. Now don't you be a stranger."

I smiled and nodded a goodbye, then went out the front door. But Mom's comment about not becoming a stranger had come too late. I'd already become a stranger in my family. My parents no longer made me feel welcome.

While waiting for the bus, my thoughts rambled around and I couldn't help but wonder what happens when someone makes a new life, as I had done by marrying James? Where do you put all that old stuff, all that entanglement with family?

The bus pulled up as a chilly rain began to fall. Determined not to take anything with me from the past, I made a pact with myself not to look back that day to see if my parents were watching out the window, the way they had done on many other occasions. No, there would be no looking back.

California Dream'n

"THE FASTER WE SAVE MONEY, the sooner we'll get to San Francisco," James said as we sat at the dinner table one night.

"I know, it's taking us too long to save money," I replied.

This was a conversation James and I frequently had. James pushed the peas on his dinner plate into a neat arrangement next to the pork chop. "Remember?" He hesitated. "Remember, Wilma, you told me about when you made extra money working as a power sewing machine operator?"

"Yeah, I remember."

"Do you think you could do it again?" Then James added quickly, "Just until we have enough money to leave?"

It never occurred to me that I'd ever consider taking another job in a sewing factory. The possibility of doing this took me totally by surprise. The likelihood that this might happen rattled around in my head while James continued to shuffle the remaining peas back and forth on his plate.

"It wouldn't be forever," James said. "I just want us to be in San Francisco as soon as possible. That's all. I wouldn't ask you to do this unless I thought it was important for both of us."

"I know." I took several deep breaths and then said, "Oh, all right." It was true. At the rate we were saving money, we'd never get to California. I would make a little more money in a sewing factory than my base pay as a file clerk. But the thought of going back to this kind of work sure didn't make me happy. Remembering those days sitting hour after hour behind a sewing machine made me slightly nauseous.

Pushing my dinner plate to one side, my appetite was gone.

James reached across the table, took hold of my hand and blew me a kiss. "If you could do that, we'd get there real fast. Let's try for August. They say that's the best time of the year in San Francisco."

I knew we would get to our destination sooner if we could pull in more money. James wasn't a big earner, but he'd gotten a raise in pay right after we were married. Now I guess it was up to me to stretch myself and bring in a few more bucks. Though I certainly dreaded the thought of going back to working on a sewing machine.

James had no problems with it, even after hearing all the stories about how hard the women worked and that after a while, how some of the women went a little off their rockers. He wasted no time in getting out the newspaper. Reading through the jobs section for me, James circled two want ads for power sewing machine operators. Handing me the paper, my eyes scanned across the ads, but nothing registered. It was as though my husband handed me something written in a language that I could not comprehend. My body went limp with disappointment.

Putting the paper down on the table, blinking several times, and then gathering myself, I again tried to read the ads. This time the words were clear enough. The first ad for a sleeping bag manufacturer seemed promising. The second ad for a ladies garment factory, way on the other side of town, presented a transportation problem. The sleeping bag place, the easiest to get to by bus, was the one we decided I would apply to in the morning.

That night lying in bed, we talked excitedly about our plans of starting over in San Francisco. We made love, sweet, sweet love and James whispered how happy we would always be. But then when my husband rolled over and fell asleep, the dark room had a sense of aloneness. Sleep did not come easily to me, but James' soft night breathing sounded relaxed, like a purring kitten. He did not seem to understand my disappointment at going back to working in a sewing factory. Maybe I didn't protest enough and that thought made me feel like a coward. But I wasn't cowardly. We both wanted to make this move happen. And then the realization struck me. This was my way of taking on an obligation for the sake of my marriage. It was my responsibility, as much as it was James', to make more money.

Lying in the dark it became clear to me that this was my first experience of what it meant to make a sacrifice for our marriage. Going back to a hated job felt all right when thinking about it in that way. Yet, remembering how tired and unhappy that kind of work made me feel, I couldn't help but regret what I was about to do.

There are no real interviews for these kinds of jobs. Someone looks at the application, sees the experience, asks when you can start, and the job is yours. These places gobbled up experienced workers, hiring them on the spot. That was that—I was back on the assembly line, this time sewing zippers into sleeping bags.

It was hard work. I had to sew the zippers into the heavy, fully stuffed sleeping bags using a large revolving table that had to be swung around each time one side of the bag was finished. The sleeping bags were heavy and the piece rate turned out to be extremely unreasonable. No matter how diligent my effort, the quota was unreachable. And my paycheck reflected the minimum wage that certainly did not please either James or myself.

After three weeks of battling with sleeping bags, we decided it was time for me to look for another job. A garment manufacturer a short bus ride from our apartment ran an ad in the newspaper for experienced seamstresses. The place made athletic jackets for high school and college teams throughout the Northwest. I had no trouble getting a job with them and it turned out that my assignment was to make the entire jacket. The procedure turned out to be difficult and tedious. Determined to learn the operation quickly, because we only had three months before our deadline to leave, I raced against the quota, which luckily turned out to be much more attainable than that of the sleeping bag company.

The factory, a small two-story shop, only had twenty-five workers—women who were a cold, clannish group. That didn't bother me; my mission was to make money, not friends.

On my first day, one woman sitting in a corner looked like someone I used to work with a couple of years ago. She appeared much older than when I knew her. During lunch hour it was my intention to go over and reacquaint myself, but when the lunch buzzer sounded, she quickly left the building before I had a chance to say anything to her. It didn't seem out of the ordinary for her to rush off like that. Many women preferred to be alone.

Several days went by before we made eye contact, and recognizing me, she said, "Well, what in the hell brings you to this hole?"

"I got married," I said. "We live down the street. This seemed as good a place as any to earn a living. What brings you here?"

"Needed a change," she said. "I forgot your name."

"Wilma, and what's yours?"

"Nora."

"It's good to see you. You hear from any of the other women?"

"No, I'm afraid I just dropped out of sight. Well, I'm headed out to my car to eat lunch. See you later." Nora turned and quickly walked out the door.

For the next couple of weeks Nora and I talked briefly before she went to her car to have lunch. Then, one day she invited me to join her.

We chatted about the weather. James became one of the topics and of course we talked about the work. Then Nora said, "You want to know why I left the other job?"

"Sure," I answered.

"Maybe you remember I had a daughter, Christine, my only child and she had two sons. Well, her son-of-a-bitchin' husband blew her brains out one night while she slept. Then the coward shot himself in the head. He had been depressed. The doctors diagnosed him with a classic case of depression. He couldn't hold down a job, Christine was doing as much as she could to make ends meet, but they were in debt up to their ears, and then their house went into foreclosure. He couldn't stand it any longer, and then one night the bastard took the coward's way out. But, why did he have to take Christine with him?"

Nora related the details of the horrid murder of her daughter in what at first seemed to me an emotionless, matter of fact manner. She avoided looking at me when she told about what had happened, but gazed out the front window of the car. Then when she turned to face me, the dreadfulness of what she had said reflected back at me in the tortured, vacant look in her eyes.

"Everyone at the old factory knew the story. I couldn't endure the looks the women gave me. Their constant gawking and the ridiculous questions they asked drove me up the wall. Some people just don't know how to keep their mouths shut. So I left the job and went some place where no one knew anything about me."

Nora reached into her lunch bag and pulled out a hardboiled egg. She banged the egg against the dashboard then methodically removed the broken pieces of shell.

The only thing I could think to say was, "I'm sorry."

"You're sorry," Nora said. "I'll never have a normal life again. That girl was everything to me. Christine was my life. I had lived only for her ever since her father died when she was a baby. And that no-good bastard had to go and take her from me. I'll never understand why he did such a thing. Not that it would do any good, but if it could be done, wishing that son of a bitch into hell would not be enough revenge for what he did. Christine's blood was all over the bedroom walls. He crept up on her while she slept and shot her in the head. What a coward, sneaking up on her in the night while she was sleeping, and their kids bedded down in the next room, too.

"Then when that creep saw what he had done, he pulled the trigger on himself. That was too easy. He should have been skinned alive."

Nora's eyes were wild with anger as she gazed out into the street, one hand holding the boiled egg while the other hand tightly gripped the steering wheel. I imagined Nora's mind vibrating with images more gruesome than I could possibly conjure, while she continued to stare out into the street as if she were in a trance.

I remained silent until the lunch break ended, and then I said, "Look, if there's anything I can do for you, just let me know."

"Do for me? There's nothing anyone can do for me," she answered, and then threw the boiled egg back into her lunch bag, opened the car door, and got out.

Nora's story caught me totally by surprise. For the rest of the afternoon the wretched tale of poor Christine kept running through my mind. Concentrating on my work for the rest of the day was not easy. I could not believe what she had told me.

That night I gave James an abbreviated version of Nora's terrible story. It interested him for a short while, but his main concern was how my work was going and if the quota had been reached.

"Yep," I said, "today I got just a slight bit over the quota. If there's no

trouble with the sewing machine, this should be a really good week."
It hadn't taken me long to acclimate to this new job. I'd resigned myself to give it my best and to just stick my nose to the grindstone and
make all the money that I could.

Each day, after that, until James and I left for San Francisco, Nora
invited me out to have lunch in her car. Each day I heard more of the
horrible details of Christine's death, and of the difficulty Nora now
had in bringing up the two grandsons, one of whom Nora hated im-
mensely because he looked exactly like his father.

"I had the walls cleaned, primed, and repainted," Nora said. "Then
one day, when I went into Christine's bedroom, blood seeped through
the paint again, the stain was there, like it had just happened. I sold
the house. I couldn't go through fixing the walls again. I thought I
was going to have a heart attack the first time I saw the room, but the
second time was worse. I couldn't stand it. It was awful, just awful,"
Nora said.

She shed no tears, but looked out the window with a blind, dry-
eyed stare. I listened to the details of Nora's story and realized she
didn't expect a response. I had become her receptacle as she continued to feed me detail after detail, expecting nothing from me but to
listen.

Now regularly at the lunch hour, Nora looked in my direction and
with a nod of her head, indicated that I was invited to join her. After
a while, I wanted to tell her, "No thanks, I don't want to eat lunch in
your car." But I couldn't bring myself to be that honest. She certainly
had my sympathy, and even though the lunch hour was miserable,
my other choice was to eat alone while being ignored by the other
women, who had not warmed up to me, even after six weeks.

"My oldest grandson is a pig," Nora said. "He looks just like his
father, and he's the most disgusting child I've ever known. He has to
get up to go to the bathroom during dinner every night. I can't stand
him."

Nora continued to tell me bits and pieces of how difficult it was
for her to raise her grandsons. Some days she retold the details of
her daughter's murder, but never with tears. She never cried, though
her eyes sometimes looked wild with anger, a look not easily forgot-

ten. Finally, when there were but two weeks left before James and I planned to leave for San Francisco, the realization hit me that this was really going to happen. Nora's story about her family was most certainly tragic, but quite honestly, I could not listen much longer to this horrible tragic tale.

* * * *

Finally, August arrived. James and I, carefully pinching our pennies, had saved enough money to make our move to San Francisco. I pitied poor Nora, imagining my old friend sitting at a sewing machine day after dreary day, putting together the same garments year after year, while constantly attempting to piece together her blown-apart daughter. I thought about Nora's grandson, the one she hated, who was a constant reminder to his grandmother—the only person left in the world to look after him—that he carried the genes of the man who killed her daughter.

As James and I loaded our possessions into the U-Haul on an overcast Oregon day, it felt as though we were leaving a tragic little cove in someone else's life. Though at this point, my happiness outweighed any sadness that was being left behind. Stowing the last box into the trailer, a twinge of guilt crept into my mind and I wondered if it was the guilt of leaving behind people with their sad lives, or did I feel guilty because I felt so happy and free.

James closed the hatch on the trailer, "This is it, Wilma," he said. "Say goodbye to the old life."

Taking a deep breath I got into the car. Yes, I thought, there would only be good times ahead.

The Mountain Gorge

WITH ALL OUR POSSESSIONS PACKED into the U-Haul trailer attached to James' Ford Pinto, we were finally on our way to San Francisco. We called it our adventure. We hadn't planned on our adventure to sour on us, but then about three hundred miles outside of Portland the engine light on the Pinto indicated an overheated engine. James quickly eased the car onto the shoulder of the road to let the engine cool down. In less than an hour we were back on the road again.

If I had not been so young and still a little tingly from being a newlywed, I might have understood earlier that my life had taken a slight turn into the unexpected on that day when the Pinto overheated. But then they say fortune telling is a game for fools.

Before we reached the California border, the road became steeper and steeper. The engine began making a lot of noise, but I paid little attention to the sounds. Assuming James knew what he was doing, I continued looking out the window, letting my mind drift, and thought about how we mapped the trip out so we'd be driving over the Golden Gate Bridge at sunset on the second day of our journey. I'd only seen photos of the bridge and tried to imagine what it would look like close up.

My mind was elsewhere when James shouted, "The engine light went on again."

"What does that mean?" I asked. It didn't seem a serious problem to me. We'd easily taken care of the engine light trouble a couple of hours ago.

"This time we're in trouble, Wilma," James said. He looked quite worried.

"How come?" I knew nothing about cars and had no idea what my husband was talking about.

"We can't stop the car on a hill. If we do, the car won't be able to pull this load in the U-Haul on this steep grade. Oh man, this is not good." The panic in his eyes frightened me. The engine light on the dashboard flashed on and off. Steam seeped out from under the hood of the car.

"I smell something," I said, trying to keep from sounding too panicked. Though at this point I had no idea how serious the situation was. But it certainly didn't look good.

"We're going to blow up," James yelled as he continued to drive the car up the steady incline.

"Stop the car. Stop the car," I demanded.

"I can't," James said, his face pale.

"Why don't you stop?" I insisted and began to feel fearful myself. A large billow of steam rolled out from under the hood. The light on the dashboard no longer flashed a warning, but now glowed steadily.

James gripped the steering wheel. "What are we going to do?"

My new husband never acted this way before.

"Stop it," I said. "You're scaring me. Pull over. Give the engine water or something." "I can't pull over. I told you we wouldn't be able to start up again. The grade's too steep for our engine." His reply came in a shrill voice.

"Well, we can't drive with the steam coming out like this. Can we?"

"Pray. Wilma, pray," James urged me loudly.

"What do you mean pray?" Before James could respond, an even larger puff of smoke poured out from underneath the hood.

"Pull over before we can't get it off the road at all," I shouted.

James drove the car onto the narrow shoulder. Once there, he leaned his head on the steering column. "I'm scared," he said. Now his voice, rather than sounding shrill, had a worrisome tone, and he began to cry.

The only other man I had ever seen cry had been Dad, when his mother died. He and his brother held on to each other, calling out, pleading for their mother to return to them. We had serious car trouble, nothing more than that and it required cool-headed thinking. Crying wasn't going to solve anything. You didn't have to be a car mechanic to know that much.

"Open the hood," I suggested. "Look and see what's the matter."

James said nothing for a while. Then slowly lifting his head and wiping his face dry, he said, "We're going to die. I know we are."

"We're not going to die. Do you know anything about fixing cars?" I asked.

James and I never talked about cars before. We talked about poetry, movies and what to have for dinner. But James never said anything about working on his old Pinto. We just got into the car and drove it places.

"I know what the problem is. It's overheated. That's the trouble. I had no idea we'd have such a steep hill to climb." With that, James sounded a little more composed. We got out of the car. "Stand back," he said and, unhooking the latch, slowly lifted the hood. A huge billowing cloud of hot steam rolled out at us. The radiator cap sizzled and spit hot droplets at us. Some scalding water landed on me.

"Ouch, that stuff's hot." I backed up.

"I'm scared, Wilma. Let's pray." James face had turned as white as a sheet, his voice trembling. Pretending not to hear him, I instead rubbed my arm to ease the sting from the burning radiator water.

James bowed his head.

From my perspective, at that moment, prayer didn't seem a way out of this predicament.

James had a tendency to be superstitious, but he had never acted like this before. Though, once, we didn't go on a drive to the ocean because that morning the battery in the car went dead. James took that as a bad omen and said he worried that if we went to the ocean, something terrible would happen to us. So we didn't leave the house that day. This overheating business with the car seemed different from his tendency toward superstition. His was really freaking out about the overheated radiator and that didn't make any sense to me.

And this thing about praying didn't make any sense either. When we got married James refused to have a religious ceremony. His parents were quite upset when James told them he was no longer a believer. Early on in our relationship James said he no longer believed in God.

"I can't hear you praying. Wilma, pray, please." James' voice now almost sounded frantic.

"I am," I lied. I didn't know what else to say. Pretending to pray made me feel like a hypocrite, yet when I thought about it, if God did exist, and I believed in the power of prayer, it didn't seem logical that a Holy entity would swoop down, pick up the U-Haul, the Pinto with us in it and carry this load to safety.

Praying wasn't big in my family. Mom was a quiet believer. Dad's beliefs were more complicated. He mostly cursed God or any entity he thought might have something to do with messing up his life. So growing up, prayer and religion was a real mixed bag. Though, as a little girl, when attending church with Grandma, bowing my head while sitting next to Grandma in her favorite pew, praying seemed a natural thing to do. But parked on the roadside with a disabled car, in the middle of nowhere, praying didn't make any real sense to me.

A cool mountain breeze blew across my face. The roadside gravel crunched beneath my feet. I looked up from my pretend prayer and saw James; his head lowered, his clasped hands trembling and this scene triggered a story mom told about grandma and praying. Mom's family did a lot of traveling when *she* was a little girl. They were part of the dust bowl migration, moving from one place to another with Grandpa looking for work and they ran into a lot of car trouble. Mom told about one time when Grandma had Mom and her younger brother and sister down on their knees at the side of the road, praying that Grandpa could patch the inner tube of the tire sufficient enough to get them to the next town. Mom said she and her siblings were all huddled together in a ditch along the side of a dusty road, Grandma leading the prayer session while cars passed by, honking horns, waving to them, with some drivers calling out, "Amen."

I didn't care how frantic James became; I wouldn't get down on my knees. As I contemplated just how hysterical my husband might become, a car stopped. Two men got out and walked toward us. I felt both suspicion and relief, at the same time, wondering if they were friendly, or if they would turn out to be the kind of men you read about in the newspaper, the kind who took advantage of stranded motorists in the middle of nowhere?

"What's the matter with your car?" asked the man in a blue plaid shirt.

"Looks overheated," his fat, red-faced companion said. The two men walked toward our car.

James unfolded his hands quickly and, leaning with one hand braced on the car fender, said, "We seem to be having trouble making it up this hill."

"You're not the only one, kid. You should see the number of cars that can't get up this steep grade. But I can tell you're pulling too much in the trailer for this little engine." The man in the blue plaid shirt spoke in a kindly manner to James. The two men looked under the hood of the car. Then slowly taking off the radiator cap, they let the last of the sizzling steam escape. They each in turn touched and fiddled with other parts of the car engine.

Then the man in the blue plaid shirt said, "You're just overheated, kid. Nothing else seems to be wrong. When it cools down, we'll put more water in for you, then you can make it up the rest of the way."

I sat in the car with the door open, my feet dangling just above the gravely shoulder of the road. James paced up and down in the dry gutter. It was hard to tell if he was praying. The look on his face troubled me. He appeared weak, not weak in his body, but weak in a way that was not clear to me. It concerned me, not that he wanted me to pray, but by the way he panicked. But it was his tearful eyes that made me uncomfortable, not that I thought a man shouldn't cry, but this just didn't seem the time or a place for anyone to shed tears.

The strangers slouched against the back of their car, smoking cigarettes. They seemed pleasant enough and I wondered if they had ever lost control the way James had. Playing in the loose gravel with my foot, it dawned on me how far from home we had traveled and that we would be even further from our roots once our journey ended. That is, if we ever got off this hill.

The man in the blue plaid shirt came back to our car. He put a hand on the radiator. "Feels like she's as cool as she's going to get up here. Let's give this engine a drink of water in and see what happens."

Pouring water from a gallon jug they took from the trunk of their car, they replenished the water in the radiator. The two strangers leaned far under the hood of the Pinto seeming to be looking deeply into the heart of our car. It wasn't difficult to imagine the Pinto giving a deep sigh of relief, rejuvenated by the drink of water.

"What do you think?" James asked. "Is it going to work?"

"Don't know, kid. Got to see what happens when we try to start it," the man with the red face said.

"Let's start it up," said the man in the blue plaid shirt. He got into the driver's seat and turned the key in the ignition. The engine made a grinding sound. He turned the key again and stomped on the gas pedal several times. A few unusual sounds came from under the hood, and then the engine successfully revved up.

I breathed a sigh of relief.

"That was one hot little engine," the man in the blue plaid shirt remarked.

"Now what?" James asked. "Will it make it up the rest of the hill?"

"Yeah, it'll make it up the hill. But you've got to gun it all the way to the top of this grade. You can't let up on the gas."

James' eyes nervously looked at the radiator under the open hood of the Pinto, then he glanced upward to the top of the hill. The strangers must have sensed James' nervousness about driving up that steep grade.

"Look, kid," the man in the blue plaid shirt said. "You want me to drive the car up the hill for you?"

"All right. It's not that I couldn't do it," James said. "It's just that this hill is so steep and, well, you seem to understand it a lot better than I do."

"Jump in the back. I'll take the Pinto up the hill for you. When we get to the top, you and your wife can coast the rest of the way down into California. How's that?"

James quickly got into the back seat of the car.

"Don't worry kid, I'll get your car up this grade. Plenty of people get stuck up here. But you're pulling too much stuff. You better rest it someplace when you get to the bottom."

The man with blue plaid shirt slammed the hood closed, then got into the driver's seat of our car. The stranger pushed down on the gas pedal slightly racing the engine. Then he slowly eased the car out onto the highway. The Pinto went up, up, up. The hill seemed to go on forever. "You kids moving?" the stranger asked.

"Yeah, we're moving to San Francisco," I said.

"Never been there myself. I hear Frisco's a pretty nice place. Always wanted to see Fisherman's Warf and maybe taste some crabs. We're almost at the top now. I've been up this hill so many times, you couldn't even count how many times it's been."

The stranger drove the Pinto slower than the rest of the traffic, keeping the car at an even speed.

"You live around here?" James asked.

"Yeah, I live down the grade and over a ways," he said.

Finally reaching the top of the mountain, the stranger pulled the car on to the shoulder of the road. "Well, kids, it looks like we did it. This is the end of the grade. From here you'll drive straight down. You won't have any problems that I can see."

The man with the red face, who had followed in the other car, pulled up behind us.

The man in the blue paid shirt got out of our car. "You're on your own now, kids," he said. "Good luck."

James switched from the back into the driver's seat. The man in the plaid shirt closed the door for James, and then he stuck his head in the open window. "Relax, kid," he said. "You're almost there. Just remember to cool down the engine all the way when you get to the bottom. You'll find a place there where you can eat and get gas. So take your time." He gave James a friendly pat on the shoulder.

Driving out onto the road, James said, "That sure was a close call. I never want to go through something like that again, as long as I live." I said nothing and turned around to watch the two men driving away. Their car turned onto a frontage road and then headed back down the hill in the direction we had just come from. We were on our own now.

"So when we get to the bottom, let's take a long rest. Okay?" James said. He didn't take his eyes off the road, his complexion turning slightly chalky again. His knuckles looked bloodless as he tightly gripped the steering wheel.

"Sounds like a good idea," I said. Then realizing that maybe we should have offered the strangers something for their help, I said,

"You know those men didn't even ask for money."

"I know. It's a good thing. We're on a pretty small budget until we get work," James said, still holding tightly to the steering wheel.

"We could have given them something."

"Forget about it," James snapped. "We don't have enough money to start doling it out to every stranger who comes along."

"Yeah, but we could have at least offered something."

"I said, forget it." Our tired old car went steadily down the hill. Then, in the distance, like the stranger had told us, we saw a gas station and restaurant. James parked the car in a shady spot under a scrubby pine tree. We got out of the hot car and headed for the restaurant. As we walked toward it, I looked back at the dusty Pinto—it looked a bit frazzled after the ordeal on the mountain. It had been a long day and I felt a bit undone by the overheated radiator myself.

James picked up his pace," I'm starving," he said.

Quickly scurrying to keep up, I wondered if all poets cried when they were frightened. If this were so, what else in the long run of our life together would be revealed to me?

A *"Be-In"*

JAMES AND I ARRIVED IN San Francisco in the summer of 1966. From that first day when we crossed the Golden Gate Bridge and unloaded our possessions from the U-Haul, the world looked like a cauldron, with humanity bubbling and boiling over with excitement. Students marched in protest against the Vietnam War. Scraggly bunches of young people calling themselves hippies were everywhere. Unlike the days when my father built a fallout shelter in our backyard, society now looked as if, rather than having a bomb dropped in its midst, the world seemed to have exploded from the inside out.

It wasn't just the outside world that seemed to have changed. The relationship between James and me had also begun to take some unexpected twists and turns. The problem wasn't that I always did the wrong thing. According to James I just never seemed to do the right thing. After less than a year of marriage, it sure felt like the honeymoon was over.

We had only been settled in San Francisco a couple of months when we met Greta, a short, plump, middle-aged woman living in Sausalito, who liked to be called "Mammasan." She took James and me under her wing, introducing us to her friends. It didn't take long before James and I were part of a large circle of people.

One evening as we sat drinking with Greta, listening to selections from her jazz record collection, she asked, "How'd you two like to help me start a business?"

"What kind of business?" James asked. He sounded curious rather than interested.

"I have several ideas," she said. "Kind of a service for the rich, like house watching and dog walking. Then, I've seen a lot of unattended Laundromats in the area. Why not offer to come in several times a week, wipe off the machines and mop the floors?"

She then turned her attention to me. "Wilma," she said, "how would you like to set up a seamstress shop? I'd provide the capital to get the business off the ground, while you make the clothes. We'd offer super mod dresses, classy mini skirts, that kind of thing. How does that sound?"

Greta settled back in her chair and took a drink of whisky. The ice cubes tinkled. It was seven o'clock in the evening, which meant Greta could drink all the booze she wanted. She followed the golden rule of no cocktails before five o'clock, which was her way of preventing becoming an alcoholic. Greta stuck to her word, never having a drink before five, though after that golden hour, Greta was rarely seen without a glass of something in her hand.

"Why us?" I asked.

"Because I like you two. You're young and you've got a lot of energy. Wilma, I know you don't like working in the garment factory."

She couldn't have been more right about that. I had gone back to working on a power sewing machine, only because James and I decided it was the quickest job I could find. James settled for a position in the stock room of a college bookstore. Neither of us was happy about what we were doing, but if this was a race, there's no doubt I'd be the unhappiest.

"You'd sort of be working for me," Greta continued. "I'd pay the bills, set up the collateral, and you'd be working toward the partnership. You could move in here and we'd turn the living room into a workshop."

James poured himself another drink. "I like the idea. It's not exactly my ideal job, but maybe I'd find a little more time to write poetry."

"Yeah, you might," Greta said. "What about you, Wilma? You like the idea, too?"

"I'd like anything that would get me out of the factory."

"Partners," Greta declared in a tone of finality. She slowly tipped her drink until the ice in the glass came clinking down against her teeth, then set the glass on the table with a firm thud, she said, "Okay. We got a deal."

A week later, James and I moved in with Greta. It didn't take long to set up the sewing room while James worked out the other details of the business. From that point on, we did pretty much everything together with Greta and her friends, Kitty, Hank, Bill, and Connie. Everyone made James and me feel as though we were old friends.

Greta liked having young people around, and San Francisco was hopping with all kinds of youthful activity. Between the free music concerts in Golden Gate Park and street theater presentations all over the city, just about every block of this hopping place had something interesting going on.

One morning Greta announced, "There's going to be a tremendous gathering in Golden Gate Park today. You want to go to a 'be-in?'" she asked.

"What's a 'be-in?'" I responded.

James gave me an irritated glance. Everything I said lately grated on his nerves.

"It's a happening," Greta said. "I don't know exactly how to explain it. A lot of people get together. There's either free music or theater and there is always speeches protesting the war."

"Don't you read the papers, Wilma?" James snapped. "Be-ins are going on all over the world." He shook his head, then, raising an eyebrow, he looked at Greta and shrugged his shoulders.

"When we get there, Wilma, you'll see," Greta told me. I couldn't figure out if she was protecting me or siding with James. But I knew she noticed James' impatience with me, and now since we lived with Greta, she was getting a pretty good picture of our marriage.

* * * *

Once Greta said, while I made a sandwich for James, "Let him make it himself, he's a big boy now." Continuing to prepare the snack, I worried about not doing the right thing for fear of losing my husband. It had gotten that bad. I took the sandwich into where James sat watching TV. Though I said nothing at the time, I wanted to tell Greta that my marriage pinched me like a poorly fitting pair of shoes. When we arrived at the be-in, hundreds of people milled about on the open field.

"Wow, look at all those folks," Greta said. "I knew there'd be a crowd, but I didn't expect quite this many people."

"They're all against the war?" I asked, trying not to sound too stupid. James gave me one of his, "Are you from another planet?" looks. This time he said nothing.

"Yep," Greta replied. "That and they want to hear the free music."

"Too bad Kitty and Hank couldn't come today," James said.

"They said they'd try to get here," Greta said. "That's if Kitty's parents left early enough. I doubt they'll be able to make it, though. Hank's not going to break his neck to get to something like this. It's not his thing."

A small group of people shouted, "Hell no, we won't go." Others joined in and soon the entire crowd chanted, "Hell no, we won't go." I shouted, too.

Someone on the stage called out, "All right, you people, what do you want?" "Peace!" the crowd responded. "When do you want it?" "Now!" the crowd shouted. "You're a beautiful audience," the man on the stage said. "Now let's get started."

The chanting continued for a short while longer until a guy with an electric guitar came on stage and played a mournful, howling collection of notes that almost sounded like a human scream. A drummer beat out a thunderous blast of noise. Then music leaped off the stage at the audience. Everyone moved wildly in rhythm with the music. People waved picket signs displaying peace symbols and anti-war slogans.

A dense fog hovered above the park. Trees, the young tall, slender ones and the ragged bent bows of old conifers, disfigured by storms and time, stood along the edges of the thickly grassed polo field.

A man and woman standing next to me, both wearing long flowing garments, swayed back and forth in rhythm to the music. The woman stood in front of the man. His arms wrapped around her, his fingers locked together just below her breasts. Her head lazed against his torso. I wanted James to hold me that way, and to sway with the music. We hardly touched anymore unless we were in bed. Maybe now, with so many couples holding each other, James might feel affectionate, too.

Stepping in front of him and easing my body into his, it seemed an obvious statement. He gave me a slight shove forward. "Watch where you're stepping," he said. Then he moved to the side. "I can't see. You're standing in front of me."

Embarrassed and hurt, I scooted next to Greta.

"Too bad Kitty's not here today," James said. "This is her kind of thing. I don't know if Hank would like it, but she'd love it." James stood on his toes, craning his neck to look around the crowd. "Isn't this great? I've never heard anything so beautiful."

I said nothing and swayed to the music.

More people continued to arrive. The bands played louder and louder until the air felt dense with the growing musical energy.

"You know," Greta said, "if they dropped a bomb right now on this crowd, they'd get rid of all the liberals in this town."

"You're right," I agreed. Though Greta may have only been joking, my response was to look up into the sky, check out the horizon for any low flying plane overhead. There weren't any. Music and anti-war speeches went on all afternoon. The speakers, though brief, riled up the crowd for a short period of time, but then when they left the stage, it still wasn't clear to me why people protested so much against this war, or why we even had troops in Vietnam in the first place. Until now, truthfully, the war hadn't occupied much of my thinking. It angered me though to hear we were sending our boys to other countries to be killed.

There was a pungent odor in the air. The couple next to me passed a hand-rolled cigarette back and forth. Though this was my first time smelling the stuff, it didn't take me long to figure out they were smoking marijuana.

Several people walked passed carrying sticks of incense. The smoke snaked through the crowd, adding another element of odor to the music. Taking a deep breath, closing my eyes, music and colors undulated rhythmically inside my head. It no longer mattered that James wouldn't hold me. He can go to hell, I thought. The exotic air engulfed me, lulling me into a feeling of contentment.

When the concert ended, a woman dressed in a hooded, long black robe passed in front of me. Her face covered in a white, pasty theatrical make-up gave her a ghostly appearance. She moved slowly, methodically as though perhaps she was gliding slightly above the ground. When the woman passed I saw that she had pinned to the back of her robe the poster of a child terribly burned by napalm. I had seen this poster frequently displayed in bookstores and other places. This disturbing image never failed to give me the shivers.

Beyond the child's face now, though, and in another visual plane were the trees, the fog and the shuffling of youthful humanity. The image of the screaming, wounded child held tightly onto my mind, as though the spirit of the poster had tentacles and my mind became the rock it clung to. The image stuck tightly to me; holding on, smothering my vision, muffling sounds. A foul taste seeped from under my tongue. The war was thousands of miles away, and yet seeing the poster of that terrified child in this pastoral setting, brought me strangely to the front line of the fighting. I felt helpless thinking that children were burning alive. In wartime, children, women, men, everyone might just as well be pieces of wood. What is the value of a human life when we sit watching the news on TV callously eating our evening meal? The eyes of the child in the poster burned themselves into my mind. What had she done, what could anyone have done, to be treated in such a horrible manner?

The foul taste continued to seep from under my tongue as though the saliva had turned to poison. I was about to spit the unpleasant taste from my mouth, when James shouted to me, "Have you ever heard anything so wonderful? I swear this is the most exciting thing I've ever heard."

The image of the burning child still clung to my vision. I couldn't respond to James.

He turned to Greta. "Those bands had some sound, didn't they?"

"Yeah, but I still prefer jazz. Rock music leaves me cold," Greta replied.

"How could you say that? We heard masterpieces today," James said with an insistent tone.

"I wouldn't go that far," Greta grumbled.

"You're kidding. They were great. I've heard some of this on the radio, but to hear it outside, live—this was special."

"Okay, so you liked it. Doesn't mean I have to like it too, does it? Let's go. I'm tired. The fresh air's knocked the poop out of me."

On the drive back to Sausalito, James sat up front with Greta. All the way home he raved about the music, and he remembered the names of every group. "I'm going to get all their albums," he said.

Greta glanced at me from the rear view mirror. "You all right, Wilma?" she asked. "You look pale."

"I'm fine, just tired."

Driving across the Golden Gate Bridge, I looked out at the Pacific Ocean. Something about the day reminded me of home. Perhaps the dampness of the fog that hovered over the park left me with a familiar northwest chill. As we neared the middle of the Golden Gate Bridge, needing a distraction from the image of the child, I wondered what my parents were doing at that very moment. It felt odd to think about my family. They had not been in my thoughts for many weeks. But there was something about the image in the poster that joggled a faint recollection of what my father said years ago, about the world being a terrible place in which to bring children. He said, given a chance to do it over again, he'd have never been responsible for any new life on this earth. Until that very instant, the full meaning of what he said had eluded me. For some reason that comment never seemed related to my existence. Dad said a lot of scary things and not all of it made sense. Now his words came to me as though for the first time, and I realized that Dad meant he regretted bringing my sisters and me into the world.

The pewter-colored turbulent bay below me, the well-manicured bridge, strong, relentless, James talking on and on about how much he liked the music, while my father's regrets that I had been born made my head feel unbearably heavy.

Sitting in the back seat of Greta's car, the image of the crying Vietnamese child burned deeply into me and into an old and forgotten nameless wound. The unpleasant taste in my mouth grew so strong that it became an odor. And I could smell my tired disillusioned father, sitting in his undershirt at the breakfast table, drinking his morning coffee and smoking cigarettes, all the while wondering was my father wishing he'd had no children. At that moment the world seemed insane. I could smell and taste the insanity. The contradictions, broken dreams, beautiful children turned into torches; and my own marriage, now a broken promise, once again overwhelmed my mouth with bitterness. I looked straight into the eyes of the wounded child, and whispered, "What do you want me to do? Please, leave me alone."

Slowly the image of the child loosened and slipped away.

"I sure could use a cocktail." Greta's comment startled me. So lost in my thought, it felt as though I were alone in the car. By the time Greta pulled into the driveway, the sunset had shattered the sky into a vibrant arrangement of colors. A brilliant orange light glowed above the trees in the backyard.

Once we got into the house, Greta remedied the foul taste in my mouth when she handed me a double shot of whisky. "Mmm," I said, and closing my eyes, there was only blessed blackness.

Betrayal

DON'T ASK ME WHY I denied it for so long. Maybe it was magical thinking that things would eventually work out, that perhaps someday James would love me again.

Then one night, James said, "Wilma, I can't keep it inside any longer. Kitty and I are in love and we've been seeing each other whenever we can."

Those words stung as if my husband had literally flung shards of glass at my face. At first, I sat silently, frozen, bound by anger and hurt, trying to absorb what he had just said. But this announcement didn't come as a surprise, not really.

"I love Kitty," he said again. His words hurt as much the second time as they had the first. "I hope you can understand how difficult this is for me." His words were directed at me, though his eyes avoided mine. It seemed to me that James had a slight look of bewilderment on his face. I got the distinct impression that James felt as if he was the victim.

"Yeah," I replied. Finally words came to me. "I can see how hard it is for you."

"It is. Believe me, Wilma. I love you, too." This did not sound apologetic. "I can't live this way," he said and this time James looked at me. From the first evening we met at one of Greta's dinner parties, it was easy to see that James and Kitty were attracted to each other. Kitty agreed with everything James said. At least that was how it looked when she bent forward intently, listening to his every word.

Kitty, the sweet one, the friendly one, the one whose husband frequently bragged about Kitty, his creative, spirited wife. He said she had gotten her nickname, Kitty, because, even as a small child, she was as gentle as a kitten. If you ask me, she seemed more like an alley cat.

In the beginning it had been fun hanging out with Kitty and Hank. Even though James and I had so little money—and we were younger than they were by at least ten years—that didn't seem to bother anyone. Though it didn't take long before things began to fall apart.

The problem started when James told Greta that once we had moved in with her, and he realized what Greta's business idea entailed, he had no interest in helping to get her enterprise up and running. I remembered the disappointed look on Greta's face. It said volumes. "I have no choice," she said. I have to ask you both to move out."

The next week James and I were living once again on our own in San Francisco. It was easy enough for me to get a job in a garment factory. James stayed home writing poetry, and supposedly looking through the want ads, searching for the "right" kind of work. "I can't play these games with you any longer, Wilma," James told me now, relating his story as though washing his conscience clean of the guilt would make it all right. "I lied to Greta. And I lied to you."

All the time he was supposed to be out setting up the business for Greta, he said, "I was with Kitty." There was a sincere, compassionate look on his face, a look that would soon become an ultimatum.

At the dinner parties with Hank and Kitty, James spent most of the evening talking to Kitty. Or he would dance with Kitty, telling me, "Hank never dances and Kitty likes to dance, so I dance with her."

I'd sit and watch them. Hank, even though he was not supposed to like to dance, would ask me to join him on the floor. He moved stiffly and needed a couple of drinks to loosen up, but he danced.

* * * *

One evening, several months after we'd moved out of Greta's place, and before James' confession about his affair with Kitty, Hank and Kitty invited us to dinner. After the dishes were cleared from the table and their two young sons were sent to bed, Hank put on a record of slow dance music. James asked Kitty to dance with him. I looked away.

"Want to dance?" Hank asked.

"Sure," I said. Hank slid his hand around my waist. He had a firm, strong body. His hands felt large across my back. James' hands had begun to feel weak to me. There was no longer a feeling of comfort in my husband's embrace.

Resting my head on Hank's shoulder we swayed slowly to the music. Hank pulled me closer, nuzzling his face into the crux of my neck. This startled me. My first instinct was to get out of his embrace.

Hank must have felt me tense up because he said, "Don't worry, everything's all right." He brushed his lips against my ear while we swayed to the music. The song ended, and though we did nothing to be ashamed of, I felt guilty. A married woman shouldn't behave this way.

Looking around the room I wanted to dance with my husband, but James was gone, and so was Kitty.

"Where'd they go?" I asked.

"For a walk, I guess," Hank replied. "They went out the front door, just before the last song ended." There was an angry tone in Hank's voice. He knew. We both knew and yet said nothing.

A slow, blues guitar cried out from the speakers; a throaty singer, pleaded, "Baby, baby, baby, please help me. I need you."

Hank took me in his arms again. My initial response was to resist, but being held, even if only for one song, made me feel wanted. We stopped dancing. Still holding me in an embrace, Hank picked up his glass of wine from the table. He swallowed some. Then touching the glass to my lips, he tipped it slightly for me to take a sip. He held the glass between us and, bending down, he kissed me softly. I tried to move back but he held me firmly.

"Don't go," he whispered. "I'll try not to do that again. You're just so delicious, I can't help myself."

I didn't resist any longer, pretending it was Hank's strength that kept me tightly held to his body. It was my own loneliness that kept me locked in his arms. Hank took another drink of the wine, then put the glass to my lips. I sipped the alcohol as if I were a small bird in his arms. Hank set the drink down on the coffee table and taking me into his arms, pulled me close to his body. His hot breath against my neck made me weak in the knees as the singer on the record pleaded for relief. We continued to hold each other. We were no longer dancing. This was for real. There was no pretence about what we each wanted.

"Damn, I could eat you up right now, you feel so good," Hank whispered. "I swear I want you more now than I've ever wanted anything."

"I can't do this," I said.

"I wish you could. You know it would be fine," he whispered. Sliding his arms tighter around my waist, he bent down and kissed me. I knew we should not be doing this, yet going against my better judgment I let myself be carried away in a delicious moment of passion while the music in the background begged, "Help me, baby, help me. I've got'ta make you mine."

Though desperately wanting to go farther, I pulled away. "I can't," I said and sat on the couch. A surge of anger swelled up in my chest. Where was James? Had he seen Hank and me kiss? Did he even care? It hadn't been that long ago that James and I had taken long walks at night. We no longer talked about those times, and now I sat waiting for him to return from a walk with Kitty.

Hank placed another record on the turntable and, as he turned away from me, in that instant his expression changed drastically. The narrowness in the corners of his eyes made him look mean. The muscles in his jaw line throbbed as he tightly clenched his teeth. Hank sat down on the sofa beside me, swallowing the remaining wine in one gulp.

Pouring more wine into the same glass we had shared a few minutes earlier, he said, "It still smells of your lips." He took another drink, eyed me, and winked. "You're one sweet woman. Why the hell does that man treat you so cold?"

I hadn't expected him to say that. "What do you mean?" I asked, not sure how to respond.

"Well, he screwed around and messed up the business with Greta. So she kicks you two out. Instead of the both of you getting jobs, he talks you into working, while he stays home and writes his lame poetry. You ever really read any of that shit he writes? Who does he think he is? Hell, you're working your ass off in that garment factory and he's sitting home writing poetry." Hank spit these words at me then took another drink of his wine.

"I like his poems," I said with a determined tone. "And I was the one who decided to work." But I lied. Hank probably knew this wasn't the truth. But continuing with my story, I said, "He'll get a job in a couple of months."

James made me angry. James hurt me, but I defended him. He was my husband.

* * * *

Several weeks later, James would tell me about his affair with Kitty. Yet that night when Hank and I danced so unashamedly close, we said nothing about any suspicion that our mates were deliberately excluding us, or worse, that they were falling in love. How do you begin this kind of discussion? Should I tell Hank that his wife's perfume frequently dots my bedroom pillow? Do I mention to Hank that when I told James about this unusual happening, of smelling Kitty in our bedroom, he laughed and said, "It's your imagination working overtime."

Yet, the smell hung in the air of our bedroom, taunting me. It was not my imagination. And I wondered that if this odor of Kitty could talk, it would have said, "You foolish woman, can't you see what's going on? Tell that cheating man of yours to get the hell out and don't come back."

What would Hank have said if he knew that I took shallow breaths at night as I tried to fall asleep, so as not to smell my husband's deceit? The week before James told me about the affair, Hank and Kitty came to our apartment. Kitty sat cross-legged as usual on the floor while James read his latest poetry out loud.

At about midpoint in the evening, James said, "Wilma, why don't you show Hank your drawings." I took Hank into the back room—a room not much bigger than a closet—that was now my studio. Despite the size of the room, it had a particularly large window on one wall that looked onto the Mission district. I took out my drawing pad. The drawings were old, so old that I couldn't remember making them.

Hank touched my hand. "I was a cad," he said. "I'm really sorry if I upset you the other night. I was all worked up, I guess."

"That wasn't such a good night," I agreed, and wondered how long this game would go on.

"How about a little kiss to make up?" he asked, giving me a mischievous smile.

"Sure, why not. I can always use a little make up kiss now and then."

Hank gently put his lips on mine. His kiss touched me in a hidden place where my deepest sadness lived. As our lips touched, I wondered if Hank could taste the tears I shed in secret earlier that evening because now Kitty's perfume seemed to be in every room of our small apartment. I wondered did Hank cry? Would his tears leave a salty residue on his lips?

We stood in the dark, in what had been at first a friendly brushing together of our lips and found ourselves locked in a kiss for survival. Feelings—raw, angry, hurt feelings—raged up in me. My knees felt weak. We clung to each other as if we were about to fall from a cliff. Our mouths filled with each other's tongues and saliva, aching with desire, or from the pain of a broken heart, desperate to replace that pain with passion. Hank pulled me closer and quickly closed my studio door. This time, I would not refuse him. I could not. I needed to be loved. I needed someone to want me, to hold me, to tell me I was worth something.

I moved against a wall, looked across the room and out the window. Clouds rolled past like giant ocean waves.

"You're beautiful," Hank said. "I want you."

Pressing me to the wall, I no longer resisted.

He fed on my breasts, sucking and biting hungrily, and I served him my soul as I let it seep out from my flesh and into his mouth. I ached for relief. Hank pulled up my skirt and, in the instant that he pushed inside me, I no longer felt the hurt of a marriage that had failed. I only felt passion. Then it was over. Hank's sweating brow, our heavy breathing, the pounding of my pulse beating, beating, beating, exploded in my ears. Then Hank groaned softly and fell against me. I kissed him on the neck. I wanted to lift my hands, to touch him, but the energy oozed from my fingers. My hands hung limply at my sides. Hank and I never made love again.

The dinner parties ended abruptly after James told me about Kitty. James and I came to an agreement. He could see Kitty anytime she could get away, and declaring my independence, it was no longer necessary to explain my whereabouts. At that point it seemed like a good solution to our troubled relationship. A great deal of damage had been done to our marriage, if you could call it that. It didn't take long before our cold relationship turned bitter. I could no longer bear to look at him. His weak, pale, poetic body repulsed me. I moved out and rented a room near Castro Street. Once again a free woman, I enrolled in evening art classes. It was nearly impossible to rid myself of the resentment I felt toward James, but I sure as hell had become a lot wiser.

Hank was no longer in the picture, though he called several times—he said to see how things were going for me. I believe the real reason for his calls was to report to me what had happened in his marriage.

"Kitty and I are going to make another go of it," Hank said the last time he called.

It was a brief call. After wishing him luck and hanging up the phone I went to bed. James was no longer in my life and it didn't matter to me what he did. The damage had been done and my rage had turned to numbness. Pulling the covers over my head, my only desire was to sleep forever.

The Devil and the Crab

ONE EVENING AFTER WORK I went to Fisherman's Wharf to buy a crab for dinner. I got on the Van Ness Avenue bus, which let me off a couple of blocks from my destination. San Francisco has no real seasons, but in the spring the days stay light longer, and the ocean's current pushes a saltier smell ashore. I stepped off the bus. The bay stretched out in front of me, a gray, turbulent sheet of water. It had only been a couple of months since my separation from James and it didn't take me long to feel comfortable with living alone.

It was an easy walk to the wharf. I knew a shortcut through a back alley by the new mall under construction. The sun had begun to set. Streetlights fluttered on, casting deep shadows along the streets. Mounds of bricks and large piles of sand blocked much of the sidewalk forcing me to be mindful of where I stepped. One window on the top floor of the newly constructed building caught the dimming sunset and glowed a warm, inviting amber light, while the other windows looked like cold, black holes.

"Hello there," a voice called out from the vacant building. A vague figure of a man holding a briefcase stood in a boarded-up doorway of the building. A shadow fell across the top half of his body. Only his legs and part of the valise were visible. Stepping out of the doorway and walking toward me, he said, "I need assistance."

"With what?" I replied.

His face came into full view as he moved out of the darkness and stood under the streetlight. He was a clean-shaven, well-dressed, distinguished-looking older man. Probably a lost tourist, I decided. Tourists were always asking for directions.

"Well, you see, I'm opening a stationary store on the second floor of this mall. It would be much appreciated if you could help me. I'm looking for advice from a young person like you, who might use the store." He put his briefcase down on the ground and pointed to a second floor window.

"I don't know anything about stationary stores," I replied.

"You don't need to know anything about stationary stores. I just want your opinion on its location. That's all," he said.

"Haven't got a clue about that kind of thing," I said. No way was anyone going to get me into that dark building, especially a stranger.

There was no longer a reflection of the sunset in the window on the top floor. Now this window also looked like a gaping black hole. At either end of the block, bright streetlights shone as though it were daylight. Crowds of people walked along the wharf. But no one walked on this particular street.

"Find someone else, I can't help you," I said and began to walk away.

"Wait, don't go," the man said in a determined tone. "I want a young person's opinion. Someone like you."

He stepped forward. I thought he was about to grab my arm.

"No, I'm not going into that building with you," I told him, thinking that sounded like a final statement, and that he'd leave me alone.

"Oh, now I see," he said. "Look, I am a married man with a couple of kids. I wouldn't do anything wrong," He smiled, but rather than looking friendly, he appeared to be offering me a challenge.

"I'm sure you are, but I'm not going in there."

I wondered why I didn't just walk away from this stranger. Yet, I continued to stand there, talking to him on this dark, deserted street. A shiver went up my spine thinking about going into that darkened building.

Then the briefcase caught my attention. What could be inside? A shot of fear raced though me imagining it contained instruments of torture. Why all of a sudden were these frightening thoughts coming to me? In an instant, I visualized my death, my body lying among the scattered rubble of the construction site. Then realizing that when he first came into view, he looked like a spider suspended in the doorway. Now as he moved toward me, cautiously, it appeared as though this stranger was trying to lure me into his web. Standing just outside of his reach, the thought occurred to me that this might be a clever tactic to entice me into his trap. While I resisted, he played the absolute innocent.

In a fraction of a second, I imagined myself, a victim, tangled in a web constructed of my own stupidity, locked in a stinging dance of death with this stranger.

"Get someone else to give you an opinion," I said, finally wrenching myself away from his hypnotic spell, my only desire at that moment was to get away.

"Wait, wait, I won't do anything wrong. I only want your opinion," he shouted after me.

I kept walking quickly, and only once reaching the end of the block did I dare to look back fearful that the stranger might have followed me. He was nowhere in sight. Another dreadful thought entered my mind. What if this stranger slithered back into the doorway, watching, waiting to lure another unsuspecting victim into the building? My heart pounded, but I felt a deep sense of relief arriving at the well-lit end of the block.

"You fool," I berated myself in a half whisper. "Why did you even stop to talk to that guy?"

Throngs of people moved about on the street, shoulder to shoulder, pointing at the mounds of cooked crabs. Steam from the large cauldrons of boiling water floated around the different cooking stations giving an eerie look to the darkness that had settled onto the bay. Sweaty men, smelling of cooked seafood, called out for the tourists to buy their crabs.

Maneuvering my way through the crowd, the smells and the excited talking filled my ears with a sense of the living.

From a mound of freshly cooked crabs I picked out my dinner, a large, bright orange indigenous crab with a full set of claws and legs. The fishmonger turned the crab over for me to get a complete view of my purchase, a female, with a broad underside tail closely hugging the contour of her belly. In one swift motion, the fishmonger pulled back the tail, lifting it firmly at the point where it joined the back shell, and pulled off the belly section. Steam burst out of the crab's body. Juices dripped into a sink. The steam from the crab quickly disappeared into the night air, adding to the fishy smell of the wharf teasing and taunting both tourists and seagulls.

The crab was quickly rinsed, with legs and claws dangling in a limp pose of resignation. Once the crab had been wrapped in newspaper and shoved into a plastic bag, my dinner was ready to be taken home.

Walking back to the bus stop, my intention was to definitely by-pass the dark street where earlier the businessman had confronted me. There was no way of avoiding the building under construction, but instead of the short cut, it seemed a better idea to take the longer route this time and stay on the lighted path. Walking past the building, I imagined the man still standing in the doorway. By now my imagination had turned this stranger into a very dark figure, perhaps he was the devil. With that thought, my mind went wild again. It was impossible to keep myself from distorting his image. He became a nonhuman creature, a messenger from hell, who could take whatever appearance necessary to capture his victims.

I wanted to stop thinking. I was scaring myself. Had he actually been the devil? Had the devil come to tell me that it was my time to die? Maybe that was the way these things happened.

I realized that my logic might be a bit off-center, because at that point fear rather than clear thinking had taken over. Glancing quickly up at the top-floor windows, my breathing now uneven, my heart racing, I quickly turned away fearful of seeing the stranger looking down at me. Fantasies flooded into my brain at full throttle. What if he came after me, or followed me home?

I quickened my pace.

Reaching the bus stop and rushing to the lamppost, my aim was to seek comfort in the light. It wouldn't be long now before I would reach my home where behind a locked door my crab could be eaten without the fear of a devil intruding. The blame lay in the shadows. They excited my imagination. The evening had grown quite cold and thick fog crept up from the water's edge. Leaning on the cold metal of the lamppost, I wanted to touch something warm and comforting.

I heard footsteps. The long shadow of a man came up the street, barely visible in the fog, moving toward me in steady, even strides.

My heart pounded in my throat. It's him, I thought. He's coming to get me.

Frozen in place, fearful of every shadow, I could not divert my eyes as a man dressed in a dark suit, carrying a briefcase, approached closer and closer. My mind raced into the future and wondered if his mere touch would end my life? Will there be a sharp sting, causing me to fall to the ground lifeless and everyone will think I died from a heart attack? My pulse raced faster as the apparition came closer.

When the stranger reached the glow of the streetlight, the man, totally unaware of my fear of him, walked past without saying a word. He walked through the lighted area then back out the other side. He continued to walk up the block, disappearing into the foggy night.

I felt foolish, though the absurdity of my visions continued to frighten me. My mind had gone out of control and by the time a bus pulled up, I jumped on, grateful to be traveling away from that place. Several times glancing out the window, my heart nearly stopped when we passed someone wearing a dark suit and carrying a briefcase. Another time while the bus idled at a stoplight, a man in the car next to us at the intersection looked up at the bus. Our eyes met and thinking that he looked just like the stranger, my heart nearly beat out of control. Repeating over and over, "Nearly home, nearly home," helped to calm me somewhat, but after transferring from the bus to a trolley and a quick short walk up the block from Market Street to my place my nerves were frazzled.

Once inside my apartment, it took no time to lock the door, though out of a macabre curiosity I pulled back the curtains just a little way to peek out to see if the stranger waited for me on the street. The street was empty. Relieved to be in my own place and behind a locked door, my mind would not let me have peace for long.

Unwrapping the crab, the aroma of the sea touched me gently, almost as though a soft stroke from a hand reached up reminding me about what had happened earlier that evening. Again the image of the stranger came to me, and wondered if anyone could elude death. Looking down at the crab I wondered if this might be my last meal. Would there be a knock at the door, with the stranger standing on the other side, waiting to take me?

I picked up the crab. The legs broke off easily. Cracking a juicy claw open with a nutcracker, the succulent meat easily pulled away from the shell. The crustacean tasted salty, like the ocean. Sucking the meat from the legs, the empty carcass parts were soon piled neatly in one corner of the newspaper.

Eating took the edge off my fear, and soon the stranger no longer felt like a threat. I licked my fingers and began to methodically open the crab's body. Crushing the tiny compartments that hid the carcass's most fleshy part, I picked out the long fibrous meat using the end of the crab's legs. It always seemed a shame that the poor crab comes with the tools of its own demise. Diligently digging into the little compartments, the precious tidbits easily came out. Licking my fingers again, a trickle of crab juice ran down my arm. Paying it no mind, I continued to eat the feast that had possibly brought the devil to my door.

Picking out every last bit of meat from the crab's body, the remains lay scattered on the newspaper. I lifted up the body once again, inspecting the ruined shells to make sure that nothing had resisted my search. Sucking long and hard on one section and then sticking my tongue into a tiny compartment with the desire to find any hidden morsels still left in the carcass. Nothing remained of the crab but shells, crushed, mangled and sucked dry. I had been sitting on the couch, using my coffee table to dine on. Totally sated by now, I slumped back onto the cushions.

"That old devil's going to have to come and get me," I said, "because I can't move." Sliding my legs up onto the couch, closing my eyes, sighing deeply and thinking what a perfect way to die. Without realizing it, sleep came to me, softly.

In the morning, much to my surprise and pleasure, I had lived through the night and wondered if I actually had thought I'd pass away in my sleep. The sun radiated brilliantly through the curtains. The room reeked of crab, but that didn't matter. During the night something had been resolved. The weighty problems that gnawed at me during my marriage were gone. Not only did my mind feel unburdened, but my limbs now moved effortlessly as though somehow I'd become lighter during the night.

Quickly closing up the newspaper, I rolled all the broken pieces of crab together and carried the bundle out the back door.

"The cats are going to have a good old time with this garbage today," I thought as I dumped the package into the trashcan.

The garbage was in the alley just outside my back door. Looking around, there was nothing out of the ordinary, no lurking stranger, and no signs of attempted forced entry. Nothing had been disturbed. There was no devil. With a deep sigh, I walked back into my apartment. It felt great to be alive.

Brushing my hair back from my face, the odor of crab was still on my hands, even though they'd been washed several times by now. The odor didn't bother me. A beautiful warm sunshine poured through the kitchen window and without thinking twice, I grabbed my drawing supplies and headed for the park. Stepping out into the sunshine, today, nothing in the universe frightened me. After all, hadn't I outsmarted the devil last night?

* * * *

Two weeks later, James came to see me unexpectedly. We had been separated for three months with very little contact. When he walked in, it didn't look like he'd changed much. We talked about the unseasonable hot spell and the anti war demonstrations on the campus where he now worked in a bookstore.

When our trivial chatter had lapsed, he said, "I want you to come back." His head bowed, and his voice slightly shaky.

"What do you mean you want me back?" I asked. This was totally unexpected.

"Wilma, I'm sorry. I don't know what got into me. Please forgive me, please." Tears quickly rimmed on his lower eyelid and then ran down his face.

I felt manipulated. He made me angry. Blood surged up my neck, and heat rushed to my face. "How dare you come crying to me, after all you've done," I snapped.

"I really want you to come back. It'll be different this time." He ignored my angry comment, wiping at his tears. He managed a smile. Then walking over to me, he took my hand in his, and said, "Please come back." He rubbed the top of my hand. Leaning forward, he kissed me tenderly on the mouth. His lips were warm and soft, but something about his touch felt cold.

Perhaps it was my old anger and hurt that left me feeling this chill. Yet even with this coldness, as a wife I felt duty bound to make the marriage work. So that night we entered once again into the role of a married couple. Though in the back of my mind a voice whispered, "No! Not now. I'm too happy to be married to you." But instead, I remained silent. Maybe these words were not in my conscious mind. Maybe I was just used to being the good girl, the good daughter, the good wife, and so I acceded. I went back to our old apartment.

We made love and kissed throughout the night. But a shift had occurred in our relationship. It was difficult to tell—because of the closeness of our bodies that first night—if it was James who had changed, or if it was me. Nothing was clear to me that night, nothing at all.

A Piece of Bread

I HADN'T SLEPT WELL FOR several weeks. Hippies had moved in next-door, and they played loud music all night long. James refused to ask them to quiet down; he liked the songs, he said, and appreciated the high he got from the marijuana smoke that drifted from their apartment.

So, I trudged off to work in a sleep-deprived funk. Sitting at my power sewing machine at the beginning of each day, waiting for the buzzer to sound, the chill of the early morning San Francisco fog cloaking my shoulders and a dull pain throbbing in my temples. The factory floor held the dampness of the night before and my sewing machine felt icy to the touch. By the first coffee break the place warmed up and the chill in the air turn sultry from the steam of the presser's department located close to where I sat.

The sewing factory, as large as a high school gymnasium, quickly filled up with women: young women, older women, women from every corner of the world, all of us now sitting, row after row in front of sewing machines with mountains of fabric piled everywhere.

By now I knew my job so well that I could have worked blindfolded—though performing these tasks with eyes closed would certainly have been punished with a needle in the finger. Injuries of this sort were common and even when a worker paid close attention to her task, racing against the piece rate quota put each woman at risk.

A needle had gone through my finger more than once. When it happened, I kept calm and removed the needle, usually without too much damage. I knew of women who had ripped their fingers wide open when they jumped from the shock of the stabbing pain as the needle hit the knucklebone. Helena, the woman who sat at the machine next to me had a scar on the side of one finger from a needle that looked as if the digit had been sliced by a razor. It was boredom that made the job dangerous, not the actual sewing. A seamstress needs to be watchful because the monotony of repetition lulls the worker into a state of mindlessness, until she is performing her task like a zombie, unaware of time, place or person. That's when the job becomes the most dangerous.

Finally, when the morning buzzer rings, every sewing machine in the place is turned on. The building explodes with a frenzied sound of roaring motors. At the same time, there is the familiar sound of snapping fabric as the pieces of garments are flipped under the needle, each woman bent over her machine, hands working at an inhuman pace.

About a month ago, without thinking too much about it, almost as unconsciously as I sewed, poems began to float through my mind. I had never thought of myself as particularly good with words—James was the poet. But the verses poured out of me nonstop, line after line while I sewed. I quickly scribbled down the poems on the paper lining that divided each dozen of fabric pieces sewn together. I had seen this paper lining thousands of times before, but now, instead of discarding the paper I used it to write down a rhyme, a phrase, a word, a feeling. Day after day, I would sew and write, sew and write.

I felt as if I were going insane, trapped by the boredom of my work and now a suspicion had begun to gnaw at me that James was seeing another woman. We had only gotten back together a few months ago after a trial separation. During the time we had lived apart my evenings were taken up with something enjoyable every night after work. Now I came straight home from the garment factory, cooked dinner for the two of us, playing at being the good wife. But things had turned cold again between us, the way they had before the separation. Instead of our relationship getting better, it had gotten worse. So, I pushed myself to work harder, and wrote my poems. Some days, the written verses were merely angry words scribbled down onto the paper—they were raw, painful feelings, feelings that I could not somehow get out otherwise.

The two women who sat on either side of me; Helena, the woman with the big scar on her finger and Sarah, a Jewish woman from Poland, said nothing about my writing. They were both older than me by about twenty-five years. But in this line of work all the women were the same age; we were all old. During our breaks we discussed cooking, the weather, and sometimes we did a bit of gossiping. Mostly we talked about our work but neither one of them ever mentioned my frantic writing.

Helena and Sarah had worked together for nearly ten years. I was the newcomer. Sarah was a frail, sickly looking woman with a gray tint to her flesh and a sad downcast mouth. Helena, a husky woman with a jovial disposition had taken it upon herself to help Sarah by hefting both of their large, completed bundles of work into the bins that transported them to the next station. Until now Sarah had not said anything to me about her past though everyone knew that she was a Holocaust survivor. Her entire family had died in a concentration camp; she had lost a baby son, her first husband, her sisters, and parents. She always wore long-sleeved dresses. Though once, when she reached up to change the thread color on her sewing machine, the sleeve of her dress slipped down exposing several inked numbers on her arm. It startled me to think what these numbers meant and I quickly looked away.

Helena usually stepped out for a quick smoke after we came back from our lunch break leaving Sarah and I to sit at our sewing machines waiting for the buzzer to sound. The last couple of days Sarah had looked more tired than usual. She hadn't said much lately, though in the time that we'd worked together, I'd learned that she got this way from time to time.

But on this particular day Sarah turned to face me. The overhead florescent light caught her in such a way that she appeared even paler than usual. The blue spider veins that traveled across Her nose and chin looked all the more prominent and her small dark eyes looked angry.

"My dear," Sarah said, and she grabbed hold of my arm with icy fingers. "If I told you how it really was, you would not believe me. No one would believe me."

The bitter tone in her voice caught me off guard. I turned to face her. She had never spoken to me in this way before.

"I lived in a ghetto in Poland," she continued. "I saw many miserable sights. But, when they brought me to the concentration camp, I saw people on the inside of the camp looking out at us. I searched the eyes of the crowd, looking for answers, but none would come. The looks on those faces watching us through the fence went beyond my imagination."

"When we entered the compound, our clothing was stripped from us. We were publicly humiliated and threatened. They gave us clothing that was either too big or too small, making us look foolish and ridiculous. Frightened, confused, I had no idea what would happen next. After an hour of being in the camp, I looked like everyone else. I was no different. Just one hour. It doesn't make sense, but it's true. I had become like those pairs of eyes watching when we entered the camp, waiting, not knowing who would live a day or an hour longer." Sarah's eyes focused on me as though she were in a trance.

"I made a friend there," Sarah said. "We helped each other in any way that we could. With precious little food, blankets, or hope, anything that we could do for each other was appreciated. We slept together with twelve other women on a long wooden bed, crammed together like sardines in a can. Yes, that was the way we slept. Someone would die, they'd be taken away, and someone else would take their place. You didn't think much about it, it was just life."

Sarah stopped talking for a moment. She turned away from me and glanced at Helena returning to our workstation, bringing with her the strong odor of cigarette smoke. Helena didn't say anything. Grabbing a heavy bundle of unfinished garments she set it down in front of Sarah. Helena bent down and picked up a few fallen scraps of fabric around Sarah's chair and then sat at her own sewing machine. Helena glanced at me, and then looked away. I got a feeling that Helena knew what Sarah was telling me.

Sarah glanced at the bundle of work, and then her dark eyes once again focused on me, and she continued with the story. "One night my friend saved a piece of bread from the evening meal. We were always on the verge of starving and she didn't know if she was going to have anything for breakfast, so she put the piece of bread behind her head when she went to sleep, to save it.

"The next morning I tried to talk to her but she didn't answer. She had died in her sleep. People were always dying there. Once, in the bathroom area a woman sat and sat on the bucket. Finally, I gave her a little nudge and told her to hurry, that she couldn't sit there all day. She fell over, dead. It was that way so much of the time. You never knew when it might be your turn.

"I felt bad my friend was dead, but for her it was over. I still lived. So I took that piece of bread she had put behind her head and ate it, breaking off small pieces, like a bird will do. It swelled in my mouth and felt soft, warm. The taste brought back memories of a time before this madness, a time that tasted sweet through all the difficult struggles. I clung to this bread, as though that one crumb was life itself. But it tasted bitter. And that was the way life was in that place. What went on was real, but I still don't believe it."

Sarah's eyes dug deep into mine. "Why?" she asked. "Why did those things have to happen? Why did I survive and everyone else died?"

I wanted to say something, yet could not think of a thing to say. Her haunting questions made me uncomfortable. "I don't know, Sarah. I don't know why those things happened."

"You don't know. No one knows." Sarah picked up a piece of fabric, turned her back to me, and began to organize her work.

The buzzer rang. Each woman rushed back to her sewing machine. Like racehorses at a starting gate, rearing and kicking, ready for the lunge forward, all the sewing machines were turned on at the same time. It was easy to envision the minds of these women floating off into the world like phantoms, while they sat trapped behind their machines, mindlessly competing with yesterday's quota. I saw Sarah like a thin wisp of gray smoke floating above us all, searching for her family through mounds of bodies, her angry eyes raking through the soil of the earth looking for answers.

From that point on Sarah told me many stories about growing up in Poland, about her family and how hard they worked, but mostly she told me about what it was like in the camp. Each time she told these stories I didn't know how to respond. What could I say?

Helena continued to lift bundles for Sarah and along with me she would listen to Sarah's stories. We would listen but neither of us could answer the ever-present question, why.

The stories made my problems with an unfaithful husband seem trivial. Yet, I could not help but feel depressed about what was happening to my marriage. James told me he needed two nights out a week and that I should take my evening art classes again. The coldness that grew between us hurt, almost as though it were a bruise. Secretly wishing him dead, I wrote several poems mourning him.

Then, one evening before we went to bed, when the deceit and mistrust had grown to such a point that I could stand no more, I said, "This is not working between us. I want out."

James said nothing at first. He looked intently at his fingers, as if they contained a collection of words that could be used to tell me another one of his lies. "You're right," he said finally. "I'm not happy either."

Neither of us cried, pleaded, or promised to change. Our marriage was finished. That night I tried desperately not to touch James as we slept. Yet, in the morning we were in each other's arms and James' head lay on top of a nest of my hair.

We said very little to each other in the next couple of weeks. My love for James had withered. It was now encrusted with anger and regret. Blaming myself for having the failed marriage, I could not wait for him to leave.

Before James moved out, he confessed that he had taken up with one of the women from next door. They planned to get an apartment together. While at work sewing the dozens of pieces of fabric together, the pain of having a ruined marriage became unbearable, and I wondered how I'd be able to live with the hurt and disappointment.

Sitting at my sewing machine each day, I could not bring myself to tell Sarah that I had thrown away a husband while she still mourned, after almost thirty years, the dead husband of her youth. So I worked harder, scribbled my poems, and listening to Sarah's stories until one day I understood how Sarah had survived. She had endured the horrors in her life because the days just kept coming, one after the other, no matter what happened.

The Gift

"I'M PREGNANT," I TOLD JAMES over the telephone.

My call to him, I realized when considering why I even bothered, was out of courtesy.

"What are you going to do about it?" was his response. He sounded curt. It wasn't difficult to detect his disinterest, even perhaps anger. He was so good at projecting blame onto others.

"I'm going to keep the kid," I snapped.

Before our last break up, we'd made love carelessly once or twice, hurriedly getting close, then recoiling again, rolling away from each other to opposite sides of the bed. Even quarrelling couples sometimes have sex. Our lovemaking, if you could call it that, had been tinged with bouts of curiosity. Could we fall in love again? The night we decided to separate, I asked James, "What would you do if I were pregnant?"

"Having a kid would be groovy. We'd share raising it," James assured me. I should have known better. "Maybe something'll happen," James now said, "and the baby won't be born."

When I heard him say these horrible words, a clap of thunder exploded in the back of my head, in a place where I evidently stored a great deal of anger—because at that moment thousands of small pieces of old, sour-smelling feelings came spewing out of me.

"I hate you," I shouted. "You don't care about anyone but yourself. I'm just sorry that the baby's yours."

I slammed down the receiver. I spit out the tears that ran down my face and into my mouth.

Throughout the next months I continued to go to work, though starting with my second month of pregnancy the routine changed dramatically. I'd get to work, clock in, then before getting to my sewing machine, I'd run to the bathroom, where I'd throw up. It wasn't the violent up-chucking like that of the flu, but it was an involuntary gagging that got out of control, releasing a stinging green-tinged bile that carried with it all of my undigested breakfast.

Several days after telling James about the baby, I stood at the sink in the ladies room after completing a bout of vomiting, a cool, wet paper towel pressed against my forehead when Gloria, the floor supervisor, came in.

"You all right?" she asked.

"I'm fine." But I wasn't, not really, and I began to cry. Lately my crying was involuntary. The tears came in irregular sessions throughout the day, never knowing when they would appear.

"It'll be okay," Gloria said, touching my arm with a gentle, comforting stroke.

"I'm pregnant, and I'm divorcing my husband," I managed to say between sobs.

"Oh, I'm sorry." Taking me in her arms she held me until I finished crying.

I doused the paper towel once again with cold water and dabbed my temples trying to cool my throbbing head. All the while, Gloria leaned on a sink, looking out into the room with a blank stare.

I'd seen that look on her face before. In fact, since Gloria had returned from her vacation several months ago, she'd frequently been the topic of conversation among the women with whom I ate lunch. We didn't know what had happened while she was away, but something was going on with her. Some days she got a faraway look in her eyes and stood for several minutes gazing into space. Previously her habit had been to run all over the factory, moving about like a mad woman, making sure production kept up at an even flow.

"You know," Gloria said, "there are times when you think you'll never stop hurting. There are days when you truly don't believe you'll be able to live through another hour. You do though."

"Yeah, I guess," I replied. Gloria turned on a faucet. It looked as though she was going to wash her hands. She turned off the water then looked at me. "I went home to see my mother on my last vacation," she said. "While I was on the airplane, she put her head in the oven and committed suicide." Gloria continued with the story, her eyes vacant, and her face expressionless. She talked as though the incident was about someone else's mother. "She didn't come to the airport to meet me," Gloria said. "That wasn't so unusual. I took a taxi to her home and that's when I found her lying in the oven, dead."

Gloria sighed softly. She looked away from me, then cleared her throat and continued in a mater-of-fact tone. "She'd been depressed for years. I guess she just got tired of living with it. I thought I'd never recover from her suicide. But I am, slowly."

Gloria's eyes fogged over with what I could only imagine was clouds of memory. I suspected at that moment she again saw her mother's head in the oven.

"I'm sorry," I said, wondering if this was Gloria's attempt to cheer me up. It hadn't. How could it? Her story only made me feel sadder and more confused. Now I was not only wallowing in my own emotionally tangled life, but every workday I'd be reminded of Gloria's miserable life, too.

We went back out onto the main work area. I sat at my sewing machine trying to focus on my work as if I hadn't heard Gloria's tragic story. But this sad tale of Gloria's mother's suicide made me feel worse.

The rest of the day, instead of Gloria running between the seamstresses the way she usually did, checking our work, or carrying bundles back and forth to the inspection station, she sat at her desk fiddling with paperwork, frequently looking off into space.

I now knew what she saw. Even though she talked as if she was healing and that her mother's suicide no longer bothered her that much, it was obvious that she was not only lying to me, but to herself as well. I added Gloria to my theory that the oppressive, relentless noise of the sewing factory, noise that should have been loud enough to blot out tragedies did nothing to relieve personal pain. Nor could the oppressive repetition of the work eclipse the wretched images that incessantly slid across the back of a seamstress's brain. Nothing could.

* * * *

The last time I saw James he looked like a hippie. He had a beard now. When we first met he greased his thick wavy hair slick with Brylcreem. These days his mass of hair went wild in an untamed frizz.

He and his new girlfriend moved into an apartment near Haight and Ashbury Streets to be closer to the action.

People, young and old, flocked to San Francisco like migratory birds. The newspapers were filled with stories of runaways. Parents advertised in the newspapers for missing teenagers to return home. Photographs of the missing were taped to light poles. Cryptic messages scribbled at the bottom of the photos pleaded for their son or daughter to contact them.

While window-shopping in North Beach I met a store clerk who left a husband and several children in the hills of West Virginia to come to San Francisco seeking a new life. She wanted to open a coffee shop where people could read their poetry. The city was amuck with searchers, experimenters, and explorers. Everyone was looking for something.

One day, while I waited for a bus on a perfect late summer afternoon, a middle-aged woman put a quarter in my palm. Before I could respond, she quickly crossed back to the other side of the avenue. I thought she would hurry down the street and away from me; instead, she sat on a fire hydrant. A man stood beside her, an arm around her shoulder. The woman sobbed uncontrollably. The man turned his back to me, shielding the woman from my view. I wanted to go to her, to see if she needed help. My bus pulled up. The situation was so bizarre. I decided to do nothing and hopped onboard.

On the way home, I thought about Mom. I knew she worried about me. Would she have put money in the palm of a stranger, a young woman who maybe looked like her daughter?

The days dragged on. I gained weight. My belly stretched in ways that seemed impossible. The mound in the middle of my stomach grew bigger and bigger. Long red lines formed on my thighs and at my waistline. Thankfully the vomiting eventually stopped. Now there was constant movement inside me. Often after eating my belly would get the hiccups. Sometimes there was so much activity going on inside me it felt like a bowling ball was rolling around inside my tummy.

Eventually I became accustomed to living in this condition. I could have probably gone on living this way forever. Then, one night, the quickening that I'd been experiencing over the previous weeks—the teasing of the muscles, tightening and then relaxing again (a tune up, the doctor called it, for what was to come)—turned into an intense grabbing pain that took my breath away. It was no longer a mystery now about how it would feel like to go into labor. It felt as though a choking harness had been thrown across my belly. It was easy to realize at that point that delivering this baby was going to hurt and it was going to hurt plenty.

The contractions remained twenty minutes apart for several hours. Then they abruptly came ten minutes apart. I called my neighbors, who had promised to take me to the hospital. Everyone in the apartment building wanted to be notified the minute the real thing happened, but there was no time to let everyone know.

The worry, the loneliness, my impending divorce, they were all forgotten on the ride to the hospital in the neighbors' Volvo, where the slightest bump in the road became a crushing blow. The pain became unbelievably intense. I grabbed my belly, then my back, trying to locate the source—to press it, to rub it, to try to ease the contractions. Nothing worked. It felt as though my entire body was giving birth. My head throbbed. Maybe the baby would come out through one of my ears. That was such a stupid thought, but right then the most peculiar things made sense in my pain. Or, maybe, I would spit the child from my body. Perhaps, desperate to free us both from this torture, I'd have to pull the child out myself. And I wondered if the baby was in as much discomfort as me.

Thoughts of death crept into my mind as the contractions grabbed onto me with claws, sharp dragon's claws, squeezing me, crushing me, demanding that this child be released. Then a dreadful thought entered my mind that I might not live through this baby's birth.

When we finally arrived at the hospital, an attendant helped me into a wheelchair. She quickly pushed me to admissions, where a clerk took forever to fill out the forms. While waiting for her to put paper into her typewriter, I had a colossal contraction.

"Oh, God, hurry," I pleaded.

The pain caused me to stretch out in my seat until I almost slid out of the wheelchair.

The attendant put the brakes on the chair and helped me back into a seated position.

"Well, young lady," the clerk said in an accusatory tone, "you should have thought about doing the admission paperwork before you got this far along."

The pain made me go deaf for a moment. When I caught my breath again, I heard the clerk say, "We've never delivered a baby in my office yet." She clicked away on her typewriter, looked over her machine at me, gave me a cold smile and an insincere practiced wink. Some joke, I thought.

"What's your Social Security number? Mother's maiden name?"

"Can't we do this later?" I asked.

"No, we cannot. We need this information before you go in. What if something were to happen to you? The hospital is responsible for you and that little one. Now you just sit still and we'll be done in no time. Tell me, what's the father name?" The clerk held her fingers at the keys, ready to type. Reluctantly giving the clerk James' name, I felt nothing for him. It seemed such a long time since we'd met, it felt as though I had gotten pregnant by myself.

With the forms completed, my child, to the satisfaction of the hospital administration, had a father. Yet, this baby had no father; this child was mine and mine alone.

The orderly wheeled me down the hall, and as we entered the elevator I had another overwhelming contraction. The pain became my body, my blood, and my skin. The elevator doors slowly closed. We moved torturously at a snail's pace floor by floor until we finally reached the maternity ward. Dizzy, sweating from the contraction, I watched a nurse unbutton my blouse. My throat and lips were parched and greedily sucked on broken bits of ice cubes. One of the attendants laid me down on a bed with chilled sheets so cold they felt as though they had been refrigerated.

A woman brought in a washbasin of warm soapy water. She lathered my pubic hair with soft sudsy foam. Then with several strokes of a razor, she quickly shaved that part of me naked. I looked down at my crotch, stretching my neck to see over my protruding belly. The area now appeared to be a total contradiction. My hairless pink crotch looked as though it belonged to a fat preadolescent girl and not a pregnant woman. I chuckled at the ridiculous sight. But the humor of the situation didn't last long as another gigantic contraction hit. Nothing was funny after that.

A nurse gave me a shot in the butt. "This'll help you relax," she said.

It didn't take long before my mind got kind of fuzzy. Soon falling into one dreamy state after another I began to construct poems in my mind between the waves of pain.

Lying in a sweat-soaked bed, for what seemed hours, moving from one position to another with no way to get comfortable, I waited for my cervix to dilate enough for the doctor to deliver my baby. Half-awake and half-dreaming, the nurse came and went, sometimes poking her fingers into my vagina, gently, though in a businesslike manner, to see if the cervix had dilated. I felt like a Thanksgiving turkey.

"How much longer?" I asked, all the while hoping the baby had been delivered during one of these dreamlike states. This ordeal was taking far too long. I wanted to wake up, find a newborn sitting on top of my belly and be done with the contractions.

"Almost time, honey," the nurse answered. "You're almost ready." Then she wiped my forehead with a cool damp cloth before leaving the room.

I floated in and out of this dreamlike state. My mind mixed odd images with the dulled pain. All the while my child pushed, kicked and shoved, struggling to get out. At one point, I found myself standing with my sister, on a hillside. We were picking brilliant orange California poppies. We scampered up the a slight incline, laughing and rolling about on the ground in the sunny, wild garden, while Dad kneeled down to take our picture. My sister and I smiled big for the camera. The wind blew a cool breeze against my face. Then I heard in the distance, "You're ready. Time to go."

I was moved from the bed to a gurney while I continued to slip in and out of dreams. The air in the new room felt cold and dry. The light, blindingly bright, hurt my eyes. The walls were an odd white. One wall shimmered an iridescent green. Strange looking equipment lined one side of the room. I worried the doctor might plug me into one of those peculiar electrical devices.

A nurse entered the room. She carried a six-inch long needle. I cringed. She lifted the blanket.

"Sit up, sweetie," she said. "Arch your back for me, please." She brushed aside my long hair that had grown nearly down to the middle of my back. There was a strong odor of disinfectant in the room, as she rubbed a cold solution on the middle section of my spinal column.

"What are you going to do?" I shrieked. "It won't hurt," she said.

I had made all the necessary doctor visits, taken my vitamins, and eaten all the healthy food suggested, but never asked the nurse or the doctor about the anaesthesiology that would be used during the delivery.

"Just bend over," the nurse insisted, "and, whatever happens, stay still. Don't move." Then, the moment she inserted the needle into my spine, my body experienced another major contraction.

Fearful that something dreadful would result if I moved, clenching my teeth, I held my breath. When she removed the needle, I sat up straight, relieved that this part of the ordeal was over, and then laid back down. But something had gone terribly wrong. I couldn't move my legs. They had gone dead. My feet dangled over the edge of the delivery table. They were no longer a part of my body. The pain had vanished. All sensations from my waist down to my toes was gone. No one told me that this would be part of the delivery. I must have looked frightened.

"Don't worry," the nurse assured me. "It's temporary." She lifted my legs and placed them on the table, strapping my feet securely in the stirrups.

The doctor walked into the room. He stood at the end of the table, looking intently between my legs.

"It's coming," he told me.

I felt nothing.

"I hope you want a boy," the doctor said. He gave me a squint that I read as a smile.

I had a son. The pain was gone. I was totally numb. The birthing was completed in a matter of minutes. Then after a flurry of being quickly washed, a few stitches, an attendant hurriedly put me onto a gurney and wheeled me into another room, where a cluster of nurses was complaining about the heavy load of deliveries they were experiencing that month.

James came to see me in the hospital that night. When he walked through the door he looked humble, or sheepish, or guilty, or confused. He did not look totally in control, at any rate.

"The baby's beautiful," he said. "I've never seen anything like it before, honest.

What are you going to name him?"

"Daniel," I replied.

James made promises to me that evening. Not that we'd get back together, but that he would be there for me and for the baby.

"I'll help out with the money," he said. "I'll pay for a diaper service. If you need anything, I'll get it for you."

These turned out to be only words, empty promises that James felt compelled to make while he basked in his own pride of fatherhood.

James hadn't changed. He rarely gave me money. He said he earned too little, even though I now lived on welfare, while he and his lover were both working full time. The diaper service he promised to pay for would, within several months, be abruptly cancelled. "Non-payment," the deliveryman said when he picked up the last bag of dirty diapers. And would James always be there for me, or for his son? No, he would not.

When I brought my baby home from the hospital there was so much to learn about motherhood. He was so small I worried about everything. Would I accidentally stick this little wiggly person with a pin? Would I drop him? Did he get enough to eat?

Then one morning, after my son and I had been home for about a week, something extraordinary happened to me while changing a dirty diaper.

This experience might have been brought on by my lack of sleep. It could have been the rich earthy odor of Daniel's poopy diaper. Or maybe it was the light in the room, an early sunrise that stippled the walls with soft shadows—but that morning, I realized that my life would never be the same again.

"Well, now," I said, "what've we got here?"

Peeling the sticky diaper from his little pink bottom, something extraordinary happened. My hands tingled. They felt warm. There was a high-pitched hum in my ears. For a millisecond I became dizzy. Holding onto the sides of the crib, bracing myself against falling forward, instead of seeing Daniel lying in the crib, I gazed down at my own self when I was an infant. And, in that fraction of a second, I became my mother. A powerful sensation of love rushed through me, filling my veins, my head, and my hands, transforming me into someone new as I looked down at the newborn lying beneath my trembling hands.

As suddenly as this sensation came over me, it vanished.

I wondered if this had been an out-of-body experience, maybe brought on by fatigue, or perhaps it was the residual effect of the drugs that the nurses had given me. But whatever caused this phenomenon, I'll never forget that day, not if I live to be a hundred years old. I can recall that morning and see the dappled light leaking through the patterned curtains, experience the chill of the autumn air, and feel the silky texture of an infant's skin; tiny, wrinkled little feet helplessly kicking, and I remember that transformation as though the morning had happened yesterday.

This experience lasted only a second or two, yet, in such a brief time, that sensation attached itself to my fiber and became an integral part of me. Keeping my baby was an irrevocable decision, though I could have never imagined at the time what rewards would come my way. And I had no knowledge then how this child would open doors to emotional vistas that would never again be closed.

The Big One

THE BIG ONE WAS ON its way. In the summer of 1970 that's what we called the earthquake predicted to hit the West Coast and break San Francisco from the mainland.

At the time, I lived east of the Mission District in a small apartment on Potrero Hill. The building was a poorly maintained misfit, squeezed between two Victorian beauties. The place had a fantastic view. The kitchen and living room windows had a panoramic view of the Golden Gate Bridge, when it wasn't fogged in, as well as having an unobstructed vista of downtown San Francisco, all the way west to the Noe Valley. It was an incredible deal, a one-bedroom apartment with a view like that for sixty dollars a month.

My life, however, was a mess. With my divorce finalized earlier that spring, being a single mother of a two-year old and going to college, I couldn't handle much more. The last thing I needed to deal with was an impending earthquake.

About this time, I'd made friends with Marsha, a recent New York transplant to the Bay Area who lived with her boyfriend, Billy, in one of the front apartments. She was going nuts with the earthquake scare. When she heard several leading seismologists agree on four crucial days in August when the earthquake would most likely occur, she really got hysterical. She talked incessantly about the gruesome possibility of being crushed under crumbling buildings. Half of the tenants in our apartment building were now like family to her and she didn't want us to die either.

We'd all begun to hang out regularly, patched together like a crazy quilt. Marsha, thin and jittery, was an art student who lived with Billy, a mailman who looked like Jesus. Sam, a Dutchman with hands the size of toasters, lived downstairs from me. We called him our pot-smoking gardener, because though the GI bill had been paying him to study gardening at the local two-year college, most of the time he sat around and smoked joints. Gracie occupied the apartment next door to Marsha, and she played the perky, know-it-all feminist. An ex-cheerleader from Southern California collecting unemployment, Gracie boasted of being newly alcoholic and recently divorced. Carl, a deserter from the Vietnam War, desperate to have long hair, lived with Sam. Then there was me, a freshman in college studying psychology, divorced, on welfare, and the only one with a kid.

The newspapers seemed to print nothing but information about the earthquake. The *San Francisco Chronicle* and the *Oracle*, a hippy, alternative newspaper, published maps of the safest zones in the city during an earthquake. Potrero Hill, where our apartment building was situated, was made up of a natural cache of gravel; therefore, according to the seismologists this would be the safest location during a tremor. That made us a bit more comfortable, though that still didn't take away our fear.

In the evenings, after putting Daniel to sleep, everyone usually gathered around my kitchen table while Marsha read us the latest earthquake articles. Her dark Mediterranean eyes intent, her thin, bony hands trembling, the newspaper made a slight rustling sound while she read. "A sheep farmer in the Berkeley Hills stated that his herds of animals frantically roamed the hillsides, nervously bleating."

Marsha lowered the paper to her lap. She made eye contact with Billy. Her hands trembled even more, still she read on. "The dairy industry claimed that cows on farms north of Berkeley were giving less milk than usual." It seemed that even the chickens were getting into the act. One poultry farmer in Petaluma said his chickens were flying up and down, all day, while many chicken stopped laying eggs altogether.

The newspapers were having a field day with this earthquake business. Entire sections were filled with notices of special church services or prayer meetings for lost souls. Ministers went on the radio, calling for sinners to repent. Everywhere I looked, someone was either writing or preaching about a crumbling society and how this new Sodom and Gomorrah, San Francisco, would slide into the sea.

One night over a jug of wine and playing a game of nickel poker, everyone agreed we'd heard enough. We were convinced that an earthquake was on its way and that our adopted hometown was at the epicenter. So that night, we decided to head for the hills during what the seismologists predicted to be the most crucial days that the earthquake would strike. This gave us one week before the "Big One."

That next day I bought a pup tent at the Army-Navy surplus store. We pooled our money to buy food and other needed provisions. We'd leave the city in three vehicles: Sam's van, the one he lived in before moving into his apartment; Billy's Volkswagen bug; and the motorcycle Carl purchased in Hong Kong on his last R and R before deciding he'd had enough of army life.

Sam checked his vehicle's engine, changed the oil and fan belt. Billy purchased lumber to build a luggage rack for the roof of his Volkswagen. During the construction he accidentally drilled through the electrical system of the car. After a couple of six-packs and much discussion, Billy, Sam, and Carl figured out how to rewire the little bug.

Daniel, my two-year-old wonder on a trike, became a natural conveyor belt, passing wrenches, pliers, and motor oil back and forth between the men. That evening after Daniel's bubble bath, he still smelled like a car mechanic.

Poor Marsha, she always worried about something, and two days before we were to take off, she feared that she'd never finish her therapy before she died. Marsha had clung to Billy for weeks when he came home from work, begging him to cuddle with her while she wrapped herself in layers of blankets, trying to warm a part that suffered from a perpetual chill. Now, as the earthquake drew nearer, she buried herself even deeper into the woollen coverlets.

Carl, the most recent member of our community, had extended his military service twice in Vietnam. Then on a drunken and drugged weekend, after completing his second tour of duty, he re-upped for a third time. After sobering up, realizing what he'd done, Carl decided not to go back. Carl had met Sam while they were both stationed in Germany. Once Carl decided he was not going back, he slipped under the military police radar, made his way to San Francisco, looked up his old army buddy, and the next thing we knew he'd made himself at home in Sam's apartment.

Gracie was hot for Carl from the first moment she laid eyes on him. She believed a liberated woman didn't have to beat around the bush and said straight out that she liked him for his body. But something else made Carl attractive to Gracie. He was dangerous—not dangerous in that he would physically hurt anyone—but he was the kind of man who took no responsibility for his actions. That excited and challenged Gracie.

Before Carl arrived Sam told us that Carl had left a different woman pregnant after each tour of duty. He'd left one woman in Germany pregnant and, as far as Sam knew, at least one woman and baby in Vietnam. Carl denied that the babies were his. Then when he completed his tour of duty in each location, he shipped out, leaving the women and children behind.

When Carl arrived, Gracie went after him as though she was starved and he was food. I'd hear her knock on his bedroom window in the middle of the night, asking to take a midnight ride on his motorcycle.

Sam was in love with me. I did not love him. He wanted to take care of Daniel and me. But my task was to learn to make my own way. He offered to let me sleep in his van when we got out of range of the earthquake. My intention was to sleep in my new tent. He liked being high on marijuana or beer, and he was a bit of a recluse. I preferred wine, the sharp edge of reality, and I liked being around other people. He wanted to be a house painter so that he could drink beer all day. I wanted to be a psychologist.

Two days before the earthquake was supposed to strike, the seven of us headed for the hills, Sam taking the lead with his van. Billy following close behind in his Volkswagen bug, Marsha sitting up-front, wearing her New York winter coat, hunched over reading *The Golden Notebook,* with Daniel and me in the back seat looking out the windows. "See the big truck. A cow. Oh, look, there's a car just like Billy's."

Carl often revved up the engine on the motorcycle, overtaking the VW bug. Swerving in and out of traffic, with Gracie perched on the back of the bike, they'd roar past us, Carl grinning, Gracie waving to us like a prom queen on a Rose Bowl float.

We headed northeast, away from the fault line, looking for solid ground with only a vague idea of our final destination, a national park on a road map. We drove for hours until we arrived at the campsite, the eight-track tape deck in Billy's car blaring, while we sang along with Bob Dylan, "The Times They Are A-Changin.'"

We set up camp, and though we didn't feel as if we could live this way forever if an earthquake really hit, this temporary home would do for now.

Late in the afternoon, the sun settled behind a long range of hills, casting a deep chilly shadow across our camp. The air quickly cooled and I knew Marsha would freeze out here tonight. Billy knew this too, and he built a huge fire.

We'd all moved away from a situation that might have ended our lives. But I don't think we fully understood the implications of this until now. We were so busy preparing for the big escape that after we set up the tents and built a fire, we sat around our new home wondering what to do next.

"When in doubt," Sam said, "smoke a joint." And he passed one around.

During the next four days we talked, played music, sang songs, drank, played poker, smoked dope, and listened to the radio for what we believed would be the end.

I thought things would be different for us away from the city, but they weren't. Gracie had to have everything her way. It didn't matter what—it could have been cooking, childcare, or car mechanics; she knew everything. Living with Gracie in the woods turned out to be more difficult than I thought. This earthquake business made her feel all the more knowing because she'd lived through several serious quakes in Southern California and that, she said, made her an expert.

Marsha cried frequently. She made the decision to leave her cat behind. She had left him plenty of food and water, with the explanation that animals were more capable of escaping danger than human beings. "He knew what was going on," Marsha whimpered. "I know he knew. If anything happens to him, I'll never forgive myself." She stopped short of saying that she would rather die than live without him.

Marsha hovered around the campfire, day and night, like a ghost drawn to the smoke. During the daylight hours, even in that seventy-five to eighty degree weather, she wore a winter coat or wrapped herself in a blanket, constantly trying to warm a chill so deep inside her that it would take thirty years or more before that cold sadness melted away. Billy stood behind her, rubbing her back, cooing to her, telling her things would be all right. He fed the fire many logs during the day, kissed her hair and brought her chocolate chip cookies from the stash of treats she had brought to feed her sadness.

We waited around the camp, our feet lightly placed on the ground, fearful we would be able to tell when San Francisco slid into the ocean. "It's in God's hands," Billy said. And even in our heretic souls I think we each secretly hoped that our sins wouldn't cause us to pay too dearly in the afterlife.

"Far out, man," Sam would say, and lit up another joint. He dreamed his way through those four days and later said he never worried. As far as he was concerned, whatever happened was meant to be.

Gracie seemed to welcome the change and wondered what the end would be like. She laughed and drank wine from one of the two-gallon jugs she'd brought. "We're children of the Bomb," she said. "What do we have to worry about?" She was right. None of us would have been surprised if we'd slipped into the ocean.

Carl frequently sat on a boulder whittling on twigs. He spoke little and smoked a great deal of dope. He said he had to maintain the quota he had become accustomed to in Vietnam. Anytime he was asked a question, he smiled a kind of stoned glassy-eyed smirk, and said, "Far out," which could have meant, "yes" or "no," or nothing whatsoever. We left him alone to whittle, and he seemed hypnotized by the wood chips that fell to the ground.

Daniel became the mascot as he followed people around the camp. Billy took him on nature walks looking for insects, pretty rocks, and leaves. Billy explained to Daniel about God. Daniel came back from these expeditions, his pockets stuffed with all the things Billy had told him was special.

Marsha read to Daniel from the storybooks we'd brought. They'd sit close to the fire, Marsha cuddling with him as if trying to capture the small amount of warmth in his little body. He sat attentively under the blankets with Marsha, sharing her cookies, Cheese Doodles, and Ring Dings.

Gracie lectured Daniel, which she claimed was teaching. He didn't spend much time with her. But Gracie had plenty to tell me about how to raise a kid. Like Daniel, I, too spent as little time as possible with her.

When Sam threw open the hood of his van Daniel jumped into the driver's seat, recklessly turning the steering wheel. "Look at me drive," he'd call out, grinning from ear to ear.

Carl let Daniel watch him whittle. "How's it going, little man?" Carl would say and kept on whittling. I wondered if Carl ever thought about the women and children he had left behind in other countries. Then, one day, when Carl set Daniel on his motorcycle, I thought Carl looked just like a big kid himself, playing with a toy.

Daniel and I took many long walks together during those four days. Life had knocked me off balance, with the divorce and rearing a child on my own. I frequently felt as if I went through life in a daze, just getting by.

My son and I would walk to the nearest hill where we played in the stiff yellow weeds, making believe we were giants stomping on trees. When we tired of stomping, we rolled down the hill and then took turns picking the weeds out of each other's hair.

Daniel had no idea what was going on as he ran around the camp playing in the dirt. I loved to watch him. Everything about my son delighted me: his little pink tummy that poked out from under his favorite T-shirt, his soft flyaway hair that flipped about his head while he chased after white milkweed moths. Even the sound of his laughter fit perfectly with the cracking sound of the dry grass under our feet.

By the fourth day, the adults had become impatient waiting for the earthquake and weary of each other. But Daniel continued to play.

Maybe the catalyst was the intoxicating smell of the dry grass, or the heat of the day pushing against my skin and my brain—for the temperature was reaching into the nineties—but on that last day, I realized that if it had not been for Daniel, I wouldn't have found a meaning to my life.

There were no reports of earthquake activity—not even the slightest tremor had occurred—so we trooped back to San Francisco.

I unpacked my stuff, put Daniel to bed, and made a pot of tea. I had to catch up on my schoolwork. I sat at the kitchen table. The city lights were strung across the night as if stars reflected in a black pool of water.

I poured tea into my favorite cup. Thumbing through a biology book, though knowing that nothing had changed, the room felt different—there had been an interesting shift in me.

However, some things I knew wouldn't change. Gracie continued to knock on Carl's window asking for a night ride on his bike. In the fall she would become pregnant and Carl would say to her what he had said to other women, "It's not mine." Sam still smoked his joints falling asleep in his overstuffed chair. Marsha, buried in blankets, fed her cat treats, while Billy comforted his beloved girlfriend, stroking her soft curly hair and cooing, "Lovely lady."

For the first time in my life I felt safe. The danger was over. We had outsmarted the Big One. I knew we would have more threats of earthquakes, possibly even some real temblors, but that night I felt as if my son and I would live forever.

Jelly Bread

I WASN'T HORNY, BUT I was lonely. Since my divorce, the men floated in and out of my life. There had been so many men that their faces had become a blur. It was the early 1970s. No one was looking for permanency. Most of the men were chomping at the bit to get out of my life as soon as they'd grabbed hold of me. They came in, took what they wanted, and then left.

I'd just ended one relationship with a guy named Duke, a skinny, long-legged photographer who wanted a mother, not a lover. In fact, I attracted quite a few of his kind. Being a single parent made some men a bit dizzy about what type of relationship I could provide for them. My three-year-old son, Daniel, didn't need a big brother. And I certainly didn't need a second child. Then I met Pete. "I really like you," he said one day while we walked above the city in the Berkeley Hills. I don't remember how we got there, but there we were, and alone. Daniel was in an afternoon daycare and I was on a semester break. Lately Pete had become a regular dinner guest.

We walked along the rugged paths of the parkland, the strong odor of eucalyptus thick and pungent in the air, syrupy almost. We lay on a hillside, directly facing into the sunlight. San Francisco had been fogged in for weeks and the warmth of the sun rejuvenated my sense of contentedness. That was the start of our relationship. Maybe I hoped that it might be the end of my restless seeking. I wanted this burly guy to fill an empty space in my soul, a fissure really, which seemed to gape larger the more I tried to cover it over.

So that night Pete put his boots under my bed and Daniel adjusted easily to having a man living with us. But we only cohabited for maybe four or five months at the most, when Pete and I began to grow tired of each other.

Daniel, a little crumb dropper from the day he had been born, made one mess after another that were impossible for me to keep up with. These messes drove Pete crazy.

"Pick up your toys," Pete demanded. "You're a messy little boy."

"He's a kid. Leave him alone," I responded day after day.

"Don't let him eat crackers in front of the TV." Pete especially did not like to see the white bits on the carpet.

Pete said he wanted stability. His father had left the family when he was young, his mother remarried soon after, and Pete never got along with his stepfather.

"I guess I was just a screwed-up kid with a chip on my shoulder," he said one night as we lay in bed together. "I don't want to be like that anymore. I want something real in my life."

I wanted stability too, though it was impossible for me to tell what a long-term relationship with Pete would be like. But once he'd moved in, life got a little coarser. His sexy ways soon began to look lumpish and sloppy, not sexy. Now, when he did the dishes, the way he stood at the sink, knees bent, his head bowed in what looked to me a stupid, awkward manner, I felt a growing resentment at his presence in my home.

We didn't fight. We ignored each other. He disappeared. Even when he sat across from me at the kitchen table, I got the distinct feeling that he was not there.

It's funny how memory plays tricks on us. Some things can stand out so strongly—like the light in the kitchen window the morning I badly burned my hand on the stove, or the smell of an approaching rainstorm on one particularly gray day—while other memories get muddled. That's the way it was with my memories of Pete—I simply could never recall any important details. That's not true, not really. Pete left me with many memories, most of which I'd rather forget.

After what felt like weeks of living with a vacant absent man, Pete told me straight out, though his exact words elude me, that he had been sleeping with another woman. But the next thing I remember doing, and I remember this quite clearly—for it even surprised me—I spit in his face.

"Get out," I shouted. "I never want to see you again. Get out."

Pete said nothing. He backed up, not taking his eyes off me. He probably thought something would be thrown at him. I might have done just that. Or chucked an object in his direction or beat him over the head with whatever was within my reach. He glared at me and then slammed the door behind him. His boots pounded heavily on each step as he went down the stairs to seek refuge with Sam, my downstairs neighbor.

"You stupid asshole," I screamed and quickly ran into the bedroom to gather up his clothes. His shirts, his pants, his underwear, I grabbed it all, even his socks neatly rolled together in the dresser drawer. Piling this stuff together by the door, I scooped up a large armful of his possessions, including a couple of pairs of shoes he never wore, and tossed them down the flight of stairs.

They landed in front of Sam's apartment with a loud thud. Sam opened his door to see what was going on, just in time to see me throw another armload of Pete's belongings in that direction.

"You better get out of here, Pete," Sam said, and then he stepped back to let Pete gather up the items that had landed at the bottom of the stairs. Pete ran up the steps, pushed past me and grabbed his camera from the dresser along with his shaving kit. He no longer used the kit, having grown a full beard, but I guess out of habit he still thought it valuable. He looked like a man on the run, a man quickly breaking camp, as he grabbed the last bit of his clothing piled by the doorway. He glared at me, his dark eyes meaner than I had ever seen them. I knew inside him resided an angry, adolescent boy, and no matter how much dope he smoked or beer he guzzled, it would still take years to rid himself of the disquiet that lived within.

I stepped aside to let him leave, remembering a story he had once told me of pulling a pocketknife on his stepfather when they were arguing. I quickly locked the door and turned on all the lights in every room, except for the room where Daniel still slept soundly. The brightness around my home now looked startlingly unfamiliar, but I wanted no shadows in my apartment.

Things went on as they had always done in our small community, even with Pete now living downstairs with Sam. Though he and I passed each other frequently coming and going, we did not speak.

Daniel continued to visit the neighbors, dragging his trucks and stuffed animals from one apartment to another—as if each had become a room for him to play in—and Pete still from time to time played catch with Daniel. But Daniel and I were alone once more. We lived our lives without a man and frankly, that was fine with me. Men complicated my life; they took whatever they wanted and made promises. Promises that I foolishly believed. In the end I only got hurt. And so did Daniel. He was the one who, due to no fault of his own, got jerked around and left behind by every man I had let into our lives. I had enough disappointment to last me a lifetime, and who knows what damage I'd already done to my son. So I vowed to remain detached from further involvement with any men.

Things eventually smoothed out between Pete and me. Several months later we were talking like old friends again. But there was no pretence that we'd ever get back into a relationship.

"There's snow in the foothills," Pete told me at the holiday gathering of my neighbors. "You want to take a ride up there and see it? I'll borrow a car from a friend. We'll take a Sunday drive into the mountains."

"Daniel's never seen snow," I half-agreed.

"Oh, we have to take him," Pete said, and grinned. He'd had a couple of glasses of wine and his dark eyes sparkled in the dim candlelight on the table. "I haven't seen snow in ages."

I didn't want to get back together with Pete, but I could see my way clear to being friends. He'd been decent to Daniel since the break up, sometimes bringing him cookies and ice cream. I'd often wondered if the treats and games had been gifts from Pete, the grown-up man, or had these special items been brought by a part of him that never forgave his mother for marrying his stepfather. But those questions were not mine to answer, and as long as he was good to Daniel, I didn't care which one remained connected to my son.

Something that was missing from my life while living in San Francisco was a rational passing of the seasons. January in the bay area could feel like May. September could be dreadfully cold, with fog and dampness chilling a body to the bone in the morning, then in the afternoon it could be hot as hell when the cloudbank retreated back to the ocean. I looked forward to getting a real taste of winter.

Early Saturday morning, Pete came to my door dressed in a heavy winter coat. I think because he lived most of his life in the Midwest, he also missed the winter weather.

"I packed us a few sandwiches," I told him.

"Good." He kneeled down to button Daniel's coat. "Well, Daniel, you ready to see what snow is like?"

"Yeah," Daniel responded.

When we arrived at the high altitude, the brilliant white snow sparkled in the sunlight as if it were a field of diamonds. Daniel, delighted and oblivious to the cold, slogged through the knee-deep fluff.

"Let's make a snowman," I shouted and began to roll a tightly packed wad of snow across the field. Daniel watched intently. When I said, "Now you do it," he pushed at the snow as if he were a bulldozer, making a small embankment of snow rather than a ball.

"Let me help you," Pete said and knelt down. He gathered up the mound that Daniel had created and patted at it heartily until he had successfully made the bottom half of a snowman.

"I have the next section," I said and handed Daniel a rather large-sized snowball. "Put it on top," I told him. "That's the snowman's tummy."

When Daniel plunked the large ball on the growing creation, I handed him another hardened handful of snow and Daniel gave that to Pete.

"That's the little guy's head," Pete said. "See?" Pete put the last snowball on the slightly tipsy looking snowman.

"Daniel, our snowman needs eyes, a nose, and a mouth."

I scrounged up a few dried leaves and twigs from a nearby tree while Daniel and Pete patted at the snowman's tummy and backside to make it look a little more even. I had never seen Pete have so much fun and it seemed as though he was truly in his element playing in this winter terrain.

Daniel repeatedly fell in the snow just for the pleasure of rolling around to see the indentation he could make in the white stuff.

I handed the leaves and twigs to Pete. "Here you go, Van Gogh."

Pete grinned and constructed quite a comical face with the debris. Then he took off his own wool knit hat, put it on top of the snowman's head and stepped back to admire his work. The little white fellow looked a bit like it had a shrunken skull under the familiar black watchman's cap. The snowman's eyes tilting slightly inward gave it a rather sinister appearance.

Pete took out a pack of cigarettes and stuck a smoke into the strange little white man's mouth. "There you go, old buddy," Pete said and saluted our new frozen friend as though it was one of his military buddies.

The sun slowly disappeared behind a grove of trees. We now stood in deep shadows. The wind picked up. Our clothing was soaking wet. We were freezing cold, and our teeth began to chatter. We were all shivering. Daniel's lips had begun to turn blue.

"Say goodbye to the snowman," I said. "Let's get to the car and warm up."

Daniel waved to the snowman, and we tromped through the snow back to the parking lot. Holding hands, with Daniel in the middle, Pete and I lifted my snow-caked son above the ground and let him skim across the surface of the snow. He called this flying. He giggled and laughed all the way back to the car, despite the freezing cold. Pete turned on the engine and set the heater to full blast.

I unpacked the sandwiches and poured Pete a cup of hot cocoa from the thermos. I had brought a change of clothes for Daniel. We wrestled with his wet trousers trying to get them off. The cold stiff, slightly frozen fabric refused to cooperate. Finally, with a lot of whining and complaining, the trousers were removed. Gooseflesh crawled up Daniel's plump little legs. Miserably uncomfortable, he didn't stop crying until we'd managed to wiggle him into a dry set of clothes. He then sat on my lap eating his jelly sandwich while I rubbed his body to speed up the warming process.

The heat from the afternoon sun had turned the snow on the roadways into a messy slush. Big puddles of gray mush spread across the parking lot like a dirty lake.

"The mountain air knocks me out every time," I said and finished the last of my hot cocoa.

"Yeah," Pete responded. "What do you say, little man, time to go home?"

"I made a snowman," Daniel told us.

"Yes, you did," I replied and put my empty cup into the bag with the trash. I adjusted Daniel on my lap. Hopefully, I thought, he'll sleep most of the way home.

Pete drove out of the parking lot and onto the main roadway, heading back to the city. The late afternoon sun reflected a blinding bright light. Pete put on his shades as we all settled back for the long drive home. Daniel snuggled into my lap. I leaned my head back onto the neck rest. Pete had borrowed his friend's brand new Chevy, and I was sure that we would have to go through all the crevices in the upholstery when we got back to San Francisco to remove any crumbs that we might have left behind.

"Nice day," Pete said.

"Yeah, it was a nice day." I didn't think we ever had a fun day like this when we had lived together, but, yes, this had been a very pleasant day.

From time to time, we made big waves of slush on either side of the car as we drove through deep puddles of melted snow.

"I'm going to have to take this car to the car wash before I give it back," Pete said.

"The road's a mess," I responded. Then just as I said that, a large wash of muddy water splashed up onto our windshield. A speeding car racing past caused a big wave of slush to freeze onto the glass.

"Shit, I can't see where I'm going," Pete shouted.

I looked down at Daniel now sound asleep. I pulled him closer into my arms. And, before I managed to say another word a loud crashing sound vibrated in my ears. It was like an explosion. The world went dark. I opened my eyes. The windshield was now shattered and broken, looking like a giant spider web spread out across the glass. I looked down at Daniel. Droplets of blood dotted the top of his head. Something warm trickled down my right cheek. I touched my face. Blood dribbled into my mouth.

"What happened?" I asked. Had I fallen asleep? Was this a dream?

I looked at Pete.

A huge cut on his lip gaped open like a sliced exotic fruit, "Oh, my God," he called out.

Daniel, my sweet baby, continued to sleep, thank goodness, with no marks on him. He looked fine, except for the blood that continued to trickle onto him from what I now knew was my bloody wound.

This was not a dream. Blinded by the slush on the windshield, Pete had hit a parked car on the side of the road.

An ambulance arrived. Paramedics buzzed around our car. And yet Daniel slept. I could not wake him. His breathing, slow and steady, showed no sign of trouble, but still he would not open his eyes.

The next two weeks were a nightmare. Glass had to be removed from my forehead where my head had pushed through the front windshield; stitches were laced across the top of my hairline, and a metal pin put in my ankle because the impact of the crash had broken the tip of the leg bone where it joined the ankle. All this resulted in a couple of days' stay in the hospital—and all the while Daniel hadn't awakened from his state of listlessness. He cried and whimpered constantly, they said, while he remained in a somnolent state.

Finally, when the doctor released me I immediately went to Daniel. I hadn't seen him since the accident. It horrified me when I first saw him. He was in a crib that looked like a cage. Enclosed behind the bars, my poor son sat on the hospital sheets, whimpering like an animal. He shed no tears, but made an unfamiliar dry, raspy sound. I took him out of the crib and sat with him in a rocking chair by a window. Hugging him close we rocked for hours. But Daniel continued to make that terribly frightening sound, not once sleeping or moving from my arms.

I could not cry. I was too terrified. What had I done? The hoarse sounds coming from the back of Daniel's throat vibrated on my breast while I hummed lullabies into his soft little ears. Nothing soothed him. He continued to whimper. We sat that way for an entire two days. Though he slept off and on, he never stopped making that little crying noise, even in his sleep.

"He'll be okay, he just needs time to heal," the doctor assured me. "Your son had a serious concussion and there's a slight skull fracture, but in time he'll be fine." So I rocked and hummed and waited another day, but still my little boy did not change.

I heard from one of the nurses that several people had come to see

Daniel while I was hospitalized. One of the visitors had said he was Daniel's father, but my ex never contacted me, and I certainly didn't have the energy to get in touch with him.

Pete left a message at the nurses station several times, though he just kind of drifted away after the accident. The afternoon of the third day, three plainly dressed women came through the door. Each woman carried a Bible.

Although not wanting to be preached at, I managed a smile.

"Would you like us to pray with you?" one woman asked.

My vision became blurry with tears. I hadn't cried, maybe because of the pain medication prescribed by the orthopaedic doctor. But when I saw the three women join hands and bow their heads, I closed my eyes, too, and wondered, who do you pray to when you no longer believe in God? And though I had been feeble and fallen from the fold, as my grandmother would have said, I found the words and begged for forgiveness for the sake of my son and for him not to be punished for my sins and for my son to be healed. Lightning did not strike me.

One of the women touched my shoulder and said, "Have courage, my dear." Then they each touched Daniel on the head, and, without saying another word, walked out of the room. I waver on the subject of guardian angels. Though since that time, I now believe that powers exist in this world that are more mysterious than any of us can explain. Because within a half hour after these women left the room, Daniel stopped making that strange rasping whine in the back of his throat.

A short while later he climbed down from my lap and walked with some difficulty to the playroom. He went there on his own, purposefully walking straight to a large red ball in the far corner of the room.

I looked for the three women to tell them what he had done. The women were nowhere to be found. I explained to a nurse what Daniel had accomplished.

"I told you he'd be all right," she said, and smiled knowingly.

Daniel played the rest of that afternoon, and the next day the doctor released him. Though my son had not yet spoken a word, the medical staff assured me that this would come in time, that his speech would return and that he'd be as good as he had been before the accident.

A neighbor gave Daniel and I a ride home from the hospital. We sat in the back seat playing games. "See the truck?" Or, dangling in front of him the floppy-eared bunny that he had named Droopy, I asked, "What's this?"

Daniel said nothing, and hugged the rabbit, all the while chewing one of the stuffed animal's ragged ears the way he had always done.

When we got out of the car Daniel would not let me carry him. Insisting on walking he wiggled out of my arms. I watched as he made his way through the alcove, heading toward our apartment. He walked with a slight limp now, but the doctor assured me that this would go away with time.

Climbing the stairs, Daniel looked eager to get inside. He didn't pause to ride his trike, or kick a ball that sat at the edge of the vestibule, but marched up the dozen steps, determined to get to the top, not stopping a moment to catch his breath. Once in our apartment, he looked around then went into his room, gathering as many of his favorite toys into his arms as he could manage and carried them over to my bed.

After unloading all of his precious possessions into a big tumbling pile, he took my hand and pulled me toward them. I sat next to the collected toys, waiting for him to choose the game. Cars. He wanted to play our driving game.

Taking the car he gave me, the red one missing doors and tires, I pushed the toy along the edge of the bed. Then, playing the car game the way we always had, I ran the small vehicle across first his right knee, then up his thigh and over onto his other knee. He patted his chest, and I drove the car up over his tummy and across his rib cage. He bent down and kissed the red wreck of a car.

We played with every toy that he had brought to the bed, then when all the familiar games had been completed, we lay on the bed, the toys scattered everywhere around us. I closed my eyes, exhausted from the day's ordeal.

Several minutes later, a little hand touched my face.

"Hungry," a strained, raspy, little voice sounded in my ear.

I opened my eyes. Daniel sat facing me. He patted his stomach. "Hungry," he said again, this time slightly stronger than before.

"Jelly bread?" I asked.

He nodded.

We got up from the bed and went into the kitchen. He opened the refrigerator the way he always liked to do, so that he could pick the jelly he wanted in his sandwich. Meanwhile, I took out the loaf of bread. We sat at the kitchen table. Daniel's little bare feet dangled underneath. He kicked them back and forth. His mouth smeared with grape jelly and wearing a milk mustache, a little pink tongue licked at a blob of the purple delight that sat on his upper lip.

He smiled. "Good."

A Little Love Story

TONY AND I HAD BECOME acquainted while volunteering for the United Farm Worker's Union. Labor organizer, Cesar Chavez, had been working to get an initiative to validate the union on the ballot in the up-coming November election. Tony and I were assigned to canvass throughout the Avenues, a middle-class community in the flatlands of San Francisco, an area that runs several miles along the Pacific coastline. I had a car by then, a big Chevy station wagon that had been dubbed "The Tank" by my friends and neighbors, so my volunteer assignment, in addition to helping with the actual canvassing, had been to drive my designated group to our various locations.

"We could fit a pretty big crew in that car of yours," Melanie, the volunteer coordinator said when she took a look at The Tank.

"Most people I know drive VW bugs," she continued as she directed a family of farm workers; a mother, a father, and their teenage daughter, and Tony, who was the group leader, to all get into my car.

Unlike the rest of San Francisco, with its blistering hot days in September, the Avenues is a chilly place this time of year. A heavy fog bank rolls in around mid-July and usually doesn't retreat until almost Thanksgiving. Tony had just moved here from New York City and being used to warm autumn weather, had worn only jeans and a work shirt. The farm worker family, also unprepared for the cool weather, only wore lightweight summer clothing.

While we ate our lunch in my station wagon, we all shivered and rubbed our hands together trying to get warm. But once we'd finished eating, we went back out into the foggy afternoon, doing what we had set out to do. By the end of the day, all fliers were delivered and we brought back four full pages of signatures.

Daniel, now nearly four years old, had spent the day in a makeshift childcare center in a corner of the temporary headquarters of the union located in a local Catholic church in the Mission district. By the time I returned, Daniel was more than ready to see me.

"Mommy, Mommy," he called out as he ran to greet me the moment I walked through the door. Daniel had most likely been watching the entrance for some time, waiting for my return.

"He's been missing you for quite awhile," the volunteer teacher remarked as Daniel hugged me at the knees.

"Hey, sweetheart, I'm back." I lifted him up in my arms. "Did you eat?"

Daniel nodded then waved a ragged corn tortilla in my face.

"He's a good eater," the teacher said. "Spaghetti, beans, rice, cookies. He ate everything, and he's been munching on that tortilla for half an hour." The teacher rubbed his little back. Daniel grabbed my neck, hanging on tightly. I knew he wanted nothing further to do with Miss Rodriguez.

"He's a good boy," she said. Then she blew him a kiss and went back to where other children were waiting to be picked up by their parents. Tony stood behind me. He cleared his throat.

"This is my son, Daniel," I said.

"Hi, Daniel," Tony said, though he didn't sound very enthusiastic. "You didn't say you had a kid." Tony smiled.

I knew what he was thinking—"A kid. No way am I getting involved with her."

I smiled back, even though I now felt a tortilla flapping near my ear as Daniel held tightly onto my neck. He would not look at Tony.

"Well, then," Tony replied as though I had asked him a question. "I promised to help out with dinner this evening—see you around." He turned, without saying another word and walked toward the kitchen.

"That's the way it goes," I muttered under my breath then gave Daniel a kiss on the cheek. "Let's get Mommy some dinner."

Daniel wiggled out of my arms. He took my hand, and led me to the line forming outside the kitchen doorway. When my turn came to receive dinner, Tony handed me a plate heaped with spaghetti, salad, rice, beans, with a tortilla lying across the top of all the food.

Leaning over the counter, almost in a whisper Tony said, "I didn't know you had to warm up the tortillas. I was giving them out cold and no one would take one. Then someone told me to put the tortillas on the grill before serving them. Yours is warmed."

"Thanks," I replied.

During the canvassing, we learned we had friends in common—Glenda, one of the teachers from Daniel's childcare center on the college campus. She'd introduced Tony to her husband, Walt, and now they hung out regularly.

That following Monday morning while Glenda helped Daniel take off his jacket I told her, "I met a friend of yours last Saturday. Tony."

"Nice guy," she responded.

"Yep," I replied, and that was all we said regarding Tony. I forgot all about him. Well, sort of. I'd made a vow to have nothing more to do with men. From my experience, they were only trouble. Though Tony's long mutton chop sideburns, his warm brown eyes, and the way he so unashamedly sang along with the music on the car radio melted a little spot in my heart. There was always a nagging question in the back of my brain that questioned whether I'd ever meet someone who'd care about my son and me.

Then, several days later, Glenda stopped me as I rushed into day care with Daniel, close to being late to class. "Wait," she called out to me. "I got something to tell you. Remember Tony?"

"Yes," I said.

"Well, Tony thought you were married when he saw you with Daniel. But when Walt said that you weren't, Tony sounded interested. What do you say about that?" Folding her arms across ample bosoms, Glenda gave me a knowing smile and said, "How about you? You interested, too?"

"I don't know. Men are more work than kids."

"He's a nice person," Glenda insisted. "Give him a chance. The four of us could go out together."

Standing around talking to Glenda was certainly going to make me late for class. I looked at the clock above the doorway. "I've got to get going." I gave Daniel a kiss on top of his head. "We'll talk after my classes."

That afternoon arriving back at the day care Glenda was sitting on the floor next to Daniel, a huge mound of blocks spread out in front of them. Daniel had a reputation for letting a stack of blocks only grow so high, until he could stand it no longer and then he'd knock it down. His pleasure was not in the building, but in the eventual tumbling over.

"Time to go home," I said.

Daniel ran to his cubby, took his jacket from the hook. Ready to go home, Daniel handed me the artwork he had done earlier that day, a very abstract glue and paste portrait of a jack o'lantern pumpkin head.

"So, what do you say to Japanese food and a Samurai movie on Saturday night?" Glenda asked.

I smiled. "Walt's idea of a fun date?" I asked.

She smiled, too. "Yes. It's his way of celebrating Halloween. We're too old to go trick-or-treating."

"Sure," I replied. "I'll go. What the heck, I'm getting tired of cartoons and solitaire, anyway."

"Good," Glenda said. "Come by about six, and we'll have a glass of wine before we head out."

This fix-up date with Tony didn't particularly thrill me. I didn't need a man around. Rather than a man, what my life needed was more sleep, greater study time, not to mention a larger supply of patience with my son. And a little more money could certainly be added to this list. So far, I'd learned that having a man around gave me none of those things.

Over soba noodles, teriyaki chicken, and a good dose of Samurai sword fighting, Tony and I got along surprisingly well. He wasn't a great fan of Samurai movies, but went along with Walt's suggestion for a fun evening.

After the movie, we stopped off for ice cream.

"I know of a Halloween party in Bernal Heights," I told them as we sat in a dessert shop eating banana splits and chocolate sundaes.

"Not me," Glenda said. "I've got to get up early tomorrow."

"Me, too," Walt replied.

"I'll go," Tony said. He shrugged his shoulders. "I've got nothing to do tomorrow."

Halloween in San Francisco is like Mardi Gras in New Orleans, with outrageous costumes and parties everywhere. Parking the car a short distance from the party, we could hear music from Santana's latest album blasting out into the night. Fake spider webs, strewn about on the hedges along the entranceway gave the house a sloppy rather than sinister look. Rubber bats dangled from elastic thread, bobbing up and down above our heads as we stepped onto the porch. When we got into the place it was easy to see that all the rooms were far too crowded to dance and most of the food had already been eaten, except for a few misshapen cheese sandwiches and a couple of dried-up, crusty-looking devilled eggs. Two warm beers sitting in a bucket of melted ice failed to tempt us.

"Looks like the party's over," I said. "Sorry."

"That's okay, I'm getting tired anyway."

"I'll drop you off at your place," I offered, and we headed back out the door to the car. There would be no kisses, or any, "Why don't you come over to my place and have a cup of coffee." The only thing I intended to offer was friendship.

We drove to Tony's place. When he got out of the car, he asked, "What are you doing tomorrow?"

"Going to the zoo with my kid."

"Mind if I tag along?"

"All right," I agreed. "Ten-thirty? But this time dress warmer. The zoo's out by the ocean and you know how cold it can get out there."

"I'll be ready," Tony said. I detected more enthusiasm for the zoo than when Tony talked about the Samurai movie.

Daniel had spent the evening with a neighbor. The little guy was deep in sleep when I arrived to pick him up. Each day he seemed to get heavier. As I scooped him up, his limp sleeping body felt as though he weighed as much as a fifty-pound bag of potatoes.

Climbing up the stairs to my apartment with Daniel in my arms, fatigue hit me full throttle. I knew my son would be up early in the morning. After tucking Daniel in for the night, exhausted, I crawled under the covers. There was not even a pretence that I would read a word in the chapter assigned for my psychology class.

The next morning, like clockwork, Daniel got up just as the sun was coming up. Before Daniel, I would have fallen back to sleep and dozed until noon. Not anymore. Now with my eyes half open, I listened to Daniel scoot a chair across the kitchen floor, making his way to the cupboard where we kept the cookies. Unsupervised, who knew what he'd get into? So, dragging myself from the bed, I was thankful that I had not stayed out too late the night before.

"No cookies this morning, Daniel," I said and took him down from the chair. "Today we're going to the zoo. Remember? You want to see the monkeys and the seals?"

"Monkey faces in the zoo. I'm going to see monkey faces in the zoo," he sang over and over as I prepared fried eggs and toast.

After packing several jelly sandwiches we got into the car, and drove to Tony's apartment on upper Mission Street. Tony was waiting outside for us with a denim jacket slung over one shoulder.

"Hi," I said as he opened the rear door to climb into the car.

"Hi. Great day for the zoo," he replied.

"Remember Daniel?" I asked.

"Sure I remember. Hi, Daniel, how are you today?"

"This is Tony," I told Daniel. "He's going to the zoo with us."

"What's your favorite animal?" Tony inquired.

"Monkeys and ah-ahs," Daniel said, friendly but cautious as he looked at Tony from over the back of his seat.

"What's an ah-ah?" Tony asked.

"You'll see," I said.

The fog had almost retreated back into the ocean as I drove up over a hill that featured a panoramic view of the western edge of the city where the zoo was located.

"It's going to be nice and hot today," I observed.

"Good." Tony seemed quite comfortable in the back seat looking out the window.

Once I parked the car and we were about to get out, Tony said, "You got a tennis ball or something back here to play catch with?"

"Yeah, I think so. We usually have something, though it's not always so easy to find."

To be honest, the back of my station wagon had become a repository for dirty laundry. I'd fill up a pillowcase with soiled clothing and then haul it out to the car. When left with no other choice but to go to the Laundromat, I'd make a big deal out of washing clothes. We'd take toys for Daniel to play with, and we'd eat fish 'n' chips from the local fry shop.

Tony pushed a few bags of clothing from one side to the other. "I found one," he said, and crawled out of the back seat holding a bright yellow tennis ball in one hand. "Doesn't look like I'll need a coat to-day," he added, and just before he closed the door he threw his jacket onto the back seat.

I took the ball from Tony and put it in the bag with the sandwiches. "Everyone ready? Let's go see the animals," I said.

We always went through Daniel's special gate, because this was the gate located closest to his favorite animals, the ah-ahs. And it didn't take long before we heard the familiar barking of seals in the distance.

"Ah-ahs," Daniel shouted. "I hear the ah-ahs."

"The what?" Tony asked.

"Seals. That's what he's called seals since his first visit to the zoo. There's always someone by the pond with a bucket of fish for the kids to throw at the seals. This has got to be one of Daniel's most favorite things to do in the world."

On a platform near the entrance to the seal's pool stood a man with a big bucket of slimy little fish. He was waiting for a child to come along to help feed the hungry animals.

Seals, baboons, elephants, giraffes, we fed them all. Then it was time for us to eat. Tony bought French fries and soda to go with our jelly bread, and then we each had a scoop of ice cream sandwiched between two deliciously chewy oatmeal cookies. Daniel needed a good sponging off after finishing his dessert. Even though I did my best to clean the ice cream from his hands and face, he was still pretty sticky for the remainder of the day.

"Where's that ball?" Tony asked. We had exhausted all the animals that would hold Daniel's interest in this hot afternoon sun and he had begun to behave as any three-year-old would when his boredom and fatigue set in—that is, he whined and complained.

Taking the ball out of the lunch bag, I handed it to Tony.

"Want to play catch, Daniel?" Tony asked.

Daniel stopped crying, and we moved into a shaded area of the park.

Tony tossed the ball to Daniel, a gentle underhanded toss, which hit square in Daniel's cupped hands.

"Okay, throw it back to me," Tony coached, standing slightly bent over, hands in front of him as though he were a catcher waiting for a magnificent pitch. Daniel pulled his arm back, his short fingers splayed as far around the yellow tennis ball as he could manage, and he let the ball fly. The ball landed directly on its intended mark.

"This kid's got a great arm. Good job, Daniel," Tony said, and once again threw the ball back to Daniel.

I sat in the dappled shade of a huge eucalyptus tree, watching my son play catch with a man I knew so little about. The only thing we knew about Tony so far was that he was a transplanted New Yorker, a student with an interest in politics, a friend of friends, and that he seemed to be a gentle, unassuming man. In fact, Tony probably told me more about himself than some of the men I'd dated for months.

Most of the men who came into my life had little patience for playing with Daniel. "That's enough, Daniel," a majority of them would say after a short game of catch. "No more playing." Then they'd collapse and complain about kids having too much energy.

"Here, Wilma, you play, too," Tony said, tossing the ball to me.

We'd have stayed longer, playing on the grass, except the fog rolled in from the ocean and the zoo became covered in a chilly, damp cloak of mist. The animals sat more quietly in their cages as we passed them on our way back to the car. The cheery zoo that we'd seen earlier in the bright sunlit during the morning now looked foreboding as fog crept across the walkways and seeped into the cages. The animals retreated back into their concrete bunkers, moving away from the chill of the approaching evening fog.

My car, too, became a welcome refuge against the cold that had descended onto the area.

"I had no idea California could get so cold," Tony said as he quickly put on his jean jacket.

Daniel, exhausted from the day's activities, quickly fell asleep as we drove back to the Mission District.

When I pulled up in front of Tony's apartment, he said, "I'd like to see you again."

"I have mid-terms this week, and I'm afraid next weekend is a laundry weekend. If you want to hang out with us there, you're welcome. But be warned, it's not a lot of fun."

Laundry was my least favorite task, and I put off the tiresome job as long as possible. But if I didn't get to it soon, I'd have to start buying new clothes for Daniel and myself. That certainly was something my tight budget could not allow.

"I don't mind," Tony said. "I'll bring my wash, too."

Doing the laundry with Tony turned out to be great fun. Usually Daniel quickly became bored. He'd whine and complain once he'd finished reading the children's books that we had brought. He'd refuse to play with his toys. Before the laundry was finished I'd usually run out of patience, energy, and ideas to keep him occupied. Tony, on the other hand kept coming up with great ideas to keep Daniel busy while we talked.

"Daniel, you run to the door and back, I'll count and see how long it takes you," Tony said as he and I sat on hard plastic chairs in the middle of the Laundromat.

Daniel took off, his little legs moving as fast as he could make them go.

"One-two-three-four-five," Tony counted.

Daniel returned to where we sat, hair tousled, his shaggy cut bangs clinging to his sweaty little brow, grinning from ear to ear. "How much?" Daniel asked, nearly out of breath.

"Seven," Tony said. "Seven seconds. Want to do it some more?"

"Yes," Daniel said eagerly.

"Okay, on your mark, get set, go!"

Daniel took off running again, headed for the door. Then he quickly ran back to us. This was certainly Daniel's kind of game. He could keep this up until he dropped. After about twenty minutes of running back and forth, that's exactly what he did. He plopped down on the floor at our feet, still grinning, though if his legs could have endured more, he would have continued to run.

"It's time for fish 'n' chips," I said.

"Me, too," Daniel called out.

"We'll go get them," Tony said. He took Daniel by the hand and led him out the door. Fifteen minutes later they returned, and we were eating soggy fries and greasy batter-fried fish doused with malt vinegar off the pages of the *San Francisco Chronicle*[1].

When all the clothes were dried and folded, we headed back home,

Just as Tony got out of the car, I asked, "You want to come to dinner tomorrow night?"

"Yes," Daniel quickly said, as though the invitation had been extended to him. Tony and I laughed. "How can I refuse an invite like that? Sure, I'll come."

I had a bit of housekeeping to do before Tony arrived the next day. Not that I thought he'd mind a messy apartment. But it was for me. I wanted to feel more together. During midterms housekeeping is last on my list of things to do. Daniel's toys were scattered all over the floor. My books and papers carelessly cluttered tabletops. Even the chairs were encumbered with schoolwork. It was past time to clear the messes. Tony coming to dinner gave me a good excuse to get the job done. Another reason for order had begun to push at me, too. I needed to have a talk with Tony, a serious talk before the situation between us went any further.

Tony arrived, right on time, a kite in one hand and a bottle of Chianti in the other. Tony stepping into our lives had taken me quite by surprise. Determined not to make another mistake with a man, it was time to tell him where I stood, not just for me, but also for Daniel's sake.

"Hey, Daniel, next weekend we can fly this kite in the park," Tony said as he handed the colorful plastic bag to Daniel.

"A kite, for me?" Daniel looked at the gift with intense curiosity.

"Yep, and next week we'll put it together and throw it in the air and watch it fly." Tony handed me the bottle of Chianti.

"Want to see my toys?" Daniel asked, and grabbed onto Tony's hand. "Sure, unless your mommy needs help in the kitchen."

"No, it's fine. The food is almost done."

Daniel wasted no time in escorting Tony into his bedroom. Then while I set the table and removed the food from the stove, I heard

Daniel making his familiar truck and motorcycle engine sounds. Then I heard an unfamiliar voice in the mix, a "beep, beep," I'd never heard before. It was clear that Tony had been drawn into the car-chasing game that Daniel liked so much.

"Dinner's ready," I called, and soon we were all sitting around the table eating. Daniel ate eagerly, making his usual mess with the spaghetti and red sauce. After dinner while I bathed Daniel, Tony volunteered to do the dishes. When these chores were finished, we played and read to Daniel until his bedtime.

When all was quiet, I plunked down onto the couch and put my feet up on the coffee table. At that moment I felt more tired than I had ever felt in my life, and I said, "Oh, man, I'm tired."

"Me, too," Tony responded.

I didn't know if Tony thought my fatigue was an invitation to go to bed, though it wasn't. And I knew that now was as good a time as any to tell him where things stood with me. "I have to set something straight," I said. "I'm not looking for a one-night-stand. I'm not even looking for short-term relationships. I play for keeps. I've had too many screwed-up relationships and they're no good for Daniel. If you're not serious, I'm not interested. I can't say it any more plainly than that."

My words did not seem to shock Tony. He didn't flinch. There were a few awkward moments of silence, and then he said, "Well, we'll just have to see where this thing goes, now, won't we?"

If I'd said this to some of the other men whom I had met, they'd have been out the door before I finished the second sentence. But Tony stuck around. He came back the next week and the week after that. He brought us gifts; a coffee cup, a bag of Mexican pastry, a new toy dump truck, a box of crayons.

Then one Saturday morning Daniel looked up from his breakfast cereal and asked, "Can Tony be my daddy?"

What do you tell a fatherless child? Do you tell him his dad abandoned him, had given him up for women, booze, and rock 'n' roll, leaving an empty spot for the little one to fill with whoever came along? No, these are not words you throw at a child. Though at that moment, anger, a sharp, mean anger jabbed at me, not just because

I felt abandoned, but also because my son felt a need to fix our lives, his and mine.

"Well," I said. "What do you think Tony would say if you asked him that?"

"I don't know," Daniel replied. He lifted a spoonful of cereal to his mouth. Milk dribbled onto his chin.

That afternoon when Tony arrived and while he, Daniel, and I were playing a game of Shoots and Ladders, Daniel said, "I want to ask you a question."

I held my breath, realizing what he was about to ask. Should I stop him? Would the wounds that my son carried only become deeper if Tony turned away?

Daniel, determined to take this thing as far as he could, said, "Don't laugh." "I won't laugh," Tony said.

"Promise?"

"Promise," Tony replied.

Then without further hesitation, Daniel asked, "Would you be my daddy?"

The room went silent for a millisecond while a voice inside my head screamed, "Why did you let your son put himself in a position to be hurt again?"

Then Tony said, "Well, Daniel, you can't rush these things. But you know what? It sounds like a very good idea. I've never known any-body who asked such a big question. You're really a special person." Tony ruffled Daniel's hair and gave him a kiss on the top of the head. Tony looked at me. "What does Mommy say?"

And though I might as well have been reaching for the stars, I wanted it, too. We both wanted Tony in our lives. Daniel had popped the question, now was I ready to say yes?

The Drunken Widow and the Moose

WINTER NIGHTS ARE LONG IN Alaska. The sun comes up mid-morning and goes back down early afternoon. From October until March the days seem to descend rather than rise. To ease the darkness, and to relieve the loneliness of widowhood, Pearl went to bed most nights in a drunken stupor, her whisky bottle on the nightstand next to an empty glass perfumed with drink. This night she had been in a deep, uneasy dream when a loud crashing sound startled her awake.

"Oh, Lord, I'm sorry," Pearl cried out. She sat up quickly, too quickly, making her dizzy, confused and setting her heart pounding.

"Who's there?" she shouted. Girt, Pearl's miniature black poodle, barked from the front room where the dog spent most nights sleeping on Pearl's old recliner.

"Who's there?" Pearl called out again.

A second thunderous crash answered, this time sounding as though someone had thrown hundreds of rocks at the metal siding of her trailer. Pearl rushed to the front of the house, where the noise had been coming from. Pretty Boy, the young parakeet Pearl kept in a cage near the TV, frantically beat his wings against the sides of his cage. Another bang thudded as Pearl removed the cover from the bird's cage. This time the noise sounded as if someone had rammed into her trailer with a car. Girt continued to bark hysterically, frantically scratching at the door.

"What on earth's going on?" Pearl shouted. "Girt, hush up! I can't think." She turned on the yard light and before she was able to look outside, something hit the side of her trailer again. She pulled the curtain back from the window and there stood the cause of all this noise.

A moose. A hungry moose had clambered onto Pearl's front porch and was eating the bark off the scraggly tree that grew alongside her trailer. Pearl watched as the animal took big bites from the tree and with each bite gave a hearty yank so that the branches, full of ice and snow, banged furiously against the trailer. Girt went wild again, barking.

"Girt, will you shut up," Pearl shouted.

The moose took another pull on the tree and this time it sounded as though an avalanche had struck the trailer.

"I can't stand to listen to this all night. Will you shut up, Girt, before I feed you to that moose." The dog continued to bark and jump at the door. "You little coward," Pearl said. "We'll see just how brave you are in a minute." Pearl grabbed the dust mop she kept in a closet by the stove and went to the door. Girt, not much bigger than the dust mop, stood by the door barking out her threat.

"Get out of the way, Girt. Go on now, get." Pearl scooted the little dog away with her foot, then slowly opened the door a crack. She peeked out to make sure the moose was not standing on the other side waiting to get in. He wasn't. The moose foraged with his backside to his hostess.

"Don't you kick me, you danged old moose," Pearl said softly. She opened the door all the way and then shook the dust mop furiously at the creature. "Get out of here!" The moose didn't budge but continued to chew the bark he had pulled off the tree. Pearl shouted again, "Get out of here, you! Go on, get!"

The moose just kept chewing the bark. Girt, the true little coward that she was, stood behind Pearl barking even louder than before. Pearl took aim and hit the moose square on the rump with her dust mop. In the freezing night air, a cloud of debris from the cotton strands swarmed around the moose's behind like a sudden sparkling of pixie dust. But the moose did not budge. Instead, he took another bite of the tree. The skinny little winter-weary hardwood shook violently and again its saddened limbs banged against the outside wall, the noise echoing throughout Pearl's home.

Girt's bark was now even more shrill and insistent, while Pretty Boy continued to furiously flap his wings against the cage. Pearl took another swing at the moose, hitting him once more on the rump. The moose turned around this time, his long, dumb face evaluating Pearl as he chewed the bark.

"You better not charge at me, you bugger," Pearl said. Clenching her teeth, Pearl took yet another swing at it. This time she smacked him on the top of his right front quarter. The moose did not budge. Pearl didn't see anything that she could do to get the moose to move short of shooting it, and at that point she contemplated getting her husband's old hunting rifle out of the back of the closet to do just that. The moose must have sensed this, Pearl thought, because he stopped eating, looked at Pearl, snorted a couple of times with long streams of vapor trailing from his nose, then turned and trotted off through the snow, leaving moose droppings behind on the bottom step of the porch. Girt cautiously came out onto the porch, all the while yapping insults at the departing moose. Pearl watched the moose for a short while to make sure he was on his way. Then she went inside and closed the door.

Girt continued her racket. "Will you shut up," Pearl shouted at Girt, and went to Pretty Boy's cage. The poor bird had flapped his wings against the cage the entire time. Pearl opened the cage door and managed to grab hold of the bird. She held him tightly. His tiny heart beat rapidly in its little chest cavity. Pearl softly stroked the bird's head. She blew gently on his fluff; something she had learned would always calm him. He had lost a couple of his wing feathers, and several minutes later, when she returned the bird to his cage, she thought he now looked a bit lopsided.

Pearl sat down on the couch. The excitement with the moose in the middle of the night had worn her out. When Girt jumped up on Pearl's lap, still barking, Pearl pushed the dog back onto the floor. The pup tumbled down, landing on its feet.

"Shut up, you fool, it's over," Pearl snapped. Girt sat on her haunches, just out of Pearl's reach, wagging her tail, panting, whining, and watched Pearl's every move. "Oh, come on," she said, and patted her lap. The little dog jumped up onto Pearl and enthusiastically licked at the old woman's hands.

"That was a close call." Pearl ruffled the dog's jowls. "I thought for sure we were goners." She kissed the dog on the forehead. "You told that old moose a thing or two, didn't you?" Pearl scratched Girt behind the ears. "Nothing like a moose attack in the middle of the night to sober a person up. I must have been dreaming because I thought for sure the devil was on my tail."

Girt, a delicate framed dog with curly charcoal fur, wagged her tail. She looked intently up at her mistress. Pearl thought the dog, not a full-blooded poodle, had to be a mix of a couple of other high-strung breeds because the little animal got hysterical so quickly. She'd been a gift from one of Pearl's daughters six years ago when Roger, Pearl's husband, passed away and Pearl moved up to Alaska to be near family. Pearl hadn't wanted a dog, but her daughter insisted that it would take away some of the loneliness. So she agreed to take her, not because she wanted one—she didn't want anything to take care of any more—but to make her daughter happy.

For Pearl, adjusting to widowhood had not been easy. She had never felt so alone in her life. She'd been through other emotionally hard times, of course, like most folks she knew, but nothing compared to the loneliness she experienced after Roger's death. And it had happened so fast. For years she had listened to her husband complain about his stomach, though he never did anything about it except take antacid tablets. Then, when he finally did go to the doctor, he'd been diagnosed with cancer and six months later he died. Nothing was ever the same again afterward. Pearl had begun to drink in the evenings, during the last stages of Roger's cancer, to "calm her nerves" and to make the approaching loneliness somewhat more bearable.

By the time her daughter brought Girt to live with Pearl, drinking had become a regular part of her evening routine. Over the past six years, Girt had witnessed the whole progression. The dog had not eased the loneliness much, and Pearl began to drink earlier in the evening. Soon, she took a little drink at lunch, and now she poured herself a drink right after breakfast.

Pearl explained to Girt, as though she were a real person, "The drink's only something to keep out the blues." Girt wagged her tail and looked at Pearl as if comprehending every word. "Well, Girt, we've seen it all now, haven't we?" she said, pushing the dog from her lap then standing. "As long as I'm awake, I might as well have a drink."

On her way to the bedroom Pearl passed the front door. She peeked out through the curtains to see if the moose had returned.

"Doesn't look like he'll be back anymore tonight. He sure made some racket, didn't he?"

Girt sat on her haunches, ears perked, tail wagging. In the bedroom, Pearl reached for the bottle of whisky. "Oh, no," she gasped. "It's empty!"

She knew the bottle had been almost empty, but she didn't remember drinking it down to the last drop. She went into the kitchen and rummaged through the cabinets, pushing aside cans of vegetables, soups, a plastic bag of pasta, a box of coffee filters, looking for another bottle of Scotch. She found none.

"Girt, I drank it all up," she said, turning the empty bottle upside down, desperate to pour another trickle into her glass. "Now what? Nothing's going to be open for hours. Why'd that old moose have to come tonight and make this mess for me? How am I going to get back to sleep?"

Pearl sat down at the kitchen table, sighed deeply, and lit a cigarette. "Girt, I sure could use a drink right about now," she said. She salivated looking at the empty bottle on the kitchen counter. A wave of disappointment quickly turned into panic.

Girt sniffed along the door jam then stood at Pearl's feet wagging her tail.

"You're a stupid mutt, you know that," Pearl said. "I want a drink, Girt. I want one real bad. It's a long wait till morning. Why don't I keep an extra bottle around?"

She gave a chuckle that resembled a sarcastic snort. "I keep drinking them, that's why."

Pearl got up and stood in front of the coffee maker. "Well, Girt, I can't sleep and now, thanks to the moose, I'm sober, so I might as well make a pot of coffee. What am I going to do? This life is driving me nuts. Girt, you haven't a care in the world. You've no idea what it's like to be lonely, do you?" Pearl bent down and scratched the dog behind the ears. Girt went limp with pleasure.

"Maybe some music will make me feel better." She turned on the radio. Only one station broadcast this time of night, an all-night country-western station. Pearl tuned it in, poured herself a cup of coffee, and lit another cigarette. The music was a slow waltz.

"Isn't that a pretty tune?" she said to Girt, who had curled up on the recliner again. "I used to be such a good dancer." Pearl sat at the small chrome dinette set in her little kitchen area. "Something just got into me when I heard music," Pearl said, and she began to tap one foot in time to the waltz.

"The music lifted me right out of my seat, and I couldn't stop dancing."

Girt perked up one ear. She watched Pearl's foot for a minute or two, then put her head back down on her paws and closed her eyes. Pearl listened to the music, smoking a cigarette and drinking her cup of coffee. She opened the curtains to look at the tree the moose had been eating. Shreds of torn bark hung like rags from the sides of the bedraggled oak. She closed the curtains. Wistfully looking toward the cupboard, Pearl said, "I sure could use a drink." She sighed heavily. "You're a fool, woman. You know that." The familiar music began to soothe Pearl as she continued to tap her foot to the beat.

"Roger and I used to dance to this song." Girt lifted her heavy eyelids in response to Pearl's voice. "Oh, I loved to dance with him. People used to tell us how good we looked together."

A different song began to play. Pearl got up with the cigarette in one hand and began to dance in time to the music. When the music stopped, she put the cigarette into the ashtray, and stood, as if waiting for someone to ask her to dance. And then in her little kitchen, a young man, someone she had not seen in years, walked up to her. "May I have this dance?" he said. She closed her eyes, and when she began to move in rhythm to the music she remembered how Roger whispered in her ear, "Dance a little closer, Pearl."

Girt had begun to snore, the way she did when she was deep in sleep. Pretty Boy stood perfectly still on a perch in the corner of his cage, his head tucked under a weary wing.

"A lot of men wanted to dance with me, Pearl said." She slowly moved from the kitchen to the living room then back again to the kitchen.

"One night Roger got into a fight with someone who'd asked me to dance because he thought the guy was honing in on his territory. That was before we got married. I never touched liquor back then. I didn't want to stop dancing to have a drink."

The sky had begun to glow a lighter shade of blue. Even though the sun would not be rising for several more hours, Pearl knew morning had arrived. She didn't know how long she had been dancing.

"Maybe I'll try to sleep now," she said, and put her coffee cup into the sink. Picking up the empty whisky bottle, she threw it into the trashcan. "There," Pearl snarled, "That's where you belong, you dirty son of a gun."

Hearing the angry tone in Pearl's voice, Girt looked up quickly. Then closed her eyes, put her head once again on her paws, as Pearl went back into the bedroom.

Pearl lay down. A favorite dance tune played in her head. The music soon became a lullaby, and she remembered Roger's soft caresses when they were first married. These memories visited Pearl now in her sleep, in her dreams, in the long Alaskan night.

Don't Let Go

IT WAS BLISTERINGLY HOT THE day I almost drowned. The sand on the beach scorched my bare feet. The blanket sucked up the rays from the sun. Every time I moved I had to hold still while my body temperature cooled the new spot.

Earlier that morning, Tony and I and our two kids had gone to the seaside. A storm out at sea had churned the Atlantic coastal beaches into a frothy mess. The wind whipped sand into the air in great gusts, stinging us so badly that we had to leave. Our other alternative was only a several miles drive to an inland lake set in the middle of a state park where the oak and scrubby pine trees would most likely keep out the wind.

Arriving at the lake, the air was deadly quiet, peculiarly still, as if we had traveled into the eye of a summer storm. The water in the lake stretched out flatter than usual. The few seagulls flying overhead, wings outstretched, glided across the sky as though sliding on blue ice.

We weren't the only family that had decided to come to the lake that day. I had never seen the park so crowded with kids splashing in the water or running back and forth in the sand, chasing each other.

One family, several blankets away from our spot, had children who whined and complained no matter what the mother gave them to eat. They wanted ice cream. The mother told them they'd have to wait. The ice cream truck would be coming soon the exasperated woman promised them. The scrappy children continued to complain making the heat all the more unbearable with their shrill, unreasonable whining.

Daniel, our independent eleven-year-old son, jumped into the lake before I'd even managed to straighten the last corner of the beach blanket. He dived deep into the water, disappearing like a porpoise. Tony hit the water next. I watched him swim back and forth along the rope at the far end of the designated swimming area of the lake. He swam slowly, slower than anyone I'd ever seen. If you watched him it appeared that his feet only slightly kicked through the water, because most of his leg action was way down deep. Tony would swim for another half hour before he'd need to take a break.

Julia, our daughter, took a quick drink from a container of orange juice and then ran to the lake, solidly planting her chubby butt at the edge of the water. She was greased from head to toe with suntan lotion, though I knew there would undoubtedly be some places on her body that I had missed. Tonight, these would flare up as if she'd been scalded, causing her to whimper until a cooling aloe plant leaf was smashed and the slimy juice smeared on the tender area. She was completely oblivious to the possibility of sunburn, and she splashed, making the best of all the water around her. In the winter, she lived in the bathtub, preferring to bathe rather than watch TV. I looked for gills on her. I found none, of course, and she did not appear to have scales or fins, either.

Tony finished his long swim and came running toward me, sloshing through the water. He ran across the hot sand, each step accompanied by an "ouch, ouch, ouch" as he rushed to our blanket.

Julia came hurrying after to join us. The sand didn't bother her feet. After two weeks of vacationing, she had developed a tolerance for the burning sand. She fell between us on the blanket, her sandy bottom facing the sun. "Take me out into the water, Daddy," she pleaded.

Tony had promised to swim with her to the rope and let her kick around. She was fearless in the water and had been swimming since she was a baby. I remember when she first began to walk, how she would run into the water to be with her father and brother. She'd be standing in water up to her neck before I could get to her and though she hadn't learned to swim well yet, she'd still try to get out to the deeper water where her brother played catch with Tony. Everyone in my family swam, except me.

Tony could only sit on the blanket a few minutes. He hated being in the sun near water doing nothing. He had to be in the water. The half-hour swim was easy for him to recover from. His family had a history of heart trouble and he was determined to do everything he could to stay healthy. So he swam three to four times a week at a local pool in the city.

After a short break, Tony jumped up from the blanket. "How can you stand this? The heat's intolerable. Come out into the water." He picked up a tennis ball to play catch in the water and then reached down for my hand. Julia was up in a flash and they both looked at me.

I resisted the water. It was not a natural place for me. I needed to have control over my environment, and the water, the deep water, made me uncomfortable. I went out with them sometimes, and once I was there, I always had a great time.

I took Tony's hand and the three of us ran quickly across the hot sand to reach the water. The edge of the lake was obscenely warm. Stepping farther into the lake, where the water was cooler, and a slight chill crawled up my back.

"Farther out it's even cooler," Tony said, and I cautiously went deeper. I was up to my knees. Daniel saw us in the water and, with two large hand-over-hand strokes; he was in water shallow enough to stand. He then ran, lunging at the water in great splashing strides to reach us. He, too, had been swimming since he was about four years old. Neither of my children has a fear of the water. I'm proud of that.

Daniel playfully grabbed at the tennis ball. It fell out of Tony's hand. They both flopped onto the water after it. The neon yellow ball rolled away and bobbed up and down across the top of the lake. Julia dived for the ball and took hold of it. Tony burst out of the water like a great hairy whale. He shouted, "Throw it here, Julia."

She pulled her arm back as far as she could and threw the ball to her father.

"Ha, ha, I got it," Tony shouted as he caught the ball. "Now you're in the middle," and he playfully dunked Daniel.

Daniel came up quickly, and even with a mouth full of water managed to sputter, "I'll get you for that."

Tony threw the ball back to Julia. She made a good catch before Daniel reached her, and so began the game of monkey in the middle. On land or in the water, Tony played ball. He loved having kids, too.

He said it was like having a whole gang to play with. The only problem was that the kids never wanted to stop and Daniel and Julia could outplay Tony every time.

"Come on, play with us," Tony shouted to me.

I was standing in water up to the middle of my thighs, toes solidly planted in the sand. I raised my hand signalling I'd catch the next throw.

Julia had the ball again. She made a good toss, right to me.

"Aha, you thought you'd get this, didn't you," I mocked Daniel, as he came rushing at me. I quickly threw the ball to Tony. I had a good arm. Tony caught the tennis ball easily.

Daniel acted like a corralled wild horse, lunging at each of us, trying to catch the ball. Finally, Julia threw a misfire and Tony couldn't catch it. Daniel dived, sank deep under the water, and came up laughing, ball raised in the air like a prize.

Tony plunged into the lake and glided like a fish to the middle of us. "Don't get used to being out there," he said to Daniel.

Back and forth, we all traded places and took our turns at being monkey in the middle. Even me. I was cautious and didn't dive for the ball, so most of the time I ended up being in the middle the longest. After a while, maybe a half hour, we were tired.

"That's enough," Tony announced. "We'll play again later." He paddled over to me. Daniel fell backward into the water and swam away submerged, headed for the edge of the lake where several days ago he had seen schools of little fish. I knew he was hopeful of catching a couple in his hands.

Julia returned back to her sand piles at the edge of the water. Several little girls Julia knew were digging along the shoreline. They needed help with their project. They called to her and waved gleefully as Julia came sloshing toward them.

Tony put an arm around my waist. "Let's go out deeper."

I hesitated and said nothing. We kissed a quick, friendly kiss. Tony kneeled down in the water as though he was proposing to me. Lowering myself into the water I sat on his knee. I trusted him. I always trusted him.

"You'll be fine." His words lulled me into a sense of security. Maybe

I depended on him too much, but he made me feel safe. I wanted to be in the deep water with him. We stood. Tony held my hand and we walked out into the cooler, deeper water. The vitality returned to my body that the hot sun had robbed. Tony had taught me to float and we moved to a place where I could just touch bottom.

"Don't worry, I got you," he said. "You'll be fine."

I loosened my grip on his shoulder. White spots remained where my fingers had pressed into his skin.

"Good, relax," he said. "Look up. The sky looks different when you're in the water."

Leaning backward into the water, my head gently undulated in the wake of a passing swimmer. Tony held me close to his body. My weightlessness and the undulating cool water made us feel sexy. The water moved between us and through our legs in a slow current. We'd never had sex in the water, though we'd talked about it. A large plastic ball rolled past us. Tony gave it a shove.

He grinned and said, "Let's go farther out."

"No, this is far enough," I said, and dug my toes into the sand. We went through this all the time. Tony wanted me to feel safe in the water and he hoped that someday I'd learn to swim. He loved the water and yearned to share the experience with me. But I was afraid. I had learned to be afraid. My fear was not rational. I knew that. My parents never went swimming and kept a close watch whenever my sister and I were near water. The water was a monster that gobbled up children, even strong grown men, they said. Never trust it.

Tony worked against my parents' grain and enticed me. "It's fun in the water. You can be free. I know if you ever learned to swim, you'd love it."

Over the years I'd gone into deeper and deeper water with Tony. Now we were at the rope that marked the farthest edge of the swimming area of the lake. My feet just barely touched bottom. There was no shield from the summer sun in the open water. The heat beat down onto our heads, while the water cooled our bodies. My hair, stringy and wet, licked at my neck and shoulders like long wet tongues. It was peaceful at the rope. The laughing and shouting of the people playing along the shoreline was sucked back into the water. Or did the sound of the voices float several feet above the water on its own independent current?

Where I bobbed up and down with Tony, it was quiet, lulling me into an even greater sense of relaxation. I playfully kissed him on the ear and brushed up against his penis with one knee. He grinned, and we let our bodies glide across each other.

Standing on my tiptoes, I was the farthest out I'd ever been, but it felt safe and, if so many people hadn't been in the water swimming, throwing balls, and floating past, I wondered if we might try to make love. Then it happened. In less time than anything I'd ever experienced, I was under the water. I grabbed for Tony, but he wasn't there. The air suddenly vanished. The sun no longer beat down on me. Nothing was familiar, but the coarse sand under my feet. I tried to jump up, but I couldn't reach the surface of the water. I opened my eyes. The thick green of algae clouded my vision. I grabbed at the water, pulled on it. Why wasn't I able to come to the surface? I thought drowning people had three chances to call for help. I had none.

People all around me laughed, played ball, and shouted to each other. I heard their muffled voices everywhere under the water. No one knew I had fallen beneath the surface of the lake. I could feel the slant of the sand basin under my feet, and I began to walk, pushing against the water, headed for the shallow end. Listening for my children's voices. Did I hear a Julia calling to her friends? Were my children close by? Could I touch them?

The heaviness of the water dragged on me. Lifting a leg to take a step was nearly impossible to do. Putting my foot back down onto the sandy floor was even more difficult. Digging my toes into the sandy bottom, the water pushed hard against me.

The water vibrated with echoes of laughter and talk, but it silenced my voice. Someone splashed nearby. Bubbles came from beneath my feet, wobbling lazily up my thighs making their way to the surface. I tried to take another step, this time using my arms to push back the water. Move forward; move forward, I kept thinking. The water was so thick, so green. Where was everyone? How far had I walked? Was I holding my breath? Was I breathing? Was that Julia giving orders to her new friends?

Julia, can you see me? I'm trying to get to you. See Momma. Look, honey, can you see me? I need your help. Call Daddy. Daniel, look for me, please, look for me.

I kept walking, digging into the sand with my toes, grabbing at the water. No! No! No! I won't die. Damn it. I'll get there. I'll fuck'n get there.

Then, as though swooped up by an eagle, I was pulled to the surface.

Tony had me around the waist. "Are you all right?" he asked.

The air was clear, hot and thin. Gasping for breath, sucking water deeper into my lungs, I coughed even more. My throat was on fire. I couldn't talk for the coughing. I grabbed him. My eyes stung. The sun blinded me. A beach ball bumped into us and floated away again. Tony didn't move from me. With one swimming stroke, we were in water shallow enough for me to stand with my head above the surface. I dug my toes deep into the sand, realizing I was almost there. Goddamn, I was almost there. I kept coughing. I must have unknowingly tried to breathe under the water. It felt as though I had been holding my breath, but I hadn't been.

"We fell into a hole," Tony said. "I didn't mean to let go. You all right?" With every cough a sharp pain sliced my throat. There was a ringing in my ears. It was difficult to tell if I had gone deaf or if the sounds around me no longer registered in my brain. Julia sat at the water's edge, piling wet sand on her legs. All the little girls were lined up on the shore alongside, their little feet poking out of mounds of sand like pink sea plants wiggling in a tidal pool. I walked past her, still coughing.

"You all right?" Tony kept asking. I couldn't talk for the burning in my throat. I sat on the blanket, trying to catch my breath.

The ice cream wagon came driving up at that moment. Screaming children rushed out of the water. Parents dug into beach bags looking for money. Impatient, cranky children cried, "Hurry, hurry, I want ice cream."

Julia and Daniel rushed up to our blanket. My coughing continued.

"What's wrong with Mom?" Daniel asked.

"She went under the water," Tony replied.

"Don't worry, Mom, that happens to me all the time. You'll be okay," Daniel said, not taking his eyes off the ice cream wagon. Tony picked up his shorts, took out two dollars, handing one to Julia and one to Daniel. I was still coughing as they ran off to get in line for ice cream.

Finally, my coughing slowed.

"So, you all right now?" Tony asked.

"What happened? Why'd you let go of me?" I demanded, clearing away some phlegm in my throat.

"I didn't do it on purpose," he said.

We had another week left of our vacation, and I knew Tony wondered if he'd ever get me back into the water again.

That night, Julia had a little burned spot above her hipbone, where the swimsuit had rubbed the suntan lotion off. So tired from playing all day at the lake, she didn't make too much of a fuss. Daniel zonked out in bed with a comic book across his chest. With the house cooler than it had been during the heat of the day, but still too stifling, Tony and I rolled from one side of the bed to the other, trying to get comfortable.

Then he whispered in my ear, "Hey, girly, you want to go swimming?"

Clearing my throat I asked, "How deep's the water?"

"Won't know till we get there. You want to go?" He pulled me close.

"Sure," I said, and we swam out to the deep end together.

A Son's Story

IT WAS A RARE SUNDAY. Daniel had consented to come to dinner at his grandparents. Sunday dinner in their Bronx apartment had become a tradition, and my mother-in-law went all out to prepare Daniel's favorite food, hoping to entice him back into the fold. Sitting next to Daniel, with one arm slung around his shoulder, I gave him a quick hug, something I learned to do since his teenage years when he had made it quite clear that he no longer wanted his mother to hug him. I'd devised a non-hug embrace, which consisted of a sturdy grab around the shoulder, a quick squeeze, and then a fast retreat.

"How've you been?" I asked. We hadn't seen or heard from him in over a month.

"I'm fine. But my stomach's acting up again," he responded. "Heartburn."

"Maybe you should see a doctor," I replied.

"Nah, it'll go away."

"Maybe it's stress," I suggested. This was always a delicate discussion. Over the years, talking with my son had become difficult. For Daniel, growing up meant pulling away from his family.

"Maybe," he responded. "But right now my life just feels messed-up."

Had he taken the bait? Could we talk about what's been bothering him? Would he talk about his feelings, something he rarely did except after a huge burst of anger? Six months ago he had dropped out of college. Since then he hadn't been able to hold onto a job. I felt he was drifting away from me. With any attempts I made to move closer to my son, to grab onto him, to help him, he only retreated further away from my reach.

"You ever think about going back into counseling?" I asked cautiously, knowing this was treacherous territory for us to talk about. Usually we got hung up in the everyday battles of why he hated school, didn't see the need for college in the first place, or why he quit one job after another because he couldn't get along with his bosses. Tony and I constantly ended up squabbling with him about how he had to start getting his act together, try to keep a job and to stop spending money the second he had it in his hands.

It was only a matter of time before I expected Daniel to tell me to butt out of his business. Instead, he leaned over and in a soft voice said, "I've been thinking about taking a trip to San Francisco."

This didn't surprise me. Not really. Deep down I knew Daniel thought about a past that had never been resolved. But Tony and I had lulled ourselves into believing that we were not a stepfamily. We rarely talked about my first marriage in San Francisco. Maybe we even pretended that it had never happened. But the past somehow wrangles its way back to you. Deal with it or not, it'll still pop back into your life, usually when you least expect it. How many times had this come into my mind? But life was simpler, more manageable, if we just became the family that I wanted and forgot about what had happened all those years ago.

My first marriage had been a disaster. The separation came about before we knew there was a baby coming. But Daniel had been there tucked away in my belly when I trotted down the hill heading for the lawyer's office to file for a divorce. Daniel had been there as an infant wrapped in a blanket, sleeping while the judge granted the final decree for the divorce. Daniel attended college-campus childcare centers when I went to class. At home he sat half-watching cartoons, half-observing me on the days I wept out of frustration and anger. When Tony came into our lives, Daniel had been there, too. And to my delight, Daniel had liked Tony so much he had asked Tony to be his father.

"You going to look for your father when you get there?" This was a tentative question, though I already knew the answer.

"Yeah, but I'm afraid," he said.

"Afraid of what?"

"Maybe he's dead."

"Why are you afraid he's dead?" This same thing had crossed my mind more than once.

"You know, Ma," Daniel said, "it feels as if he's dead. Why didn't he contact me? So, in my mind, it just seems natural that he *is* dead."

We had never talked this way before. The subject seemed taboo. Though here we were, having Sunday dinner with Tony's parents in the Bronx, thousands of miles from San Francisco, talking about a topic that made us both uncomfortable. I had never really gotten over the feeling of being deserted. My son, too, felt deserted, and thinking that James, my ex-husband, was still with us after all this time made me angry.

"Hey, you two," Tony said from across the table. "What's the matter?" Tony gave me a quizzical look. He knew something was going on.

"I'm fine," I said, wondering if anyone else had heard what Daniel and I were discussing.

Tony's mother put a platter of poached salmon on the table. The aroma of the meal momentarily broke my reflective mood. The room came alive with happy people clinking silverware as they talked excitedly while munching through a veritable parade of dishes.

"Grandma really outdid herself this time," Daniel said, and quickly dug into the food.

"I love you very much," I said to Daniel. "I always tried hard to do what was right." These words were spoken straight into Daniel's ear, for he was not looking at me, but busily eating.

How many times had I felt a need to apologize to my son for giving him the worst biological father in the world? Hadn't Tony made up for my mistake?

"Look, if you feel that you have to get in touch with your father, then that's what you have to do. Whatever you decide is all right with me." Taking a slice of salmon, these words reverberated in my head and hoped I could live up to my promise.

Several days later, Daniel telephoned. "Ma," he said. "I looked online and found James' address. I tried to write to him, but I can't do it, the words won't come. Could you help me? Would you write him for me?"

Daniel had given me courage to live during some of the lowest points in my life. If I were to live for myself alone, there had been days when I might have decided to end it all. But having a child forced me to push on. Now my child was asking for my help to do something that until this moment seemed impossible. There would be no refusing him.

When writing the first draft of a letter to James, there was a heavy smug tone. The carefully worded message explained Daniel's desire to see this stranger, who years ago, had tried to strangle the life from me. We had a happy life now, happier than I had ever imagined possible. The communication told of all the wonderful things that James had missed. But this was not the letter Daniel had requested me to write. This letter was for my son, not for me.

Stuffing my hurt and anger back inside, tucking everything away again in the dark musty past to be dealt with at another time, the revision of the letter to James was on behalf of Daniel. It was not a smug or angry letter. It was merely a request to meet.

Mailing the letter felt like sending smoke signals from the top of a mountain. Dropping the envelope into the mailbox was quite empowering, and I wondered if we'd ever hear from him.

Two weeks later, Daniel telephoned. "I got a call from James," he said.

"You're kidding," I answered.

"He's going to call again in a couple of days. He said he'll pay for my airplane ticket to San Francisco. It's really strange, isn't it," Daniel said.

"At least we know he's alive." I felt a little lightheaded. Secretly I hoped James had died and that the letter would come back marked "deceased," like in the movies. Then everything would have made sense; the years of silence, the reasons for toys not sent to a son at Christmas time, or the birthday songs never sung over the telephone by an absent father. *That son of a bitch better not hurt Daniel, or I'll kill him this time. I swear I will.* I kept these feelings close to my breast and listened to my son.

"It's pretty exciting, isn't it?" he said. "Imagine, I'm going to San Francisco."

A month later, Daniel left for the West Coast. He got on an airplane with hundreds of questions tucked away in a carrying case that had been made from his childhood fantasies; his mothers tears; a stepfather's love; and his jealousy of Julia, his half-sister, whom he thought got all the breaks. All these things, and probably many more that even a mother could not fathom, stretched across a skeleton of time, evolving with Daniel year by year, slowly building around his life like a fragile, lacy shell. My hope was that he would find answers with a father who had been lost to him. I wondered if anything so elusive could ever be found again.

During the two weeks Daniel spent in San Francisco, Tony and I worried that James might try to whisk Daniel away from us. My fantasy was for Daniel to hate James as much as I hated him, even after all these years. I had tried not to influence my son. Though it was impossible to think that my feelings hadn't affected him to some degree. I had a desperate need for Daniel to believe that it wasn't my fault, that my attempt to make things right in my marriage with James fell on deaf ears. It was a miserable wait for the visit to come to a close. We all wanted Daniel home again.

One night while we cleared the dinner dishes, Tony said, "I'd forgotten Daniel isn't my biological son. James has no rights to Daniel. I raised him. We're the ones who rushed him to the hospital when he had an ear infection. I changed his pants that time in the department store when he had diarrhea."

Tony scrapped the bits of leftover food from the plates into the garbage pail. He leaned against the stove, the dish and fork still in his hand. "I love him as though he were my own skin, my own blood; I love him as though he were my own life. No matter what, I'll never stop loving him."

Tony abruptly stopped talking. He put his arm around me. "Whatever happens, I know that this is what Daniel needs to do. It's time to come face to face with this man. It's not good for him to live with a ghost."

* * * *

The airport was crowded. It was one of those intolerably humid New York summer evenings when Daniel returned from his visit with

James. Tony, Julia and I stood off to one side watching the travelers walk past. Julia held my hand. She had not said much about her brother's visit to San Francisco, but Tony and I knew that her silence was an expression of her concern. She's a lot like Daniel in that particular way. They were both quiet when they were upset. Tony is the one who talks, babbles really, when things bother him. Talking seemed to settle his nerves. The rest of us hang onto our words, afraid of what we might say, perhaps not so comfortable with making our feelings public.

The plane arrived late. When Daniel finally disembarked, we strained to spot him in the long line of people trailing past us. Daniel saw us first. He waved. We all waved back.

While we waited at the luggage carousel, Daniel told us how tired he was and how it had taken him several days to adjust to the west coast time difference.

"Now," he said, "I'll have to adjust all over again to another time change. But, I'm happy to be home and I'm not interested in traveling again for quite awhile."

During the ride home, Daniel said, "Meeting James was like meeting a stranger. Oh, I know he really is a stranger. Maybe at first, seeing him was all that I wanted. Somehow, though, it wasn't enough. In the end, seeing him made me feel empty. I don't know what I wanted to happen, but I guess James and I will just be friends."

Daniel had wrestled with a missing father all his life, even though we rarely, if ever, talked about James. Now it sounded to me as though the flesh and blood person had been a bit of a disappointment compared to the fantasies Daniel had undoubtedly bottled up over the years. I wondered if my son would ever find what he was looking for.

After we reached the house, Daniel became quiet. He leaned against the dishwasher and said, "You know, Ma, James said some things that were pretty upsetting. I don't know if I should tell you."

"Tell me only what you feel comfortable with," I said, knowing very well that I wanted to hear everything, no matter what the cost.

"James said he never loved you. He said he didn't know why he married you." A sad look moved across Daniel's face.

"You're kidding? He said that to you? He had some nerve telling you that." Surprisingly I was unhurt by what Daniel had just said, my concern was for Daniel and how hearing that affected him.

"I asked him," Daniel continued, "if, since he didn't love you, and he was moving out, how come you got pregnant with me? He said I was an accident."

"I can't believe he'd tell you that." My first instinct was to curse James; to rant, call him every name in the book, because after all these years, he had not learned how not to hurt people. But this was no time for me to get caught up in my old issues with James. It was Daniel's feelings, his hurt and confusion we were dealing with here, not mine.

"Daniel," I said, "it was the worst time for me to have gotten pregnant. But when you came along, I never once thought about getting rid of you, or of giving you up for adoption. I loved you at the beginning. I love you now. Nothing will ever change that. Never forget what I'm telling you today. You were never unwanted, never a mistake."

Daniel hugged me. Or rather, he grabbed on to me, his arms no longer those of a child, or even a gangly adolescent, but with the muscles and bones of a man. My son held me tight. Sounds, like large waves of hiccups came from his throat and he began to cry.

To hear your grown children cry is a heartbreaker.

"I love you. I always have," I said over and over, trying to soothe away his rush of emotion. Once in a while, I think about that night when Daniel returned home from San Francisco telling me that James had never loved me. At first I didn't believe it because after all, it seemed the very early days of our marriage were enjoyable. But then realized that what James said must have been true because he walked away so easily from me.

But in the end, it was James who had lost out. It was sad to think about all the wonderful moments in Daniel's life that James had missed. The hurt, the unhappiness, the anger, it all seemed such a waste of my energy when looking at the wonderful things that eventually came to me.

After that visit in San Francisco with James, Daniel became more at ease with himself. He no longer struggled with Tony and me the way he had. It no longer felt like he had to break away from us to be his own person. Julia and Daniel made their own kind of peace. They talked calmly together, if not conspiratorially from time to time, as Julia let her brother into her pre-adolescent world.

Gratefully, I forgot how difficult the last couple of years had been. Now Daniel could finally get on with his life.

Old Ghosts to Rest

TONY AND I DIDN'T KNOW if Daniel had done it on purpose. He said he hadn't. But now, even though I could not say it out loud, I wondered if I, too, would have the courage to meet up with James, after not seeing him for over twenty years.

Daniel had maintained a relationship with James after his visit to San Francisco. Then, Daniel announced that James would be attending a conference in New York City and he made arrangements for James to come into the Bronx to meet him and his girlfriend for dinner. He suggested a restaurant on Broadway across from Van Cortlandt Park, only a quarter of a mile from our apartment. James agreed.

When Daniel went to San Francisco, it never crossed my mind that one day my ex-husband and I would ever meet up again. Seeing him meant the possibility of dredging up the past. I didn't want to remember how hurtful it was to have meant nothing to someone who I had loved so dearly.

Daniel had arranged to come over with his girlfriend, Beverly, for a short visit with Tony and me before they were to meet with James.

While we waited for them to arrive, Tony and I sat around reading the Sunday *Times*. Then, out of nowhere; Tony asked me, "You want to see James?"

I laughed. "I don't need to see him."

Tony said nothing more about James. We went back to reading the paper.

A few minutes later, Tony said, "Though, you know, it might be of some importance, after all."

"Maybe," I replied, and returned to my newspaper.

Each time Tony brought up James, a curiosity needled me, while another part of me recoiled. Old hurts stretched, then yawned as though waking after a long sleep. I had packed away a lot of uncomfortable feelings over the years. They had begun to stir and wriggle around in my mind. Some seem to be saying, "Oh, yeah, I remember what happened."

Julia, away at summer camp, put me in charge of Ruth, a pet guinea pig. Our daughter had a particular way of doing things. For instance, she never liked to have dolls dressed. From the time she was very little, all the dolls in the toy box were naked. Even if the clothing had been stapled to the doll, she'd still take it off. She treated Ruth no differently than she did her dolls. And that summer Julia decided that the weather would be too hot for the guinea pig with its thick fur. So before she went off to summer camp, she cut off most of the fur from the panting animal's long shaggy pelt. When she got finished with it, Ruth's once luxurious fur coat now stuck out in jagged unkempt chunks.

I gave Ruth fresh water daily as ordered by Julia, cleaned the cage weekly and wondered what Julia would have thought about seeing my ex-husband. When she turned five years old we told her that I had been married before and that Daniel had another father.

"I can't believe that," she snapped at me. Then during the rest of the day Julia said nothing more about the subject. A couple days later, at the dinner table, Julia asked, "If Daniel has two fathers, what's that other guy to me?"

I had no idea how to answer that one, and said, "I don't know." "Well, he's related to me somehow, isn't he?" she insisted. "Somehow, I guess."

"Like all the dead relatives that I never got to meet? They're still related to me, aren't they?" Julia had her own logic.

Julia worried a great deal when Daniel was out west visiting James. One night while Daniel was away in San Francisco, as she was getting ready for bed, Julia hugged me extra hard. "I don't want you to leave me and Daddy," she whispered.

"I'd never leave you guys."

We knew she worried that Daniel would not come back home again. Now it seemed she worried about me, too.

Tony and I could do nothing to make Julia think any differently.

We were all uneasy during those days; concerned that my ex-husband and Daniel's father would now possibly enter into the circle of our family. Life had been much simpler without him. Yet, here he was, surfacing like a ghost from the graveyard. Julia, now away at summer camp, would miss the opportunity to see in the flesh a mystery relative.

Tony put his newspaper down on his lap. "I think Daniel wants us to meet James. Or he wouldn't have made the dinner reservations so conveniently close. Imagine, James will be less than a mile from here. It would almost be a shame not to see him."

"You're probably right," I said.

Tony was always so logical. "It might be good for Daniel to see you and James together," Tony said.

"What about you? You want to see him?"

"I guess," Tony replied.

"I've got to tell you though, I'm a little afraid of hurting you," I said.

I didn't know exactly what I meant by this. The possibility of an encounter with James confused me. Maybe I was worried that seeing James again after all these years, would bring back a rush of emotional pain. It felt risky.

"What could you possibly do to hurt me?" Tony asked.

"James might say something that makes me cry? I'd worry that would make you think that I still had feelings for him. I don't."

"If he does anything to hurt you or Daniel, I'll bust him in the mouth and send him back to San Francisco in pieces."

We looked at each other. We were sharing the same thought. There was no doubt in my mind that if James got out of line Tony would give him the beating of his life.

There was a time, especially during the divorce proceedings, when the thought of inflicting physical pain on James comforted me. Old fantasies came to mind when I imagined about poisoning James or running him over with my rickety-old station wagon.

When Daniel and Beverly arrived that afternoon, I announced, "Your Dad and I would like to see James, too."

Daniel didn't seem surprised. "Whatever you want. It's up to you," he said calmly. But then, that was Daniel's style, cool, reserved, and frequently keeping his thoughts to himself.

"You sure you want us there?" I asked. It occurred to me that if I were to back out, this was the time to do it.

"It's fine. Come along. The more the merrier," he replied in a chipper manner.

"Though," I added, "I must say, it does seem like you set this dinner thing up so that we couldn't help but see James. Even if we went shopping this afternoon, it's possible we'd have run into him. Did you do this on purpose?"

"Nope," Daniel said, and we left it at that. Daniel would meet with James first, picking him up at the subway station. Then at five thirty we'd all meet for dinner.

Tony and I arrived just as Daniel parked his car up the hill from the restaurant. He had taken James on a tour of the neighborhood and drive past his high school. Later we learned that they had even driven down the street where we lived. Daniel turned the steering wheel one more rotation to align the car with the curb. James sat in the front passenger seat. After all these years, he looked pretty much the same.

Tony and I got out of our car. James walked up to me and extended his hand. We touched again after all these years. I felt nothing. Then he shook Tony's hand. Daniel stood to one side, smiling. He seemed to be getting a kick out of this.

"It's great to see you," James said. "I thought about calling you, to see if you would want to meet with Daniel and me."

I smiled, nodded, and said nothing. Walking to the restaurant it was obvious that James' walk hadn't changed. His big feet, so out of proportion to his body, still made him look a bit like a T-square. His skin had a pale greenish tone. It didn't look like he got much fresh air.

One of the luckier males his age, James still had a thick head of hair, although it had all turned quite gray. His long mass of curls looked as if it had been cut off years ago and his beard was gone. His voice sounded so familiar that it startled me. For a brief moment, thousands of words descended on me like static coming from a radio speaker, all garbled; the broken promises, the hurtful comments tumbling around in my head like a storm.

Tony, Daniel, and Beverly walked on ahead, while James and I walked behind them. This arrangement felt quite uncomfortable. I wanted to be with Tony or Daniel. With every fiber in my body it felt as though my anger should still be there. But it wasn't. Despite the crush of hurtful words that had come between us, the anger was gone. That made me uncomfortable. *If I'm not angry,* I wondered, *then what do I feel? I certainly don't want to like him.*

We all sat at the table talking about the differences between the East and West Coasts. I forgot where we were, or why we were there. It was startling how much Daniel looked like James. They shared the same thin lip genes. Daniel always said that he had thin lips.

His girlfriend teased him, "No, Daniel," she'd say. "I'm sorry to tell you, but you don't have lips."

The similarities between the two was so obvious: the cut of the nose, strong, long, and broad with a knob in the middle; the jaw line solid, well defined, wrapping high, close to the lower ear lobe; the broad, rounded cheek bones.

Many times in my darkest moments, I fantasized that my son had come forth into the world without the sperm of any man.

Tony had forgotten, too, that Daniel was not his natural child. Yet this man sitting at the table with us, a man with so many facial features that resembled my son was Daniel's actual biological father. James was real, and he was alive. The situation seemed so unbelievably civilized, as Beverly would later describe our dinner visit with James. We talked about music, a little light politics. James told me about his siblings. His mother and father had passed away.

A stranger observing this scene might have thought we looked like old friends—not comfortable friends, because there was most definitely an air of stiffness. There was no mention of James never sending money to help pay for food while I scraped my pennies together, feeding my son and myself from food stamp allotments. No one questioned why he had told me that he loved me while he slept with another woman. These things all danced around in my head. Of course we wouldn't talk about these things. Everyone was on his and her best behavior, everyone speaking guarded words.

At one point during the dinner, while relating an incident when

Daniel was a small child, instead of saying Daniel's father—meaning Tony—I had instead said, "Tony."

"That bothered me," Tony later said, after we had left the restaurant. "Why didn't you call me 'Daniel's father' instead of saying, 'Tony?'"

I remembered that part of the conversation. "I did at other times," I answered, realizing how cautious we all had been.

"It's funny how it stuck out, though," Tony said. "I guess I was really listening for it."

The dinner lasted two and a half hours, though it seemed like an all day experience. The visit had been exhausting. When the meal finally ended, seeing James had been worth the effort. I'd expected to see him as a monster. If nothing else, I left the restaurant feeling confused.

That evening, when James returned back into Manhattan, Daniel and Beverly came back to our place. Beverly liked to hear stories about Daniel as a little boy. So we told stories. Eventually we talked about James and what it had been like seeing him after all these years.

When Beverly said, "He seemed like a nice guy," this almost made me laugh out loud.

"Yeah, sure," I wanted to tell her. "He didn't fool around on you when you were married to him."

Julia had been right; he had been like a dead relative come back to life, bringing with him loads of old baggage.

"I was afraid there'd be a fight," Daniel said, "and I'd have to rough up James, tell him to get out of town. Then I'd tell you and Tony to go home, that I'd see you later. Beverly and I would sit in a bar while I calmed down."

Tony laughed slightly, not at Daniel, but because he said he had somewhat of the same fantasy. "I prepared myself to bust him in the face if he got out of line."

"Really?" Daniel said, grinning. "James will never know how lucky he is that he didn't start something."

They both laughed and looked pretty pleased with themselves.

Until seeing the flesh and blood James, it hadn't dawned on me how much work I had done over the years to heal myself. Now it was clear to me that the threat of this impending visit had not been in seeing James, but in the possibility of meeting up with my old self again. It was meeting up with the ghost of who I had been all those years ago that frightened me.

I wondered, *Did that confused and sad girl who had married James still exist?*

I didn't think she did. Yet there was the possibility that she was still there, lurking somewhere inside me.

While listening to Daniel and Tony talk about how they would have struggled with James if he had gotten out of hand, my thoughts drifted back to the table and how, several times something brushed up against my arm. Looking around, there had been nothing out of the ordinary. Then, giving it more thought, I realized what it was that had touched me. It had been my old self. She poked her head out after all these years of hiding. Was she also curious? Slipping out into the open, away from her long time hiding place, this timid part of me, fearful that the past might return, did she now see that there was nothing to worry about. Sitting very close to me, not sure what was going on, there's no doubt in my mind that this dear little part of who I used to be, could now feel quite satisfied, knowing that life had turned out pretty special despite this one-time husband.

Where Are You? How Are You?

IT'S COLD IN THE BEDROOM now that the air conditioner has dried out the New York August humidity. But it's hard to sleep, thinking about my early morning flight for what I call the Upper West Coast. My travels will take me first to Washington State to see one sister, Jenny. Then, four days later, I'll head up to Alaska, for a ten-day visit with my mother and my other two sisters. The trip was set up in February, long before our daughter, Julia, decided to spend the summer in Israel.

In July, after frantic maneuvers to get a passport, ticket, as well as some last minute sketchy accommodations, Julia was gone. Our only connection with our daughter now is through cryptic emails like, "I'm in the southern desert, temperatures in the 120s, working in the kitchen. The cook hates me." These messages illuminating my computer screen are like her blood pulsing through my veins. In the instant they arrive, we know where she is, how she is. When the computer is turned off, she's gone again.

Now I have to leave Julia and my email connection to her, because my mother has become quite frail in the last couple of years. I'm called to my mother, drawn to her like a small child frightened by a mother's illness. There is an urgency, also, to be closer to my sisters. We've grown distant, not due to the miles that separate us, but because our life styles and experiences have made us strangers.

Reading all of Julia's emails one more time before leaving for the airport, I fixate on the first one. "Working in a kitchen eight and nine hours a day, helping to prepare meals for a couple hundred people." This makes me chuckle because when she was a teenager, she had to be asked repeatedly to do the dishes before she finally got around to do them.

She writes, "I'm not getting tanned, I'm getting stronger from lifting crates of vegetables." When my husband and I read this we wonder if she is complaining or boasting—or both. She had wanted to get away from New York, do something different. She's old enough now to do anything she wants, a college graduate living on her own. I send one last email before leaving on my journey. "Where are you, Julia? How are you?" Calling out to my daughter through the Internet is a cold way to communicate with loved ones.

It was agony not hearing from her for almost a week after she arrived in Israel. I was miserable, but there was no choice but to let go and wait. "Don't worry," my husband says. "She'll be fine." He promises to "save as new" all Julia's emails while I'm away.

Flying west as dawn begins to break gives the illusion that the sunrise goes on for hours. Julia is never far from my thoughts and I remember an email telling us, "I rise early every morning now, just to watch the sun come up." I wonder, are we watching the same daybreak?

Halfway into my flight, during the second refreshment service, while I'm still basking in the constant morning sun coming through the window on my side of the airplane, the captain announces that we are flying over the devastation of this summer's forest fires. The news had been filled with the fires that burned thousands, maybe millions of acres. The smoke creeps along the deep valleys of the mountain ranges like a thick fog. For the remainder of the flight I watch the wilderness of South Dakota, Montana, Wyoming, Idaho, and Washington burning as though on a toy display of the planet earth. It is interesting how insignificant the damage seems from so far away.

My sister, Jenny, meets me at the airport. Five years have gone by since we last saw each other, though I would recognize Jenny anywhere, even if her back were turned to me. She has gotten older though. I suppose we both have.

Too many years have passed between our visits. We both feel the distance time creates as we drive to her new home, talking awkwardly, dancing around in our conversation as strangers do when seeking common ground for a relationship. When we approach the house she recently bought, a house she waited years to own, I'm first struck by the lovely garden in Jenny's front yard. Roses are everywhere. Hollyhocks reach halfway up the side of the house, all in full bloom with gobs of purple flowers.

"It's beautiful," I tell her.

She smiles. "I love my garden."

The house itself smells of fresh-cut roses and delicate bouquets of lavender. That's how I would describe Jenny if I had to tell you what my sister smelled like. Her kitchen is no surprise to me, either. It's a quarter of the entire house. Jenny's husband, who greets us as we come into the house, laughs a familiar laugh, one I remember hearing almost forty years ago when they were dating. "No mystery why we bought this house, is there?" he says.

We walk out into the backyard. Jenny tells me about the roses, the Crimson Beauty, the Heavenly Sunset, the Luscious Apricot, her Satin Dreams. Watching my sister gesture with hands I used to hold as we walked to school, I'm pulled away from being a mother, and wife, and I'm drawn back into my childhood. I remember how we floated our little girl umbrellas, twirling the handles to make them spin around and around as we sent them off across a mud puddle.

My husband calls me on the second night of the visit. "Did Julia send an email?" I ask. We'd received nothing. The last email she said, "Traveling with several women—two or three from France, one from Korea—and a man, an Israeli lifeguard, who plans on attending film school later in the year."

"Where are you, Julia? How are you?" I whisper in the dark and crawl into bed, kicking the covers loose from the tight military regulation tuck. Jenny always was better at making beds than I was.

The four days with Jenny go faster than either of us thought. But if I stay much longer we will move toward territory into which neither of us is ready to venture. We are sisters, after all and if the visit is too much longer we may encounter issues that may never be fully resolved. But when Jenny accidentally forgets her handbag on a workbench in the garage, the sad mood of us parting is lightened. She has to borrow money from me to pay for the parking. Then my driver's license is buried somewhere on the bottom of my carry-on. It is needed to show the airline clerk that I really am who my ticket says

I am. Jenny and I laugh. We laugh so hard we have to dab at our eyes to catch the tears before they fall too far.

Once on the airplane headed to Alaska, in the back of my mind, in a place where the words run across my brain like a ticker tape, I remember one of Julia's emails, all in caps, the way she sent it, "I JUST WANTED TO SAY I LOVE YOU." The airplane engine revs up. We're pulled into the sky. The woman sitting next to me hands her husband a stick of chewing gum. It's a gentle, every day act that touches me.

The flight into Anchorage is one miracle after another, watching ice floes and high, snow-crusted mountains that exemplify the concept of ruggedness. I watch the frozen land passing under the airplane all the while knowing Julia, at that moment, is in a desert suffering 120-degree temperatures. One of her emails told of sleeping on the roof of a youth hostel and how she could not believe how hot it was at night, how she felt "rootless for the first time, and kind of liking it."

I have one more connecting flight before reaching the town where my mother and two younger sisters live, 250 miles west and slightly south of Anchorage. I, too, am like my daughter, traveling. But, unlike her enjoyment of rootlessness, my journey is seeking the source of my roots by visiting my mother, maybe for the last time.

Mom meets me at the airport. She looks smaller, so much more bent over than when we were last together. Osteoporosis is chewing at her old bones, eating away my mother's life. We hug. I think, as I always have, that Mom could be easily broken. She is like a fragile, cracked porcelain cup. Her body even makes slight crunching sounds when she is wrapped too closely in my arms. But refraining from holding my mother too tightly when we first greet each other is difficult. Looking at her I realize that some days I too feel old creeping closer to my bones.

In the evening when my sisters get off work, they come bounding into Mom's small apartment. We hug and kiss and jump around each other like puppies. They were preadolescents when I left home. Now, miraculously, we have become the same age and are all the same size; tall, large-boned women. They were perfect little sisters and I regret that we have let five and ten years go by between our visits.

I've been forwarding Julia's emails to them, keeping them up with her travels. "Where is Julia? How is she?" they ask once we settle down to talk. I tell them about my daughter's travels, savoring her adventures as though they are memories of my own.

They ask about my son, Daniel. "He's doing very well these days, too." There wasn't enough time in this visit to tell them all the details of my life, so in a short version I tell them only so much. We have all become adult women. Each of us has a story to tell. Perhaps if there is enough time we'll divulge these personal tales.

My visits with Mom are usually spent as a companion. Because of Mom's bad health she gets out very seldom. She'll go grocery shopping and maybe stop off for a few minutes at a local fabric store to pick up material for a quilt she's making to pass time. I sew while she sits in a recliner. We talk or watch daytime programs. Last year during my visit, she helped me make a baby quilt for a friend.

This year, Betty, my youngest sister, made a weekend reservation for us three siblings to stay in Seldovia, a small fishing village across the bay from Homer. We lounge around on the deck of the B and B that sits on stilts overhanging a river. We catnap in the brilliant evening sun and watch eagles fly over the trees, while otters playfully swim about in the water below us.

We walk, and talk, reminiscing about each other. I feel as if we are putting together a puzzle, with each of us remembering different pieces of the past. Pieces are missing from the puzzle, too, hurtful times that involve our father. Cruel and always angry, he made us forget big chunks of who we were. Those are the pieces we do not want to put into the picture.

We fit only the happy times into the mural of our childhood. My sisters tell me how I took care of them while Mom cleaned and washed and cooked and canned and farmed and tried to knit the scraps of her life together with dirt-poor remnants. They tell me how I clomped around in rain boots and danced to cheer them up on the dreary northwest, housebound days. I made puppets for them, baskets of woven paper strips, and brought books from the library for my sisters to read. They tell me I taught them to love to read in a home where our father mistrusted any written word except the Bible, and sometimes berated even the Bible for its lies.

Because we live so far apart, my sisters have only seen Julia and Daniel a few times, once at Dad's funeral when Julia was a two-year-old busy streak of fluff that got into everything. Daniel was by then a gangly preadolescent. The second time Daniel was a sturdy young man and graduating from high school while Julia had grown to be a quiet, self-conscious adolescent.

"Tell us about Julia," they ask. "She's so lucky to be traveling. She's not afraid of the world, is she?"

I tell them she is very strong-willed, and that no way could anyone keep her down. I tell them about Julia's voice. "She's got a megaphone in her throat. If anything went wrong, she'd call out so loud we'd hear her across the sea."

When we return to Mom's apartment, she tells us that she was ill while we were away. "But, I'm feeling better now." We huddle around our mother, giving her the cinnamon roll we purchased in the only coffee shop in Seldovia. She takes it. "I'll eat it later," she says. The pastry is too dry when she gets around to it, and she throws it away.

"She's working on a banana plantation in the upper regions of Israel," my husband says. That impresses everyone when I related this information. They all agree that Julia will have great stories when she returns home.

Traveling turns time upside down. What is usually short is long, and what is typically long passes by in a flash. I'm rarely hungry here because of the constant daylight in the Alaskan summer. I never know when to get tired. Looking at the calendar, I realize that I'm scheduled to leave the next day. The puzzle has not been completed, but then it probably never will be.

The visit has been too short for everyone. Mom cries at the airport. Her tears dry quickly, and I wonder, are there fewer tears in the elderly?

Mom looks like a small child standing next to my sisters. She appears to have gotten smaller. "I'll come back soon, Mom. I promise."

My flight homeward moves me from the unreality of constant daylight to the unexpected normality of total darkness as we move east and into the night. I order a drink from the refreshment cart and settle back. An hour later, the captain announces that the northern lights are playing in the sky on the left side of the plane.

A huge hazy ribbon undulates all along the horizon. I can't stop watching for the slightest change, as wisps of light float up like smoke, break off and disappear. For many miles the lights play outside the airplane windows, following us, flirting with us. Closing my eyes I see a faint imprint of my sisters and Mom, as they were when they watched me board the airplane. The image slowly fades. And then I wonder how far away are my children's travels destined to take them.

The Prize Nut

TONY AND I HAD TAKEN an early Sunday morning drive up-state. But the fall foliage, usually vibrant in New York this time of the year—with uncountable shades of yellow, amber, gold, red, and peach—were dull against the gun-metal gray sky, with stark branches bared by an early frost and heavy winds the week before.

We had to get back to the Bronx in time for Tony to watch the afternoon Giants-Cowboys football game. We made a quick stop at a rickety farm stand north of Nyack where we bought Granny Smith and Macoun apples, spaghetti squash, fat white onions with the roots and long withered stems still on, new red potatoes that smelled of dirt, and a large bag of what a sign taped to the gunny sack said were fresh fallen walnuts.

I hadn't tasted fresh walnuts since my childhood when my family lived on a farm in the Northwest. Tony had grown up in the Bronx. He remembered playing stick-ball, hanging out at the handball courts and scooting bottle caps across the sidewalk playing a game he called scully. When Tony told stories from his childhood, he frequently talk-ed lovingly about heading over to a local pizza parlor to get a slice and a soda for a dollar, which was a big treat in those days.

He said, "I didn't know there was such a thing, as fresh fallen wal-nuts."

After one of these conversations, we'd have a short discussion, the kind we've had over the years when we've learned something new about each other, even after being married nearly thirty years and raising two children.

We arrived home with a few minutes to spare before the game started. Tony made a pot of French roast coffee, while I put some of the walnuts into a bowl and set it on the coffee table. We perched ourselves in front of the TV. In no time, Tony was mesmerized by men in helmets hurtling themselves against the Astroturf trying to catch the ball.

I watch football half-heartedly; truthfully, the game bores me. In the last couple of years though, I had taken pity on Tony for having to watch the Sunday games all by himself. Not so long ago our son and daughter would have been right there on the couch beside their father counting the downs, groaning at missed passes, and cheering interceptions made by the New York Giants. But our kids have both gone off on their own now. It's just the two of us. I keep Tony company during the games to fill an emptiness we both sense as we adjust to being empty nesters.

I picked a walnut out of the bowl.

Tony clapped his hands and called out, "Okay, way to go."

I looked up at the TV. The players were helping each other up off the field. Returning back to my walnut, I placed it between the two metal legs of the nutcracker and squeezed, hard, too hard. The shell broke into dozens of pieces, leaving only a couple of large chunks of the nutmeat stuck in the crevices of the broken shells. I dug into the shells with my fingernail and absentmindedly popped the pieces of the nutmeat into my mouth. I looked up at the TV in time to see a Giant catching a long pass thrown by his teammate.

"You're missing all the good plays," Tony said.

As I chewed the walnut everything around me melted away. All that remained was the walnut and me. There was no Tony. No TV. No football. Closing my eyes, I was twelve years old again, and it was Halloween.

A woodsy odor, musty smelling, like that of newly cut mushrooms and rotting mossy logs, came up from the back of my throat as I exhaled. I had been transported in time to the farmhouse outside of the small town of Ridgefield, Washington, where I grew up. My two younger sisters stood beside me. Mom had put me in charge of them. We were getting ready to go trick or treating.

Mom was going to have another baby soon, and Karen, my youngest sister, thought we should paint a pumpkin face on Mom's tummy. That way, Karen said, she could come along with us as she usually did.

But Mom was too tired to do much of anything. I'd heard her tell Dad at dinner that night she thought the baby was going to come any day. She said, "Maybe the full moon will bring on the baby."

I put another broken piece of the nutmeat into my mouth. My sisters came clearly into focus. We were each wearing one of Mom's old dresses that she had pinned, tied, and tucked in every which way. The dresses dragged along the ground with uneven floppy hems, despite Mom's handiwork. We thought they were beautiful.

"Oh, Madam, you look so pretty," Janet, my middle sister, said to Karen. Janet smiled, her lips pursed together as if she had just swallowed a tablespoon of fresh squeezed lemon juice. This was her version of a grownup smile.

"You, too, my dear," Karen responded, pushing at a mass of curly hair that had come loose from a beret—and we all curtsied to each other. Fidgeting and impatient, my sisters and I could hardly wait for the final touch to our costumes, Mom's lipstick.

My lips tickled as she painted my loosely opened mouth with her tube of greasy red color. The lipstick had to be red or we weren't dressed up. When I blotted my lips and saw the blood red mark my mouth left on the tissue, I felt transformed into a woman.

All dressed up, unable to stand still any longer; my sisters and I twirled around in the kitchen, our skirts billowing up. Then we dashed through the house and out into the damp evening air just as the sun began to set. Halloween night, with a full moon coming, a magical time, a time when wishes came true.

"Now, Wilma, watch your sisters," Mom called to me from where she sat at the kitchen table. "Just go up the old gravel road, no farther, then come back."

"Okay," I shouted, and we ran out into a sunset that had torn the sky into ragged strips of magenta, purple, and gold. When I think about a Northwest sunset I always remember those extraordinary colors.

Our dresses smelled delicious from mothballs, deteriorating dusty fabrics, and old cologne that hung along the necklines of Mom's clothes. We smelled just like Mom as we pranced, one after the other, out into the cold air that bit our cheeks and sliced at our bare legs under the thin cotton garments. We headed for the shortcut that led through a grove of evergreen trees then crossed over a small swampy patch we called a brook. This time of the year there wasn't much mud, but if we weren't careful we'd get our dresses dirty before we even started to trick or treat.

Being the one in charge, I said, "Janet, you go first. Karen, you get in the middle and hold up the back of Janet's skirt so it doesn't drag in the mud."

"Who's going to hold your skirt?" Karen asked.

"I can take care of myself," I told her, and picked up the back of Karen's skirt with the hand that also held onto a precious old black-plastic pocketbook with one corner that had been chewed on by our dog, Cookie. With my other hand, the hand that held my trick or treat bag, I grabbed up my own skirt. We each wore an old pair of Mom's shoes, and as we made our way through the mud, stepping on rocks and clumps of grass, we managed to forge across without getting our skirts dirty at all. A dense patch of fat, feathery, sticky ferns growing at the edge of the brook grabbed at our long skirts. We pulled ourselves free and ran squealing and laughing until we reached an open hay field where we followed a barbed wire fence. The fencing penned in lazy brown cows that did nothing but stand around all day chewing their cuds, with big sloppy drool coming out of the sides of their mouths.

We shouted at the cows, "Trick or treat," and ran to where the path ended at the old gravel road. This was where we'd begin to trick or treat. We knew which houses we were going to even before we'd started out. We were expected and we knew we'd have disappointed the neighbors if we didn't show up.

The first few houses were a couple of tumbled down shacks, one in back of the other, that belonged to Delbert. All the kids who lived on the gravel road knew Delbert as a cranky bachelor. He kept a mean, lop-eared hunting dog named Boy chained up in the front yard. No one tricked or treated at Delbert's place.

The widow Johnson rented the house in back of Delbert's. The widow was a plump, jolly woman who had no children. I'd overheard someone say once that she had come to our neighborhood carrying her bad reputation with her, whatever the heck that might have meant. My sisters and I walked past Delbert's mailbox, headed down the road to do our trick or treat deeds, the gravel crunching under our oversized shoes. Boy began to bark at us. I recognized his bark. Some nights we heard him from our backyard, and the low, deep, throaty howl made me shiver.

Karen grabbed my arm and screamed, "He's go'n a get us."

"He can't get us. He's chained up," I said.

"He just sounds scary," Janet assured her.

Karen made a growling sound then barked right back at Boy. "Shut up, you stupid dog," she shouted. Boy kept barking.

Mom knew how to handle Boy. She and I had walked past the bachelor's place one day and Boy started to bark. Mom called out to the dog, "Quiet, Boy" in a tone she used with our dog, Cookie—and sometimes a voice she used with my sisters and me. It worked. Boy stopped barking.

"Quiet, Boy," I shouted in a voice that to me sounded just like Mom. But Boy kept on barking. "Quiet, Boy," I shouted again. This time, calling out to the dog in a lowered tone of voice, hopefully sounding more serious. Boy continued to bark. A giant old walnut tree stood at the edge of the bachelor's property. I picked up a walnut from the ground, threw it at the dog, and shouted, "I said, *quiet!*"

The next thing I knew, all three of us were throwing walnuts at the dog. We weren't trying to hit him, not really; he was too far away. In fact, our aim was too poor to ever reach him. The more walnuts we threw, the harder and louder Boy barked. Without realizing it, we had begun to slowly move into Delbert's driveway as we picked up the walnuts to throw at Boy.

Someone turned on the porch light and shouted at us, "What're you brats doing on my property? Get out of here before I get this dog after you." It was Delbert, his voice cracking at us like a whip.

We ran up the road screaming. We stumbled and nearly fell, holding on to each other while we ran as fast as we could in Mom's old shoes—all the while laughing. We were deliciously out of our minds with excitement.

By the time we reached old lady Worthington's, our first intended trick or treat stop, we must have been some sight, because this friendly, ancient-looking neighbor laughed so hard when she opened the door and saw us, that her face turned red, and purple veins popped out on her forehead.

When she stopped laughing, old lady Worthington fanned herself with a handkerchief she had tucked into the sleeve of her sweater. "My, my," she said, "aren't you all just beautiful." She gave us each an extra candy bar and a handful of walnuts.

Everyone in our neighborhood had at least one walnut tree on his property and in the fall walnuts were so abundant they would be left on the ground to rot. Halloween was a good time to get rid of them— a piece of candy and a handful of walnuts for all the little beggars.

After every house had yielded to our threat of tricks or treats we made our way back down the old gravel road, heading home. The light still glowed in Delbert's house. I thought Boy would bark at us again. But he must have been tired out from all the barking he had done earlier that night with many other trick-or-treaters coming down the road riling him up.

A light was turned on in the yard of widow Johnson's house. A man stood on the front porch, looking out at the road, and smoking. The cigarette glowed a faint dot of red. The man looked a lot like Dad. But what would he be doing at the widow Johnson's? Then I saw our car, parked behind Delbert's shack, the back-end sticking out. I watched the man. He went into the house, and the yard went dark.

The full moon now looked like a big hole in the sky with the sun shining through from yesterday and with my sisters in hand, we made our way back to the secret path through the woods. I decided that the man standing on widow Johnson's porch was not Dad, and that the moonlight had played tricks on me—because that night there were many shadows in the woods that I had never seen before. The trees, instead of looking black the way they usually did at night, glowed silver. The cows had moved away from the fence. They were probably chewing someplace else and I remembered Dad told me once that cows even chew in their sleep.

My sisters and I wearily dragged our trick or treat loot home. We were exhausted, but as pleased and proud of our booty as though we each held a pirate's treasure chest filled with doubloons and jewels, instead of Mars Bars, Hershey Kisses, bubble gum, sucking candy and the inevitable walnuts.

Once we arrived home our energy returned. We sat at the kitchen table and excitedly dumped the candy from our bags, piling our collection as high as we could.

Every year we did the same thing. We counted and sorted the candy, putting the chocolate bars and Kisses, our favorite, aside to be eaten first. We made a pile of caramel squares, and a mound of fancy sucking candy, which had its own hidden treasure of tart berry jellies. We stacked the bubble gum on one corner of the kitchen table and rolled all the sour balls and jawbreakers together. The different candies were put into separate dishes and lined up along the back of the kitchen countertop.

The last to be put aside were the walnuts. We gave them to Mom. That year we found several mud-caked walnuts on the bottom of one of the trick or treat bags.

"Who gave you these?" Mom demanded.

I looked at the dirty walnuts in Mom's hand and realized where they came from. Janet looked at me. She knew where they came from, too.

Somehow, during all the excitement, one of us had managed to hold on to a couple of walnuts from the bachelor's yard until we reached old lady Worthington's house. Instead of dropping the walnuts on her porch we had put them into the trick or treat bag.

Karen looked at me. She squirmed on her chair.

"I don't know," Janet answered quickly.

Mom would have been angry if she knew we threw walnuts at Boy. When Mom looked at me, I knew she could tell something had happened, but she said nothing. She sighed deeply and then washed the mud off the nuts, put them in a bowl with the rest of the walnuts. Then she placed the bowl on the kitchen counter next to the stove to help dry out any remaining moisture in the shells.

That night the moonlight came thickly through my bedroom window, but we wouldn't have a new little sister for another three weeks.

When all of our candy had been eaten, a week and a half later, reluctantly my sisters and I began to eat the walnuts, wishing they were at least a jawbreaker or a Pez. I remember coming home from school on cold rainy afternoons, the wind whipping stinging pellets of rain into a frothy sheet against the windows while we sat at the kitchen table playing the game of who could open a walnut perfectly.

Karen, being the youngest, was new at this game and that year I taught her the best way to hold the nutcracker. Her fingers were still too short to get a good grip on the nutcracker—she held the cracker using both hands, squeezing it with all her might. The winner would be the one who could remove a whole walnut from its shell. The nut had to be curly and wrinkled, missing nothing; not a single bump could be broken off. Carefully, we each worked the nutcracker with the precision of sculptors. And when a prize walnut had been pulled whole from its shell, the winning nut would be passed around the table for inspection. Triumphantly, the prize walnut would then be popped into the winner's mouth and chewed and chewed as though it took longer to eat a whole and perfect nut than it did to eat a lot of little pieces.

An explosion of cheers burst from the TV. I paid no attention and cracked open another walnut, this time more carefully. Eating it slowly, the dresses my sisters and I had worn danced in front of me. My favorite dress was the sky blue one with little white morning glories. I remembered the feel of my feet flopping around in Mom's worn-out high heel shoes, the white ones my sisters and I fought over. And I remembered the disappointment of having eaten all of my Halloween candy. I was too young then to know that someday this would be a memory.

I sat beside my husband, cracking open another walnut. The nut had so many levels of flavor and texture; the skin, acidic, had a slightly biting sting, the meat of the nut was oily. The nut ground into my molars, drugging me, and I sank deeper into my memories.

My children are grown, I'm not a kid any more—and neither are my sisters.

I watched Tony, a stranger in my childhood, as he carelessly forced the legs of the nutcracker together, while my technique was to rotate the walnut, squeezing firmly, but gently, making minute fractures in the shell, still trying after all these years to produce the prize nut.

About the Author

MARGARET MENDEL LIVES IN NEW York City and is a past board member of Mystery Writers of America and Sisters in Crime, NYC. Margaret is an award-winning author who has an MFA in creative writing from Sarah Lawrence. She has published two novels, Fish Kicker and Pushing Water. Many of her short stories have appeared in literary journals and anthologies. For more than twenty years she worked in the mental health field, though now she is a full time author. Photography is also an import part of her life and Margaret not only drags a laptop, but a Nikon D7000 camera wherever she goes. Read more about Margaret on her blog at: http://www.pushingtime. com/home/

More from Margaret Mendel to enjoy:

Fish Kicker
Against the landscape of Alaska, a solitary woman eludes a murderer, confronts her inner demons and regains custody of her daughter.

Pushing Water
It's 1939, Sarah, living and working in Vietnam, finds her life turned upside down when she discovers a murdered co-worker.

Did you enjoy *Patches*?

If so, please help us spread the word about Margaret Mendel.
It's as easy as:
• Recommend the book to your family and friends
• Post a review
• Tweet and Facebook about it